YOU
CAN GO
HOME
NOW

YOU CAN GO HOME NOW

A NOVEL

MICHAEL ELIAS

HARPER

NEW YORK • LONDON • TORONTO • SYDNEY

HARPER

A hardcover edition of this book was published in 2020 by HarperCollins Publishers.

YOU CAN GO HOME NOW. Copyright © 2020 by Michael Elias. All rights reserved. Printed in the United States of America. No part of this book may be used or reproduced in any manner whatsoever without written permission except in the case of brief quotations embodied in critical articles and reviews. For information, address HarperCollins Publishers, 195 Broadway, New York, NY 10007.

HarperCollins books may be purchased for educational, business, or sales promotional use. For information, please email the Special Markets Department at SPsales@harpercollins.com.

"The Beautiful American Word, Sure" by Delmore Schwartz, from *Selected Poems*, copyright ©1959 by Delmore Schwartz. Reprinted by permission of New Directions Publishing Corp.

FIRST HARPER PAPERBACKS EDITION PUBLISHED 2021.

Designed by Bonni Leon-Berman

Library of Congress Cataloging-in-Publication Data has been applied for.

ISBN 978-0-06-295417-6 (pbk.)

21 22 23 24 25 LSC 10 9 8 7 6 5 4 3 2 1

For Bianca, Fred and Sylvia, and Fred

Oft have I heard that grief softens the mind,
And makes it fearful and degenerate;
Think therefore on revenge and cease to weep.

—WILLIAM SHAKESPEARE, *HENRY VI*, PART 2, ACT 4

I was taking every hit from you,
You drive-by shooting son of a bitch,
I'm done. Oh whoa, I'm done.
And I'm sorry that you don't like your life
My joy, my joy, my joy takes nothing from you.

—FRAZEY FORD, "DONE"

YOU
CAN GO
HOME
NOW

Grahamsville, New York

1999

A question:
What are some things you can do to kill time while you are waiting to kill someone?
Sure. Things you can do:
Breathe.
Watch.
Listen.
Suck on a lozenge.
Things you can't do:
Smoke.
Make a phone call.
Chew gum.
Pee.
Thank you.

The man stands at his kitchen sink, looking out the window. He can't see me. I am one hundred meters away, dressed in black. The date was chosen so there would be no moon. He rinses dishes and puts them in the washer.

My rifle, on a tripod, is aimed at the window. I was taught that I will need to have his head in the crosshairs of my scope.

The bullet will travel at a speed of 2,500 feet per second. Sound travels at 1,126 feet per second. He will be dead before he hears the rifle shot.

I was taught not to close my eyes.

I close my eyes and pull the trigger.
When I open them he will be dead.
I will have killed his time.
And mine, too.
But I will be alive.
And many will be saved.
Many will be saved.
Praise God.

CHAPTER 1

Artemis Shelter for Women

I have two black eyes, possibly a broken nose, and scrapes and abrasions over my face. I also have a loose molar and a cut lip that doesn't seem to want to stop bleeding. A meat tenderizer hammer wrapped in a dish towel added three purple bruises to my thighs. "For good measure," he said.

I get in my car, drive unsteadily to a parking spot on Northern Boulevard, and walk two blocks to the shelter. I lean against the shelter's steel grille; behind it is a solid wooden door with a peephole. Above the door out of reach, there is a CCTV camera aimed at me. I ring the bell and count seconds to dull the pain. At thirty-one, the door opens. A woman looks at me and shakes her head. "I'm sorry, we're full. We have no room."

"I'll sleep on the floor."

I step closer so she can get a better look at my face. I see hers. It's about sixty, unlined, with kind blue eyes behind granny glasses. She thinks for a moment, then says with gentle resignation, "We'll give you a sleeping bag on a couch for now. I'm sorry I can't promise more."

It's okay. I'm in.

CHAPTER 2

Two months earlier

What the fuck?

I write it and cross it out.

There is no way I can enter these three words into my daily log—a thick loose-leaf folder, pages defaced with coffee stains, containing notes of interviews, arrests, observations, phone calls scrawled in ballpoint, Sharpie, and India blue-black ink. It is the record of everything related to my job as a Long Island City homicide detective: investigations, interviews, active and inactive cases, and most recently what I did on the first Thursday in October apart from my choice of lunch—a foot-long Subway Meatball Marinara with a bottle of iced tea. I ate six inches and saved the rest for later. The meatballs are still sloshing around in my stomach like wet towels in a washer. Not a good choice.

On that day, ~~What the fuck?~~ came in three visits. Before I get to them, my name is Nina Karim. I am a single thirty-one-year-old woman who likes cats, Ryan Reynolds movies, beautiful sunsets, and walking on a wintry beach holding hands with a tall, caring, lightly bearded third-wave feminist. *Yeah, right.*

Long Island City Police Log: Detective Nina Karim
October 6, 2017

10:35 a.m.: Interview with John and Melinda Steevers, 3600 Myrtle Drive, South Flushing. Their son Ronald failed to show up at the weekly Sunday-night family dinner and had not reported to his job at the Home Depot in Long Island City. There was no response to their phone calls, texts, or emails. On Monday Mr. Steevers drove to Ronald's residence at Sunny Gardens Apartments, in Queens, and found his apartment empty. There was no sign of Ronald's wife, Susan. Most of her clothes were gone. Mrs. Steevers said, "We're not interested in the disappearance of Ronald's wife as there was no love lost between us."

Mr. Steevers: "It's not our problem." Mrs. Steevers intimated Susan was capable of murdering their son. I asked them to fill out a missing persons report and told them I would follow up with an investigative visit to the apartment.

11:45 a.m.: Interview with Lawrence McDermott, Caucasian male, 25 Lancelot Lane, Northport, New York. Mr. McDermott confessed to murder but had no knowledge or memory of the person he had murdered. Mr. McDermott appeared to be sane and well dressed, and works as a risk specialist at Chase Bank in Manhattan. As ridiculous as his story sounds, I have some memory of this man that I can't quite place. I know it will come to me. (I noted his basics—see above.) After he left, I endured mild verbal abuse from my fellow homicide detectives. Apparently, Mr. McDermott has been here before. He is considered a nutcase. ~~What the fuck? #2~~

12:15 p.m.: Interview with Arthur "Artie" Crews, Caucasian male, 365 Maiden Lane, Little Neck, New York. Crews is a weatherman on KCS TV Channel 7. He asks if he could employ me on a private basis to help his son Scott find his missing cat, Bonkers. ~~What the fuck? #3.~~

CHAPTER 3

I consider finishing my Subway sandwich in the car on the way to the Sunny Gardens Apartments but instead rewrap it carefully and hand it to a homeless man zigzagging cars at the stoplight. At the Police Academy, we were taught the cautionary tale of Jack Salucci, a veteran cop who was forced by new regulations to report to the shooting range and take a proficiency exam on the .38 revolver he insisted on carrying. Officer Salucci arrived at the range, aimed his weapon at the target, and couldn't pull the trigger. His gun was jammed. Salucci handed it over to the instructor, who discovered a cement-like material encasing the hammer. There was no way it could be fired. Salucci freaked, picturing himself facing an armed bank robber, hunched behind the open door of his patrol car, unable to return fire. Further analysis of his pistol revealed the cement-like material around the hammer to be hardened mozzarella cheese that had dripped down on the weapon from the hundreds of pizza slices Officer Salucci had consumed while sitting behind the wheel of his patrol car. My own weapon, a regulation Glock 22, is strapped to my hip under one of the two navy-blue JCPenney blazers I rotate, along with four white blouses, three pairs of blue slacks, and two pairs of black rubber-soled shoes that comprise my normal work costume. I also have a formal Long Island City Police uniform: a navy-blue suit with gold braids on the sleeves for my years of service, a medal for bravery, and an American flag patch. I am expected to wear a white shirt and a tie, completing the appearance of a man in law enforcement. For miserable Long Island weather, I own a series of blue sweaters, a blue raincoat, and, in winter, a down jacket, also blue. I am just a little girl blue homicide detective; that's fine. My just-in-case weapon, strapped to my ankle, is a .38 Ruger LCR, the Lightweight Compact Revolver. I call it the NLF, Nasty Little Fucker. It's about five inches long. Apparently, it kills as well as anything else. The point is, unlike Officer Salucci, when I need to fire my weapons there will be no cement-like mozzarella on either of them.

So far, I have never had to fire either weapon at any living thing. So far.

I don't wear makeup. I have a serious interest in a man, Bobby Booth (Bobby B), the one I sleep with when our busy schedules allow—mine as a cop, his as a loan shark.

Sunny Gardens Apartments is a two-story brick building with white wood trim and flower-lined concrete paths. There is a smug NO VACANCY sign planted in the lawn. I park in a handicapped spot, place the blue badge with the wheelchair symbol on the rearview mirror. I confiscated the badge from a guy at my gym. As I passed him on my way to the treadmill, he said something *unkind* about my butt to his trainer.

Okay, a word about my body. Unlike Gaul, I am divided into two, not three, parts. Top is perfect: a twenty-two-inch waist, flat stomach, and Kate Moss breasts. South of the belt, the geography changes. My hips widen, and my thighs end in a bump that looks like it should be on someone else—on my best days, a modern dancer; on my worst, what my ex-fiancé Darren used to call "not a one hander." But Bobby loves me, and that's just fine. I say there's something in me for every taste, just not all in one package.

I followed Mr. Unkind to the parking lot, showed him my badge, told him I'd heard what he said and asked to see his handicapped paperwork. Mr. Unkind mumbled apologies, said he had a bad heart and friends in the police department. I could see that his heart was encased in a buff body, and told him it was a bad idea to use the *friends in the police department* line.

"Friends? Name one," I said.

He can't. He finally confessed he bought the handicapped-parking badge on Canal Street. Can you believe he began to cry? I forgave him and kept the badge.

My face? My favorite V. S. Pritchett story is about a woman who owns an irresistibly lovely nose and a devoted dog. A handsome gentleman woos her, but just as he is about to propose, the dog bites off the tip of her nose. The man disappears. She and the dog live happily ever after. My nose? Like hers, also missing a little piece.

The rest? I was born with a slight smile. It tends to confuse people. A tiny turnup at the mouth that makes me look perpetually happy, in opposition to my naturally discontented soul. I have been told at various times in my life by disgruntled teachers and superior officers, "Karim, wipe that smile off your face." I can't. A smile doesn't come in handy at funerals, disciplinary hearings, or breakups. But it can be disarming when I tell you that you are under arrest, move along, show me your driver's license, or, in a movie theater, *Get your hand off my knee.*

Anthony, my hairdresser, who keeps me blonde, says I have Dutch hair; he means wild and salty. If I keep it short, I will stay presentable. My eyes are blue and lively, my cheekbones prominent enough to make a difference. I have been told I look like Geena Davis or Victoria Beckham. Have they been told they look like me? I will add that I take after my mother. I have her eyes, her complexion. Looking in the mirror makes me miss her, and thus sad. I tend to avoid mirrors. Back to work.

The manager of the Sunny Gardens apartment complex is Brian Robbins, a shortish, bearded early thirties adjunct professor of psychology at Fordham. We both know the title means nothing as he works too hard teaching freshman classes and earns just a bit too much money to qualify for food stamps. In addition to being essentially disposable, adjuncts don't get tenure, health care, retirement, or offices. They are paid by the course unit; their teaching loads vary from part-time to overloaded. Brian's managerial job at Sunny Gardens gives him a free apartment in a building that is new enough not to need any serious care while Brian works on his PhD and dreams of a professorship with tenure. At Sunny Gardens, the tenants are all employed and they pay their rent on time.

Brian leads me to the Steeverses' apartment, number twenty-two, second floor, rear. Since first impressions are best gotten alone, I ask him to wait outside. Inside is an apartment of no consequence: low ceilings and clean rooms with wooden floors. There is a picture window with a view of a copse of trees that enclose a deep ravine. I wander around making simple observations. The walk-in closet has empty hangers and few women's clothes: a pair of torn jeans, a blouse, and two dresses—size two. One from Target, the other Macy's. A drawer contains a rumpled T-shirt, one pair of pantyhose, and two mismatched sweat socks. On the floor of the closet, there are a pair of flats and a lone flip-flop. She's gone.

Ronald's side of the closet contains three pairs of jeans, two khaki Dockers, a baseball jacket, a gray Gap hoodie, a John Tavares Islanders jersey, and a navy blazer with a pair of gray flannel slacks. His drawers are a mess of socks, underwear, rumpled

T-shirts, a white dress shirt, and a stack of baseball caps. There is a pair of worn Nike sneakers, and scuffed black loafers on the floor. Ronald tends toward slob, and Susan took her good clothes with her.

Apart from a few lonely ants marching around the toaster, the kitchen is spotless. The fridge holds man food: cold cuts, Ball Park hot dogs, yellow mustard, Kraft Singles, beer, a jar of pickles, a head of browning iceberg lettuce, and a plastic jar of Muscle Max. No yogurt, almond milk, probiotics, or Diet Coke. I assume Susan left first. Or, if Mama Steevers was right, Susan returned, killed Ronald, and took off. I make a note to search the ravine for Ronald's body.

Then, while my brain is in murder mode, I suddenly remember where I have seen Mr. McDermott, the man who didn't know who he killed. Six months ago, I was called to a high-rise apartment building in Lefrak City in Queens. The victim was a dancer at the Gallery, a gentlemen's club—surely an overstatement—in Manhattan. She did pole work and lap dances. Occasionally, when the manager was away, she took a customer back to her apartment for further pleasure (his). Her last customer strangled her and left her sitting upright on the couch. Two days later, her sister, a stewardess for Singapore Airlines, discovered her body. NYPD was thorough in trying to identify her clients that fateful evening, but whoever he was, he'd paid cash, and the club's CCTV cameras were out of commission. The employees were interviewed and all had the same useless response: "He was a middle-aged white man in a suit." The murder became another cold case—a victim without an advocate, a woman in a problematic profession, her interest to the homicide squad somewhere between the homeless and the undocumented.

Because she lived in Queens, our homicide department had

a piece of her. I was assigned to find out who murdered her. I subscribe to the theory that often killers return to the scene of the crime, join the gawkers behind the yellow tape to watch the parade of police and forensic and medical personnel. They like to catch a glimpse of their grim work being wheeled to the waiting ambulance. So, while my colleagues are inside dusting, scraping, and cataloguing, I take photographs of people standing outside. I may have a picture of Mr. McDermott. Back to work. I open the door for Brian.

"Okay, Brian, you can come in now. Tell me about the Steevers."

Brian is a man full of pent-up information who lectures about psychology for a living. I try not to get in his way. I know I'll get more insights into Ronald and Susan than I need.

"Ronald and Susan. Ronald and Susan. You know?"

Not a smart beginning, Brian. I don't *know* anything and I hate it when people say *You know?* On my list of speech warts, it comes right after *No problem* or people who say *Thank you* after you say *Thank you.* But I nod encouragement, and Brian continues.

"Ronald works at Home Depot; he told me he's a big deal in the paint department. He's six two, about two twenty, an ex-jock, but I don't think he'll keep the body. I can tell from the beer cans. He complained about stuff I couldn't control, like pool noise, slow Internet, and jerks who take his parking spot. He leaves at eight, comes home at six, works Saturday and Sunday, with Mondays and Tuesdays off. He gets up early Sunday to wash his Mustang GT. For him, it's church."

I laugh insincerely along with Brian.

"Sunday nights, he and Susan drive to South Flushing for dinner with his parents. Lately, I notice Susan doesn't go with him. How do I know?" *You took the words right out of my mouth,*

Brian. "My apartment looks out over the garage. Ronald customized the Mustang's exhausts, and he puts the top down. I hear the engine, look out the window—it's Ronald driving away. Alone. You know?"

I consider complimenting Brian on his powers of observation but resist.

"He's an Islanders fan. Bragged he had his boss's seats. He's a gamer. I am, too, so once in a while he drops by; we play World of Warcraft. I never heard him mention a book, music, politics, church or state, you know? That's all superficial. You want me to go deeper?"

"Ronald's missing. Go deep," I say.

"Okay. At first, I thought the guy had no qualities. He was a cliché. White male Long Island kid, finished high school, had a little community college, didn't like school and school didn't like him, lucky to have a pretty good job, loves his car, his work buddies, his Islanders, and his wife in that order. You know? At a certain point, I assumed one of two things would happen: his wife would get pregnant and he would grow up or she would leave him. But now I think it's more complicated. You know?"

I wouldn't want this guy to be my adjunct professor of anything. I decide to go crude. "Tell me, Brian, were you fucking Susan?"

It works. Brian blushes around the edges of his beard. He's smart enough to take his time to plan his next steps. It may not be the truth, whatever it is. "Look, we got into a friendly thing. If I had to fix something in the apartment, she'd make me a cup of coffee, we'd talk. She told fascinating stories. Did I tell you she was from Alaska? For me, it was exotic, you know? Windswept villages, dark days, long nights, people freezing to death on their way home from the supermarket, polar bears eating your garbage. Then one night when Ronald was at a hockey game she came down to my place and we smoked some weed. Oops."

Brian looks at me to see if I am going to arrest him for confessing to using marijuana. I ignore the misdemeanor. He continues, "Ronald had seats behind the Rangers goal, so we could see him on TV. It was safe; we knew where he would be for the next three hours. She felt guilty afterward, swore it would never happen again. But it did. I had the feeling she was so insecure that she thought sex was the only thing that would keep me interested in her, you know?"

"Was it?"

"No, there were other things. Like I said, she was exotic."

I didn't hear Brian mention love or affection, so I guess he's happy to go along with her insecurity as part of the deal. *Prick.*

"Did they fight?"

"She told me they did. You mean did I hear them? I couldn't if they did. I'm too far away, you know?"

"What else did she tell you about the marriage?"

Brian strokes his beard. He thinks I believe he is thinking.

"That was about it."

I ask him to make a copy of their rental agreement and give me a list of the names of their neighbors who live in units next to them. What did I know so far, you know? Ronald and Susan had a lousy marriage. No, Ronald had a good marriage; Susan had a lousy one. Do I care? Ronald's Mustang is in his parking spot in the garage. Actually, this is a bad sign. He's missing, his car isn't. I peek in the windows—spotless inside—inspect the tires—October in Queens means fallen leaves everywhere: his are clean; Ronald hasn't driven recently.

The Bermans' apartment on the right and Dixons' on the left aren't answering, so I knock on the floor directly below. An Indian woman in a sari cracks the door open to the chain's length. She tells me I'd have to wait for her husband to come home from work. I can hear children behind her. I say I will return. I explore the ravine. There are no dead bodies.

On the way to my car, I think about Brian and his basket of lies.

CHAPTER 4

Lieutenant Lily Hagen stops at my desk. I give her an update on my two active cases: the missing Ronald Steevers and the forgetful potential murderer, Mr. McDermott. I tell her I am looking for his photograph. She is interested in Mr. and Mrs. Steevers and their missing son. McDermott is not worth the effort, and it's not an appropriate time to mention Artie the TV weatherman and the case of his son's missing cat.

Lily Hagen rose to lieutenant and chief of detectives the hard way, before enlightened promotion, diversity programs, or hiring quotas. She didn't get the benefits of Title 1, or Gloria Allred filing sexual discrimination lawsuits on her behalf. She endured the jokes, slurs, misogyny, and occasional "good-natured" groping from her fellow male officers as a beat cop, or as a partner in a patrol car. A couple of times, it almost cost her her life when backup didn't arrive. She's a gym rat. I once worked out next to her and marveled at her strength, but we both knew her body was where it was and would stay that way. She has a husband who works in Weights and Measures for the city, a married daughter in Virginia. The only other thing I know about her is she's sixty-one years old. She will retire in four years at her present rank and won't go any higher. She is aware that every woman who joined the force after she did has had it easier. Sometimes with women police officers, this knowledge results in solidarity, sometimes resentment. In her case, it was the latter.

"I worked on feeling charitable, Nina, I really did, but it just wasn't in my bones. I think of all the shit I had to go through and how you women who come in today have it easy."

"Easier," I say. "I haven't seen any copies of *Ms.* in the duty room."

She laughs.

Lieutenant Hagen is called unkind. Behind her back, some women officers refer to her as the Clarence Thomas of the Long Island City Police Department. It's a lousy rap. She fought battles, toughed it out, and made enemies along the way. Over get-to-know-you drinks, she asked me, "Why did you become a cop, Karim?"

"TV shows. *Columbo, Charlie's Angels, Baretta—Police Woman* was my favorite. I loved seeing Angie Dickinson kick ass when I was a little kid."

"Reruns. You weren't born when it aired."

"Yes, reruns."

She downed the last of her Chablis. "*Police Woman.* I used to get shit for drinking white wine."

The thing I like most about Lieutenant Hagen is that she keeps a framed embroidery on the wall behind her office chair. In the style of American Dutch Folk Art, a tulip border encircles the words: YOUR JOB IS TO ARREST, NOT PUNISH.

Driving to Home Depot on Queens Boulevard, I make a mental list of the items I need for my apartment. Any time I can combine police work with shopping is a bonus. I imagine a new washer/dryer combo, but that isn't going to happen. Home Depot isn't like Costco, where I come home with enough pasta, Tylenol, and toothpaste to last the rest of my life. Home Depot is about fixing, improving, adding, growing plants, and buying lawn mowers. I find the paint department, wander around, and try to consider who is likely to be Ronald's boss.

Owen Kunkle—it says so on his name tag—is at the paint counter. He's got a big smile, bright blue eyes, blond whitish hair on a big frame. When he says, "Now, how can I help you?" I know he means it. He will be my friend. I open the Behr color sample booklet, where my police ID rests in the outdoor section. Owen nods, comes out from behind the counter, and leads me away to a wall of outdoor paint cans.

"How can I help?"

"I'm looking for Ronald Steevers."

Owen takes a deep breath. "Well, since he hasn't come to work for the past week, I assume he's quit. Of course, he didn't call in."

Owen doesn't seem worried about Ronald.

"Were you friends?"

"I wasn't a fan of the man, and if he doesn't ever come back it's just fine with me, and probably with some other people I could mention."

"Your fellow workers, or customers?"

"Workers. Before Ronald got here, Al Eidelman was running the paint department with a simply marvelous crew. We were loyal and dedicated, and there wasn't a color we couldn't match. Word got out to the design community. You wouldn't believe it, but we had big-name decorators coming in for paint. Al not only believed in diversity, but he practiced it. Our team was like the UN: Korean, Sikh, Afro-American, Israeli, Syrian, *moi*: your basic Midwest, apple-cheeked, farm-raised frustrated artist."

He straightens a stack of eggshell-white gallon cans. "To cut to the chase: Steevers thought we were a bunch of freaks. Before we knew it, Al was transferred to ladders, Passionara to aluminum, Danielle to power tools, Yossef and Ahmed to lumber, and yours truly in Mr. Asshole's face saying, *Take this paint and shove it*. Not really, but I wanted to. Hey, I mean no disrespect; once a cop, always a cop."

"I beg your pardon."

"Ronald was a cop before he came to Home Depot. You didn't know that?"

It is a question whose answer I am supposed to pretend to know. I prefer honest ignorance.

"No, I didn't. What do you mean, 'once a cop'?"

"Look, it's a question of authority, isn't it? Ronald was the boss. Okay, we all got it, but we're not the Marine Corps—we're selling paint; we all work together to make the customer happy. Ronald saw it as we all work together to *make him happy*. He used to say that about his wife. It was her job to make him happy. He talked about her dedication, how she had her duties, how she went out of her way to please him. She knew her place, and he used the *s* word."

I was thinking *suck*.

"*Serve*."

"No." I'm shocked.

"It was clear he expected all of us to do the same, especially the women in the department. He never came out and said those words—hello, HR—but he conveyed it, and we got it. We decided the best policy was to just keep our distance. You learned not to argue with Ronald. You know, once a cop . . ."

CHAPTER 5

At headquarters, Mr. McDermott is waiting for me outside my cubicle. I show him the photograph of the people at the crime scene in Lefrak City. He adjusts his glasses, studies the picture until he picks himself out of the crowd.

"You probably want to know what I'm doing there."

"Yes, I do."

"I live across the street. I was coming home and saw the commotion. I stopped to look."

"Anything else?"

"No."

"Do you have travel plans?"

"No."

I ask Mr. McDermott if he would mind giving us his fingerprints and a swab of DNA, and telling me where he was on the night of the murder. He is so eager to help and find out if he did kill Ms. Hwang that he offers to throw in a sperm sample. A week later, I give him the bad news; all the tests indicate he's not the killer. His alibi of dining at Orso in Manhattan followed by a performance of *The Book of Mormon* also checked out.

"Frankly, I'm glad I didn't kill Ms. Hwang, but it does look like something I could have done."

"Mr. McDermott, you will need more evidence in hand if you want to confess to murder. Anyway, I'm very busy looking for a missing cat."

"I beg your pardon?"

Sometimes it is better to sound crazy when talking to the crazy. It puts us on a level playing field. McDermott promises not to bother me unless he has better evidence with which to incriminate himself. He leaves. *Something he could have done?* The hell with Lieutenant Hagen, I'm staying with McDermott.

Finding out where Ronald worked in law enforcement involved a phone call to Home Depot human resources asking them to send a fax of his employment application. Answer: Farmingdale, New York. It is an interesting question as to why his parents didn't mention that Ronald did a four-year stint with the Farmingdale police force. Finding out why he wasn't working there anymore presented problems. Four years in, Ronald had to have been making more than he could at Home Depot. It didn't make sense as a career move, so it was a good bet that the Farmingdale Police Department asked Ronald to leave. There was nothing in Ronald's personnel file that explained why he'd left; it was just noted on his work history, along with graduation from Flushing High School, one semester at Queens Community College (you were correct, Brian Robbins of Sunny Gardens Apartments), then four years in the Farmingdale Police, two years at Home Depot in Scarsdale, a town next to New Rochelle, then a transfer to Home Depot in Long Island City, where he was put in charge of the paint department and made Owen Kunkle's life miserable. I knew the Farmingdale Police Department would be reluctant to release personnel files. Getting dirt on a cop these days is tricky. On the other hand, I might get lucky. Ronald may have made an enemy who hated him enough to tell me. I ask around the station, but no one knows anybody at Farmingdale, so it will be a cold call. On my way back, I can drop in on Ronald's parents.

Farmingdale's station house is suburban, freshly painted. Inside, at the desk, I show my badge to a bored clerk who sighs on every third exhale. I tell him I am on a missing persons assignment regarding a former police officer, Ronald Steevers. He doesn't react to the name, makes a call upstairs, repeats what I told him. He listens, then gestures to a volunteer cadet, a high school boy in an ill-fitting uniform playing Fortnite on his phone. The cadet springs to attention, suppressing the urge to salute. He reminds me of my brother, Sammy.

"Take her up to Sergeant Dickens," the clerk says.

I follow the cadet up the stairs, into an interrogation room. Metal desk, two chairs facing each other, one bolted to the floor. The cadet tells me someone will be with me in a minute and closes the door behind him. Like waiting for a doctor in an examining room, it's an excellent time to check emails, send texts, and steal bandages and Q-tips. In this interrogation room, there is nothing to steal or read. I take out my phone and pass the time with Jane Gardam's *Old Filth*, my novel of the moment, a memory of a life in Colonial Hong Kong. It is far away and exotic enough to disconnect me from any of my memories. I've managed two pages when Sergeant Dickens enters. She's a big redhead in her forties, taller than me when I stand, which makes her almost six feet. I get a firm handshake, a wide smile.

"I'm sorry we have to talk here. I'll take the perp chair."

This is generous of her. She slips into the chair bolted to the floor. "At least we can smoke."

I know this. An interrogator can get a lot of information from a suspect with the offer of a cigarette, or by withholding one. She offers me one. I accept; it is the polite thing to do.

"I try to quit, but every time I do, I gain ten pounds," she says as she lights me up.

I pass her my ID. Sergeant Dickens glances at it, shakes her head.

"You said Ronald Steevers. What did that asshole do now?"

This is turning out to be better than I expected.

"He's missing. As in didn't show up for his parents' Sunday dinner or for work. I'm mostly interested because his wife isn't around, either. Three scenarios: he killed her, she killed him, or they won the lottery and went to Miami."

Sergeant Dickens takes a long drag on her cigarette.

"I really can't tell you anything except good riddance. To Ronald, I mean."

She shrugs.

"One last thing," I say.

"Sure."

"How's your retirement package?"

"Terrific. If Ronald hadn't been fired for beating up his wife, he might have been around to collect it."

CHAPTER 6

A phone call comes out of the blue from Ernie Saldana in Maui, and it brings back memories of blue skies, ocean, and towels from the Kapalua Beach Motel where we spent family Christmas vacations. There is the first memory of my brother and me getting out of the rental car, staring in horror at the one-story wooden 1950s U-shaped building peeking out from tumbling red bougainvillea. We begged our parents to leave this icky resort and take us to a shining white hotel on Kapalua Beach—one with waterslides, shopping malls, movie theaters, and beach towels. As we walked to the front office on an AstroTurf path lined with drooping birds of paradise and blue ginger plants, my father said, "We chose this motel because it's inexpensive."

Our mother added, "The money we save, we can spend on fancy restaurants and Hawaiian shirts."

"A bed is a bed," my father said. "Do we care about an ocean view from thirty stories up?"

"Or a huge TV we won't watch?"

Entering the office, I knew we didn't have a chance. I elbowed Sammy.

"Can we buy souvenirs?" Sammy asked my father.

"Of course, my darlings. We'll fill our suitcases with fake spears, puka-shell necklaces, tiki tumblers, and polished driftwood."

"Deal," Sammy said.

"Deal," I said.

A bulging rack of brochures next to the reception desk advertised scuba lessons, hot-air balloon rides, sunset cruises, helicopter rides, luaus, river raft trips, volcano expeditions, and an adventure through a pineapple plantation on an antique train.

Mom said, "It's like a menu from Hop Sing's. Everybody gets to pick a dish."

I chose a sunset luau with fire dancers; my brother picked scuba lessons and swimming with sea turtles. Mom said she just wanted to sit in a beach chair and read Tolstoy. My father's choice was dinner at Roy's restaurant in Kaanapali. We ate dragon rolls, short ribs, and blackened ahi tuna. I still remember the sweet-and-sour honey taste of the ribs but for the life of me can't remember what a dragon roll is.

Days were spent on the beach, swimming in the warm Pacific, snorkeling, eating poke lunches we bought in Lahaina. In the evening, we went to movies and scoured the souvenir shops in the Kaanapali mall. I still have my wind-up hula dancer. Sammy smashed his shell collection in one of his meltdowns, and I never had a chance to ask my mother if she finished *Anna Karenina*.

For my father, one of the pleasures of the Kapalua Beach Motel was getting to know Ernie Saldana, the man who called me out of the blue to tell me I was a giant step closer to changing my life. Ernie was a retired police officer from Los Angeles, vague on details of his rank or experience—"Let's just say I did stuff," he told me later when I pressed him for details. Later, when I was a cop, I assumed he was in internal affairs, connected to the Rampart corruption scandal of the late 1990s that began when an officer was caught stealing cocaine from a department property room. The following investigation uncovered crimes by LAPD officers, including the framing of suspects and connections to violent street gangs. If Ernie Saldana had a hand in sending any of those cops to prison, he wouldn't be eager to talk about it.

In exchange for taking care of security, Ernie received a free room in the motel. There wasn't much to do; he patrolled the property at night accompanied by Dufus, his standard poodle. Ernie was a big man. He'd played football at Cal State and looked like he still could. His presence on the grounds was enough to discourage wayward local kids from breaking into rooms. He didn't call the cops when he did catch one. Ernie just found out who their parents were. The threat of telling them was usually enough. He ferried cash deposits to the bank in Lahaina, did background checks on new hires, and played chess with my father. I would sit next to my father and watch them play. At first, my father would tell me where to move his piece, and whisper in my ear the reason for the move: "I will let him take my knight, but it will double his pawn and he will regret it in three more moves." Eventually, he let me make my own moves. It's how I learned the game and got to be pretty good; it also cemented my own friendship with Ernie. One of these days I will tell Lieutenant Hagen that it was Ernie Saldana, not Angie Dickinson, who was my inspiration to become a cop. But that would mean telling her who I am and what I am doing on her police force.

Another memory: the drive from JFK, our Maui sunburned skin still peeling, clothes too thin for the cold of upstate New York. We lived in a two-story wood-frame house in Grahamsville, population less than a thousand people and a hundred miles too far from New York City to commute. Grahamsville was pure country; it had a gas station with one pump, a general store where you could find canned ham, hunting magazines, Powerball tickets, antifreeze, and, occasionally the *New York Times*. For everything else, there was a Walmart in Ellenville, fifteen miles away. It was dull but picturesque and had no amenities. There was a local joke the boys learned:

TOURIST: "What is there to do here in the summer?"
NATIVE: "There's fishing and fucking."
TOURIST: "What about the winter?"
NATIVE: "No fishing."

Our house straddled a flat acre off the main highway, fifty yards up a dirt road my father called the *damn thing*. In the spring the road, the *damn thing*, turned to mud. By August, the mud dried out and even a gentle wind kicked up fine dust that coated cars and colored white sneakers brown. In winter, our neighbor Harry Dill plowed the snow so our cars could come in and out. Periodically, my father promised he would pave the *damn thing*, but he never got around to it. The house was a one-story ranch with nothing to distinguish it from any of the others built by Rondout Construction in the late 1950s, except for the sign that read DR. MARTIN KARIM, GENERAL MEDICAL PRACTICE. The front door led into our living quarters, a side entrance opened into my father's medical suite. He made house calls, turned no one away for lack of money or insurance. Often, farmers paid him in produce. We were never short of fresh vegetables, eggs, apples, and, in the summer, corn off the stalk. His suite had a small waiting room with a couch, a few chairs, a playpen, and a box of toys for the kids. The magazines were *Scientific American*, *Jack and Jill*, *Time*, and *National Geographic*.

Our mother, Gloria, was his nurse, paramedic, receptionist, and bookkeeper. She had a gift of calming children facing vaccinations, and she knew how to set a broken arm, do an EKG, and take X-rays, developed in a bathroom that doubled as a darkroom. As a rural doctor, my father was on call 24/7. If one of his patients was in an emergency situation, they either came to his office or he went to their house. Our meals were interrupted by house calls, vacation plans were canceled because a baby was about to be born, and we grew up knowing that our own family needs came in second. My father was aware of this, so when my brother, Sammy, was born, he started commuting to Albany Medical College to complete his board training in gynecology. As he was finishing, a young doctor just out of his residency in family medicine wanted a small-town practice. My father sold him all his medical equipment, closed his office, and took a job at Planned Parenthood in Albany, and we began to experience a normal life. There were adjustments, of course. My mother had to find a job, and the house felt a lot bigger without the medical suite, but for the first time, we had our father to ourselves on weekends—he could help coach Sammy's soccer team and drive me to swim meets—and if we missed the bus, he could drive us to school. And there would be family vacations.

But most important, since I was too old to share a bedroom with Sammy, my father's medical office was converted into a living space for me. My bathroom still smelled of X-ray film developer, and I was occasionally awakened by a knock at the side door: a car crash survivor with a bleeding skull, a woman holding a sick baby, or a man with chest pains who hadn't heard the news that my father had given up his practice. I gave directions to the hospital emergency room in Ellenville to all of them. There was always a part of me that believed in vibes and ghosts. Living in a former medical suite, where lives had been saved, wounds sewn up, and bad news delivered, I slept fitfully, even though I was separated by only a few yards from my parents. I heard their conversations, their ambient life humming in nearby rooms. I was called to meals that had already begun. At night, I retreated to my apartment to sleep. The space was mine. I had my own entrance. I could smoke cigarettes, sneak in a boyfriend, play my music as loud as I wanted.

From my bedroom window, I had a view of the woods behind our house, a Catskill forest speckled with tall red black spruce, thick balsam fir, and slender mountain ash. Whitetail deer nibbled the tender branches of the apple tree my father planted on the edge of our property. One winter evening after dinner when it was my turn to take out the garbage, I saw a bobcat under a tree, its taut brown body against the white snow, paw raised, staring at me, evaluating me as friend, food, or threat. I wasn't afraid. I tried to match its stare. After our staring contest was over, it leaped in the air and disappeared back into the alder brush.

On another evening, under the same tree in that Catskill forest, a man aimed his rifle and sent a bullet through our kitchen window, spilling my father's brains onto the floor, splattering his blood on our white refrigerator door. Sammy and I were eating dessert—chocolate cake topped with vanilla ice cream—while our father washed the dishes. He had sent my mother upstairs.

"Gloria, darling, you cooked, I'll clean up."

My mother never heard the shot, only my brother's scream. She burst into the kitchen, saw my father lying on the floor, turned off the kitchen faucet, swooped Sammy in her arms, and carried him out of the room. Like all murders, the bullet that ended my father's life changed ours forever.

I was alone, the last human being in the world. An enormous pair of scissors had cut every string that connected me to all the people I loved and knew. My body felt like cigarette smoke.

I thought I was going to rise and be sucked out of the room through the shattered window into the dark night, but nothing like that happened. My mother came back, took my hand, led me out into the living room. She sat me down next to Sammy on the couch, cradled us in her arms and called 911. I was sixteen. My brother, Sammy, was nine.

The police searched for the killer. They scoured the forest with bloodhounds, set up roadblocks, checked gas stations with CCTVs. They brought in the FBI, the New York State Police, and expert forensic people. The killer was smart. He'd come to the shooting spot in his socks, so there were no shoe tracks; he'd fired his rifle while sitting on a painter's tarp that he'd taken with him, so there was no fiber analysis; he hadn't eaten, smoked, or drunk anything while he'd waited. No cigarette butts, no half-eaten candy, no urine passed from his bladder. The shell casing was never found. The bullet that had opened my father's skull was homemade; there was no tracing it. The killer was an expert at his profession. But so am I, and I'll find him, the *cowardly bastard*. He murdered my father and de-stroyed my family. It will not be *I alone am left to tell the tale*. No. It will be *I alone am left to get revenge, not on a dumb whale but on an intelligent human*.

I became a police officer because Ernie Saldana told me I would have a better chance of finding the *cowardly bastard* if I did not follow my passion (or was it my dream? I get them con-fused) and accepted early admission to Stony Brook, then went on to Cornell for a master's degree and a PhD in English litera-ture. Instead, I followed my rage. After high school, I commuted to Rockland Community College in Suffern for two years, got an associate's degree in criminal justice, and went on to John Jay College of Criminal Justice for two more years; had odd jobs during the application process to the Long Island Police Department, making it through their Police Academy. I did three years of patrol duty, and now, I am a homicide detective less literate but armed with a Glock. If I happen to be walking on that wintry beach holding hands with Ryan Reynolds and meet this *cowardly bastard*, I will excuse myself from Ryan, lift my flared blazer, remove my weapon, and shoot the *cowardly bastard* in the abdomen. Then I will let him catch a glimpse of his bleeding entrails before I end his miserable life with a close-up round to his heart.

On second thought, I might just let him die in unimaginable pain as I continue my walk on the wintry beach with Ryan, while the *cowardly bastard*'s screams are drowned out by seagulls and breaking waves. Then perhaps I will go back to Stony Brook and restart my life in literary pursuits. Maybe.

My grief counselor suggested meditation. I do it often. My mantra is *die, die, die*, as I remember my father on the floor, Sammy screaming at his father separated from most of his head and therefore not his father but a horror movie, unrecognizable because he had no words to comfort his son, unrecognizable because he couldn't get up and say, *It's all right, Sammy, darling. It didn't happen. I'm alive and this is a dream and it didn't happen.* None of that happened, so Sammy just screamed and screamed until, as I said, my mother came in and picked him up in her arms and carried him out of the room.

Years later, my mother said she had been in rehearsal for the murder of her husband ever since our father made the death wish list of the Army of God. The *New York Times* said it was an anti-abortion group linked to violent extremists. Linked? Like the

SS was linked to violent Nazis? Their website posted, *He that hath no sword let him sell his garment and buy one. (Luke 22:26)*, and added, *They who support abortion have the blood of babies on their hands*. Their website celebrates men who have murdered doctors as heroes. My father's killer hasn't made the list—he's still anonymous—but when he does, he won't be alive to see it, thanks to me.

My mother saw herself as a combat wife: Grace Kelly waiting for Jimmy Stewart to come home from testing a new fighter plane, or was it Dirty Harry Callahan's wife who watches him strap on his .44 Magnum and kiss the children good-bye and wonders if he will return? My father didn't consider himself a hero; he was a doctor who thought women should make the decisions about their own bodies. He respected the autonomy of women, trusted them to decide what was best for themselves and their families. His parents emigrated from Iran; doctors who came to the US in the 1950s to escape the Shah. Like them, he worked hard to become a doctor, like them, he wasn't going to let anyone tell him how to practice medicine whether it was members of the Peacock dynasty, SAVAK thugs, mullahs and their thought police, or here in America, the followers of the Army of God. I don't know his name, the man who pulled the trigger—but I will find him—the *cowardly bastard* who killed my father with a sniper rifle.

At the Planned Parenthood clinic where my father worked, the staff was taught to identify suspicious phone calls, screen people who might be posing as patients but were really trying to infiltrate the clinic. Bomb threats were common; demonstrators copied license plates and addresses of staff workers, and, in my father's case, the Army of God posted our home address on their website along with pictures of our family. Mine was from my junior high school yearbook, Sammy in his Cub Scout uniform—how did they get that? My father's was photoshopped in the crosshairs of a rifle scope. The other doctors in the clinic were also targeted. One doctor had her car firebombed; nurses and office workers were followed; they all received phone threats, hate mail; they learned not to answer their phones, removed their mailboxes, and had everything forwarded to post office boxes. The bravest ones stayed on, and no one thought less of anyone who quit. On the Army of God website, my father was accused of murdering six hundred babies. When he was killed, a shadow image of the killer, "A Warrior for the Children" was posted. Still, there was no way to connect the assassin to the Army of God. I knew some of their names—the ones inside prison and the ones who were getting out; those who had threatened or attacked abortion clinics, Planned Parenthood sites; the crazies, the zealots; their lawyers, who worked for free; the clergy who praised them from their pulpits. But I was looking for a name, and the reason I became a cop had nothing to do with Angie Dickinson.

Ernie said, "You become a cop, get to be a detective, and you will have access to criminal databases. You will be able to see FBI and NSA files, and you can check other police department files. You are looking for a name, a person who probably lives in New York State, ex-military, someone who knew how to shoot, maybe even a cop himself, but smart enough to stay clear of the law."

"I'll find him, Ernie. I will."

Once, my boyfriend, Bobby, said, "You are a revenge-seeking bitch of mayhem."

"Apologize," I demanded. "But just for the bitch part; the rest is accurate."

Sammy and I got grief counseling. I don't know how he could have been counseled for anything, much less grief. He fell into a catatonic stupor that lasted three months. When I came into his room, he'd sit upright on the edge of his bed, purse his lips, and stare into my face until I looked away. Sammy would twist his body and fall backward on to the mattress. Lying motionless on the bed, fists clenched at his waist, he'd stare at the ceiling. The meds, mostly benzodiazepines, got him moving again. He returned to middle school, where he was treated with extreme kindness, with the exception of Paul Singer, a bully who liked to whisper in his ear that Sammy's father had been a baby killer who'd deserved to die. Paul's own father was an alcoholic who beat him regularly and taught Paul the virtue of cruelty. The principal of the school intervened aggressively without the need of a threatening lawsuit from my mother. He got Paul into a mentorship program at his church and his father into AA. Paul came to see the error of his ways, and the bullying stopped.

Sammy refused to go to school, even after Paul Singer found religion and his father made amends. Sammy simply said, like Bartleby, that he would *prefer not to*. Mom got him into Jericho Pines, a private mental health facility in the Berkshires. Jericho charged seven thousand dollars a week, with a minimum six-week stay; if my mother's cousin, Dr. James Andrews, hadn't been the director of Jericho, my mother's health insurance hadn't reluctantly paid most of it, and a board of directors hadn't forgiven the balance, Sammy would not have been there with other suicidal teenagers, some of whom had experimented disastrously with Schedule 1 psychedelics, most of them just rich and crazy—pardon my nonmedical terminology.

Sammy began to violate Jericho rules by walking away and occasionally trying to kill himself by overdosing on his meds.

His doctor said, "These are *gestures*, not serious attempts. He just needs time to heal."

Unfortunately, Mom's cousin Dr. Andrews said Jericho couldn't keep him indefinitely, so we had to start thinking about alternatives. There weren't any. That's the thing about murder. You don't just kill one person; you spread death in little ripples like a pebble tossed in a pond.

Of the three of us, Sammy suffered the most; he was the youngest, and we knew his pain would last the longest. It ended when Sammy was eleven, on one of his runaways from Jericho. A woman saw him standing in the road, just below the crest of a hill, but by the time she pulled over, an oncoming cement truck driver, not seeing him until it was too late, had crushed him beneath the wheels of his truck. My mother survived Sammy's death, but not by much. Her heart stopped silently in her sleep, halted by grief and the belief that her love had failed her sweet Sammy.

I am bound to avenge my own losses—my father, my mother, but especially the misery inflicted on my little brother. The one who did this, the *cowardly bastard*, he will die at my hands when I find him.

I used to live in Eaton's Neck, an arthritic finger on the north shore of Long Island. If I leaned over the balcony, I could see Connecticut across the Long Island Sound. Jay Gatsby and I had the same view; his balcony was bigger. The beach below was accessible by negotiating a weathered wood staircase. In the winter, on my days off, I would pry knots of black mussels from the rocks at low tide. The kitchen sink overlooked the water. There was no place for an assassin to hide and shoot me.

I bought the condo with my fiancé, Darren. He bought his half from me after I didn't show up for our wedding. I tried, I really did, but at the last minute I realized I would be marrying a doctor. I couldn't do it; I had already lost one.

Darren was finishing his surgery residency at Northport Veterans Affairs Medical Center. I was just out of the Police Academy. We met cute; he was speeding, I was on training patrol—after he talked his way out of a ticket, he asked if we could have dinner. We each liked the idea of what we each did for a living. He liked that I carried a gun in my purse, and I liked having a doctor around when I wasn't feeling well. The trouble was we had impossible, opposing hours, Darren in his surgery residency and I as a rookie cop in the Long Island City Police Department with an obsession to find the man who killed my father.

Darren knew my tragic history. He was sympathetic, but he owned the soul of a surgeon: Diagnose the problem. If it's a tumor, a torn meniscus, a bum hip, remove it, repair it, and heal.

"Move on," Darren would say.

"From what?" I always replied.

"This idea of revenge." Because Darren, a *reasonable* man, had a proper civilized aversion to revenge—except in movies—*Go Arnold, go Denzel*. He viewed my desire to find and punish the *cowardly bastard* as verging on mental instability. He was right. I am damaged goods. Darren was patient in weathering my depression, my mood swings, my crying, and my rages. I alternately loved/hated him for his *understanding*, his calm, steady bedside manner. He finally diagnosed me: I had post-traumatic stress disorder. He prescribed Zoloft. I told him what I really wanted was a box of hollow-point bullets, but I would try the meds.

"I just don't get the revenge part," he said.

"You don't have to. It's mine. I own it, and I'm keeping it. I appreciate the pills, but they don't make anything go away."

Our dependence became a theme, until the one time when we weren't there for each other. He was mugged at an ATM, and I flushed the Zoloft. Things went downhill from there. In a crazy attempt to repair the relationship, he proposed marriage. Equally crazy, I accepted. Neither of us meant it. So when I didn't show up at the Queens County Clerk's Office on our wedding day, it was merely embarrassing, and not quite unexpected.

We didn't own much together. He took the TV, and I kept the Escher prints. Afterward, we advanced on the board game of life; Darren became a sought-after orthopedic surgeon while I got Detective of the Year twice. I saw his name in *New York Magazine* as one of the best hip replacement doctors in Manhattan. I wonder if he saw my awards in *Newsday*.

At the end of my senior year Wren Ballard, a social worker, drove over from Poughkeepsie and took me to a diner.

"I don't do Starbucks," she said.

Wren was thin and spindly, with a narrow, pinched face, hair in a reddish-blond bun. She walked in an ungainly tiptoe step that resembled her name—a nervous wren pecking at the ground. Later, Wren revealed it was early Parkinson's. She ordered chocolate milkshakes for us and said, "I'm a grief counselor. How can I help?"

"I don't have grief. I have rage," I said. "And I don't want it to go away."

"That's normal, but you will still have to deal with the grief."

We drank our milkshakes and she gave me a referral to Dr. Feldman, who was just out of analytic training at Albany Medical College.

"If you had the person who killed your father in the room and he was tied to a chair, and you could do whatever you wanted to him, what would it be?"

I liked that he started in the middle. But it was an easy question. I had become a student of pain, of torture, of mutilation fantasies. *Here's one, Doc; a favorite of mine. It's seventeenth-century, but way ahead of its time.*

"I would copy the punishment dealt out to the Gunpowder Plot conspirators. They were condemned to be 'put to death halfway between heaven and earth as unworthy of both.' Their genitals were cut off and burned before their eyes, their hearts removed, then the still-beating organs shown to the victims as the last drops of blood spluttered through their veins like a shut-off garden hose. They were decapitated, and the dismembered parts of their bodies hung on poles so that they might become 'prey for the fowls of the air.'"

Dr. Feldman said, "That sounds about right." He gave me a prescription for Ambien. "You'll sleep better but still wake up fucked and angry."

The days after the murder of our father, we were put up in a Holiday Inn in Kingston. We never returned to the house in Grahamsville. Kind local women packed up everything of value, both emotional and useful, and stored it until we found a rental apartment a few miles away in Hurley. We kept the shades down, the curtains drawn, and we tried to be safe. Harry Dill, who used to plow our driveway, came over at night and sat in his pickup.

"Just to maintain a watch," he said.

We really weren't in danger, as an anonymous phone caller told us after we moved in. "You will not be harmed, as your father and husband will no longer commit the murder of innocent babies. Reflect on his evil and find redemption in Jesus Christ Our Lord."

That was kind and considerate. I'll keep it in mind, just before I shoot him.

Ernie doesn't waste time on a telephone call from Maui with *hello, how are you, what's new, how's the weather?* He's on a budget, won't Skype or use FaceTime, and has important information for me.

"Nina, the Feds have a man in detention in Honolulu. He went down on a gun trafficking charge, a serious one, and he wants to make a deal. He'll rat out everybody he can for a lesser sentence, says he has the name of a guy who bought a sniper rifle from him. He called it a *baby saver*. He said this to a US attorney who remembers your father's case."

Baby saver—in the more extreme edges of the anti-abortionist crowd, it's the nickname for a Remington M24 sniper rifle that's accurate to eight hundred meters, twice the distance from the edge of the woods to our kitchen window.

I've seen them in gun shows; they go for about a thousand dollars. For my father, they spared no expense. When I looked back at the death threats sent to him with photoshopped images of him framed in the rifle's telescope sight, I wondered why they had ownership of fear. My parents lived it, and even though they did their best to hide it from their children, Sammy and I lived it, too.

Why did we have to live in fear while the people opposed to us didn't? They marched safely on picket lines in front of women's medical clinics, protected by the police, sometimes by me when I was a rookie cop. It was a duty I relished. I studied the faces of the protestors, listened for clues, random conversations. Would

I hear something about the man who had murdered my father? I wondered why they are allowed to make us live in fear and not experience it themselves? What would it take? A few random killings: a .30-06 from eight hundred meters into the head of a Norman Rockwell grandmother holding a sign showing a fetus in a jar? That might give her life-affirming colleagues pause. Or that same sweet grandmother and her well-meaning husband who cross the country in their well-meaning Winnebago Minnie to picket women's clinics as other retired couples visit minor-league baseball teams or national parks. What if I sent her a letter (no return address) with pictures of her grandchildren, their addresses, the names of their schools, innocent young faces framed in the crosshairs of a *baby saver*'s telescopic sight? Live with that, Grandma and Grandpa. My parents did.

They worried for us, for themselves. It was a part of their lives. It's why they loved the Kapalua Beach Motel. Their children were out of range.

I realize these are the musings of revenge. They spring awake at three in the morning, erasing the Ambien, accompanied by despair and loss. These musings oppose justice, law, and civilization. I know that part of me. I know the desire for revenge is barbaric. It is also the rage of a teenager. I am glad I was sixteen when my father was murdered. If I had been older, more mature, I wouldn't have that obsession; it wouldn't be imprinted in me, made permanent, that desire to avenge him.

Now I am a police officer. My duty is to find and arrest people who break the law. I agree that it is up to the state to dispense justice in every case—except mine.

"Will the Feds make a deal?" I ask Ernie.

"I don't know. I'm going to go to Honolulu and see. But I doubt it."

"Can you squeeze him without a deal?"

"If I could I would dangle him off the roof of the Hyatt to get him to talk, but that's not practical."

"I can fly out in a minute."

"I know you can, honey. Let me see if there's anything to this first."

Out of the blue.

CHAPTER 7

The Steevers house is standard: one-story brick and white wood. It occupies an eighth of an acre of flat suburban land in South Flushing, built after the war for returning GIs. The same contractor did all the houses, so they display no differences aside from the cars in the driveways, and the still-standing Christmas decorations. When the trees are in bloom, the owners may have some privacy, but right now, in these dead days of late winter, the Steevers house and those of their neighbors are exposed like white nuggets on a Monopoly board. If you part your curtains, you will have no secrets.

"Did you find him?" Mrs. Steevers asks.

"Did you find him?" Sammy asks. He speaks to me in the dayroom of Jericho Pines. It is how we begin our conversations.
   "Did you find him?"
   "Not yet, honey, but I will."
   Sammy, reassured, settles back into his chair, and we begin our game of gin rummy. I always deal first.

Sitting across from Mrs. Steevers, I am quiet. I sip the coffee she has given me and look out the picture window at the yellow, muddied lawns dotted with nubs of black snow. Spring is right around the corner. I will deal first.

"The problem is, Mrs. Steevers, Ronald is an adult. We have a protocol regarding missing persons. Children first—the younger they are, the more immediate. You've seen the Amber Alerts. Next, our priority is older people with Alzheimer's or dementia, people who wander off. Adults are at the bottom of the list. I know Ronald was a police officer in Farmingdale. That makes him a brother officer, Mrs. Steevers. We take that kind of disappearance seriously. He goes to the top of the list—mine. Tell me, did Ronald have any enemies? Did he get any threats that might have related to his past work?"

"Ronald only had one enemy. His wife."

She says it with a smile. I realize I am tired of playing amateur shrink, crafty cop, or trickster. I long for the simplicity of pulling someone over and asking politely for their license and registration while my partner runs the plates and signals to me the car is stolen. *Please put your hands on the steering wheel*; my gun is out of its holster behind my back while my partner comes to the other side of the car.

"I think you have to tell me all about Ronald and his wife."

"There's nothing to tell. She's a crazy bitch."

"Look, Mrs. Steevers, your son is missing. He left his car in the garage, he hasn't shown up for work, he hasn't used any of his credit cards or his cell phone. I know these things. I am going to presume something bad happened to him. I don't want you to lose your status of concerned parent and move into the less pleasant one of withholding information that could lead to the apprehension of a criminal. The same goes for your husband, too, if he takes the same attitude."

Mrs. Steevers looks down into her cup.

"Please tell me about his wife."

"She got Ronald fired from Farmingdale."

"How did she do that?"

"They got into an argument, she started hitting him—like I said, she's crazy. He had to defend himself. Then she went to the cops, said he beat her up."

"The next time?"

Mrs. Steevers looks at me as if I know more than she thinks. I don't. I am just guessing.

"They believed her, but she was just setting him up."

"They stayed together, correct?"

"Yes."

"Why?"

"I asked him many times. You know what he said?"

I knew the answer. *Because I love her.*

CHAPTER 8

At the station, there is a crisis. A young woman was discovered in her car on Twenty-Fourth Road, off Queens Boulevard, stabbed to death. All the detectives in homicide are assembled in a conference room waiting for Lieutenant Hagen to bring us up to speed and assign people to the case. The victim is Anita Cavastani, a thirty-two-year-old waitress at Trattoria Amalfi, which, according to Yelp, is a highly rated Italian restaurant in Manhattan. She died in the passenger seat of her own car, a 2006 Toyota, so she must have known her killer—family, husband, boyfriend, girlfriend. Why wasn't she driving? Officer Schwartz handed out photos of the victim for us. We look at them, then pass them to the person to our right, until they all end up back in front of Schwartz, who stacks them into a neat pile. We could have been looking at his vacation pictures of his wife and kids at Disney World, posing with Mickey, his smile sewn into his face, instead of a young woman slumped against the passenger door, her head wedged in the corner between the seat and the window.

Ms. Cavastani must have retreated as far back as she could, but she was still within range of the knife. There are black splotches on a thin leather jacket indicating stab wounds to the body, a flap of flesh dangling open on her cheek that exposes a row of white molars. Her hands and wrists carry red lines as she tried to parry the darting knife. There is a track of the blade against her white throat that must have killed her. The front seat is stained red with her blood. I vow, as I do every time I see human butchery, never to eat animal flesh again.

Lieutenant Hagen appoints me lead detective and tells me

to pick my own team. I will choose Linda Fuentes and Sean Higgins. Detective Higgins is a hardworking guy with a bizarre history. He went to Penn on a full scholarship, majored in mathematics, got a law degree at Columbia, and walked out of his bar exam. He informed his parents that he was only interested in a career of action and adventure. He went to Tokyo, spent a year perfecting his karate at a nasty dojo, returned to the US, and joined the marines. He served two tours in Afghanistan, and then applied to the Secret Service, who turned him down, as did the FBI, the CIA, and the DEA. Unfortunately, his parents had spent five years in the Weather Underground in the '70s, running from some of the same organizations he wanted to join. In terms of security clearance, Higgins was so dead in the water he couldn't get into the Coast Guard. The enlightened Long Island City Police Department gave him a job, and he made detective in a year. If he can ever escape his parents' sins, he might end up chief.

I will also ask Bobby B to look for any background on the victim—Lieutenant Hagen won't know about him, leaving me free to investigate the disappearance of Ronald Steevers and the serial confessor and possible serial murderer Mr. McDermott. And, if I choose, the disappearance of a weatherman's cat.

But none of this is more important than hearing from Ernie Saldana in Maui about a man who bought a "baby saver."

CHAPTER 9

I meet McDermott at Molly Blooms on Queens Boulevard. It's a pleasant Irish bar whose customers, with a few exceptions, think Molly Bloom is the owner. There's a Clancy Brothers cover band on Tuesday nights. Saul Rifkin, the real owner, lets a play-reading group use the basement Sunday nights. Since McDermott has already confessed to murder, I take that as a sign we have bonded. We can skip the small talk. We order drinks: bourbon for him, a Diet Coke for me. My lips do not have to be loosened.

"Mr. McDermott, we have another murder in the neighborhood."

"Can you tell me about it?"

"Only what you read in the papers."

"I don't think we read the same papers."

He's correct. This murder wouldn't be in his *Wall Street Journal*. My *Newsday* would have it all over the front page.

"A young woman was stabbed to death in her own car."

"Doesn't sound like me."

"What does?"

Is this sex talk? How would you murder a young woman, Mr. McDermott? What's your style?

"Can you tell me something about her?"

"She's Caucasian, twenty-three, five one, slim, attractive, teaches ESL at Roosevelt College." There are some lies in there. I hope he will correct me.

"Possible."

"Possible? Can you elaborate?"

"I will say that I have not been sleeping well."

"Is that a consequence of *possible*?"

"Yes. At four in the morning, guilt is like a strong cup of coffee."

"We're all a little guilty," I say. "Are you seeing a psychiatrist now?"

"He told me a story, my psychiatrist. Yes, I am seeing one."

I have a soft spot in my heart for elliptical speakers, but I mustn't fall for this one.

"The story?"

"It is perhaps apocryphal, but it may apply to my condition. This psychiatrist had a friend, a child therapist who had a patient, a ten-year-old boy. The boy had pushed his younger sister out their apartment window. She died. He has no memory of the event. Should he help him to remember or make sure he never does?"

It made me think of the story I would tell in response if this were a normal conversation about a man who is heartbroken over his wife leaving him. He misses her terribly, is miserable, depressed, inconsolable. He goes to a voodoo lady and asks if she can help him. *Of course, I can, darling. Would you like me to make your wife fall in love with you again or would you like me to make you forget her?*

I don't tell him this story, as we are not in friendly conversation; we are not friends. He is what I will call a cooperative suspect. I've never heard of the term, but I like it.

I say, "We will bring you the crime; when it fits it will be yours."

He smiles and lifts his drink to me.

"A deal."

I don't like where I am during this conversation. McDermott is an attractive man, aligned to artistic opportunities in New York that I find interesting. He is familiar with cultural nicknames—MOMA, BAM, the Met, Eataly. Manhattan shortcuts flow out of his conversation like playing cards flipped by a professional dealer. I see myself on his arm, in the third-row seat next to his, reading the playbill before the lights dim. There will be a Tuscan dinner afterward at Orso in the company of handsome men and smart women, some of whom might be the actors in the play we saw. That's just him trying to show me an interesting, innocent, *yes, I'll have the tiramisu* good time. It occurs to me I'd rather someone tried to rob Molly Bloom's, armed, if possible, so I could shoot the dude and change the topic of conversation. I always want to change the topic of conversation. I also want out of this meeting.

"You have my number, Mr. McDermott. Call me when you have something real to tell me. I have to go back to work."

Change the topic of conversation? Okay:

Bobby B: Like a young Denzel Washington but better looking. Taller? Blacker? The sinewy muscles of a wide receiver that harden to the touch like his beautiful cock? That part I learned later. Bobby B, who had to wear boy's belts, his waist was that narrow. When he took a seat next to me in the Long Island City Police Academy auditorium, I lost my breath. This man is so amazingly beautiful all I wanted to do for the first thirty seconds was not be engaged to my doctor. When I calmed down, he whispered, "I would love it if you would lend me a pencil."

Which could also be taken as *I love you; please lend me a pencil.* I was back in the seventh grade, sitting next to Neil Smith, trying not to look at him when he said the same words. I gave Neil the pencil and ended up doing his homework for the rest of the year. Was this police cadet named Robert Booth—it said on his badge—another Neil Smith? I hoped so. He had the looks, but unlike Neil, I found out he also had the brains. What he didn't have was a real desire to be an upright citizen. He was more into the other side. Bobby chose to be a criminal.

Or, in his own version: "When I graduated from high school, I was looking at job offers from my parents. They could place me in one of their kiosks in the JFK terminal and I could sell smartphone covers—fuck that. I had a buddy who owned an ad hoc banking institution. He had an opening for a credit counselor, aka loan shark. I told him I was considering law enforcement. He thought it would be an excellent career move as there was a lot of money to be made as a corrupt cop. They could use me to our mutual advantage."

This conversation took place shortly before he washed out of the academy, as Bobby suspected he would.

"I don't know what made me think this would be a viable career for me. Was I rebelling against my parents? I knew I could either be a cop or a crook, but I couldn't be a crooked cop."

Later, in the wake of the 2008 economic collapse, he defended his profession.

"Banks won't lend any of the money the government gave them as bailouts, so I'm just filling in the gap. My interest rate is slightly higher than payday loans, and we don't break people's legs anymore if they can't pay it back. We work with them. I do credit checks—not the kind you get for free on the Internet but the ones I get asking around the neighborhood. I'm also a job creator. I loaned some money to Adela Nubelo so she could buy a sewing machine and do piecework at home. She makes some money; she pays me off, then borrows enough for another one and hires one of her friends. With the profit from the two machines, she buys another one, and another, and soon she has a shop of women doing piecework for *bubkes*, so they have to come to me for loans. I'm a real job creator."

Bobby and I stayed in touch through my graduation, rookie year, broken engagement, and promotion to detective three years later, which we celebrated with sex and a lovely dinner in a suite at the Carlyle Hotel.

"We should do this more often," he said.

I disagreed. "It would ruin everything. I would have Internal Affairs on my ass, you eat too fast for me, I'm a country girl, and you're from Queens." Neither of us had any idea what that meant, but it silenced us until the next course.

We don't live together, but we share keys and stash enough clothes and toilet articles at each other's apartments to make it feel like we do. We say, *Your place or mine?* and sometimes I come home and find Bobby on the couch reading one of my books at his usual breakneck speed. Or one of his own for his bizarre book club whose members float on the fringes of criminality: a marijuana delivery kingpin, a disbarred lawyer, a retired bank robber, an ex–call girl who sells high-end real estate, and Bobby's bookmaker. The book group is led by a Hofstra English professor who is working off his debt to Bobby. The members refuse to read anything having to do with crime, as the arguments regarding veracity take up too much time. At the moment they are reading Salman Rushdie's *Midnight's Children*.

After dinner, Bobby and I play chess or watch movies Bobby downloads from the Criterion Collection. He is partial to French New Wave: Truffaut, Godard, and Melville. I know he sometimes imagines himself a Queens version of *Bob le Flambeur*. I prefer gentle comedies: Wes Anderson to lift me out of my darker moments, or anything with Will Ferrell or Reese Witherspoon.

In bed, I hold on to him, before, during, and after we make love. Aside from tender sex, letting me cry when I tell my sad story, and eating pizza in bed, Bobby also occasionally informs for me. Not that he would rat anyone outright, or by name, but if there is a crime he could help me with, he points me in the right direction—without naming names. If he said, *Check out the Rainbow Lounge in Kew Gardens*, it meant it was where a suspect liked to drink and I could make an arrest. The fact that Bobby was a loan shark meant I had to look the other way in exchange for information. That applies to all informants, whether one is sleeping with them or not. It is the essence of detective work. Bobby was also part of a small circle of people who knew I was looking for my father's killer, people who kept their eyes out for any information that might lead me to the *cowardly bastard*.

Bobby once suggested I go underground and into the anti-abortion movement, join the Army of God and find the *cowardly bastard*. I thought about it, but I wouldn't get any further in the movement than marching in a demonstration in front of a Planned Parenthood clinic. They have their own intelligence, too. I would be asked to leave, politely at first, and then less so.

After my drink with Mr. McDermott, I text Bobby that I'm coming over to his condo in Rego Park. We eat the pizzas he ordered. Mine is always a margherita with anchovies, his a sausage with goat cheese. I tell him about my cases. He says I should be careful about Mr. McDermott, the forgetful but self-confessing murderer.

"Don't get involved with amateurs. This guy sounds like one. Digs you, or is a cop freak, loves to hang out with the police. Ditch him fast. Ronald and Susan are interesting. I would say she killed him, but what do I know? The TV weatherman's lost cat might be your best bet."

"Who killed the woman in the car?" I ask.

"It's a confession crime. Give it a couple of days; the killer will show up."

We brush pizza crumbs off the sheets and rub our feet together under the blanket. Sex is on the horizon, but I need something else first; it comes out like this:

"Bobby?"

His hand is on my calf.

"Tell me what you like about me."

"Do I have to?"

"Yes."

"It's a matter of *even though*s. I like your laugh *even though* there's not a lot of stuff in your life that's funny."

His hand is on my knee, then behind it. Why does it feel like a hot massage stone?

"I like the way you smell *even though* you don't use perfume, deodorant, or scented shampoo."

His hand is on the top of my thigh; his fingers dance.

"I like your body, and there isn't any *even though*."

His other hand is under my T-shirt.

"I can't get enough of the sides of your breasts"—he is caressing my nipple—"or the soft lower spot just below your belly button on the way to your sweet well. Enough?"

"More. I'm enjoying this."

"*Even though* you have a funny little bump on the end of your nose, it makes you interestingly beautiful, not just plain beautiful."

"That's all?"

"No."

His hands retreat from my body, and he sits up. He locks his forehead against mine. It feels as sweet as his soft knuckle on my clit.

"One more thing I like," he says. "Your desire for revenge. It's primal, strong. I am attracted to it. Clint, Bruce, Liam *don't fuck with my family* Neeson, these are our heroes. You do bad shit to them, they don't call the cops, they don't sue—they come after you. We cheer the bad guys getting it in the chest with the .357, tossed off a building, shot sitting on the toilet. We feel better. Then society tells us it's wrong, we can't be vigilantes. You're supposed to say, *I will let justice take its course.* You don't. So that's another thing I like about you. *Even though* it's all the way to hell."

I take off my T-shirt and pull him to me.

The next morning, I wake up. Bobby is gone, the side of the bed where he slept restored to smooth, the duvet flattened, the pillows stacked and fluffed. It's as if he were never there. How does he make his exit so silently? Did I get a farewell kiss? Does our sex put me into such a deep sleep I don't witness his departure the next morning? I carry his smell and sweat to his shower. I make them disappear, like him.

Outside, it is a lousy March morning in Long Island City. I'm driving cold, waiting for the heater to kick in. I pass Hunts Point Produce Market, where workers are loading boxes of food on trucks bound for Manhattan supermarkets. They are dressed in wool caps, thick gloves, and bulky jackets. For a moment, I envy them; their lives seem so much less complicated than mine. They don't have to deal with a young woman knifed to death in her car. I recognize the cop mentality I swore I wouldn't own: I see the underbelly of life, I work in the sewer, I see the worst of people, and so on, it's just cop talk. Maybe one of the workers is related to the woman knifed in her car; the ever-expanding ripples of murder. Cops just see the stone hit the water first. We are all in this world together. As the men warm themselves around a steel-drum fire, they carry the burden of wayward teens, unpaid bills, health problems, elderly parents, addictions, and the pain of exile. I open the window and let the freezing air empty my mind.

I hear a *bing* from my purse. It's a text from Mrs. Steevers telling me she wants to share some new information about her daughter-in-law Susan. Fine, I like to share. It is followed by two more. One from Artie Crews, who still wants me to search for his son's cat; the other from Lieutenant Hagen: Found Ronald. Pick me up at the station.

Sorry, Artie. Your son's cat will have to wait.

CHAPTER 10

Lieutenant Hagen is waiting for me. I lean over and open the passenger door for her.

"Thanks," she says. "I'd rather you drive."

I will skip the details we've seen a hundred times on TV. Yellow plastic tapes, news trucks, forensics technicians in white jumpsuits, uniformed cops directing traffic, detectives standing around, freezing their asses off.

Ronald Steevers met his end in a deserted warehouse near the exit of the Queensboro Bridge. Al Zitowitz, the night watchman, accompanied by his German shepherd, made daily sweeps of the property to rouse, as gently as possible, the few homeless people who had worked their way inside, looking for a warm place to live. Al, a former homeless Vietnam veteran himself, carried cards with the names of shelters and churches in the area. As he escorted people out of the building, he gave them MetroCards and directions. In exchange, they told Al how they got inside, he would then report the broken window, jimmied door, or hole in a wall to a group of enlightened trust-fund kids who bought the building with the intent of developing it into an arts complex. They wanted the homeless out for risks of fire while they debated various solutions to the contradiction of creating a space for artists while evicting the poor and dispossessed. The window or door would be repaired, and a few days later Al would repeat the process. This time, as he was leaving, one of the men told Al he should check the basement near the furnace. Al discovered Ronald Steevers, standing erect, his body duct-taped to a handcart that had transported him to his final destination.

"You own this one," Lieutenant Hagen says. Translated, it means that aside from solving the homicide it is also my responsibility to visit Ronald's parents to tell them their son is dead. Whatever Ronald's sins and shortcomings, his errors, his arrogance, even beating his wife, none of it added up to a reason to wrench two parents out of their comfortable lives into the horror and endless sadness of a child lost, grown or not. I would have to tell them this. It is the part of my job I never learned how to do. Then, after I have informed the parents of the death of their son, we will try to find out who killed him.

My colleagues are thorough, but not in a hurry to find a murderer. This deed is, according to preliminary opinions from the professionals in the white jumpsuits, the work of an extremely careful person(s). There is no murder weapon, no shell casing, and the bullet that went into the back of his brain just above the cerebral cortex was dug out with a scalpel. We are left with Ronald as he exited the world. The only possible clues might be that the person(s) who did it knew how to use a scalpel (a surgeon?), or where the duct tape was purchased and by whom (impossible), and to make matters worse, there are no witnesses, no swatches of clothing to dangle over the noses of bloodhounds to course over the plains of Queens. Then again, the Long Island City Police Department doesn't have bloodhounds.

Ronald's death was carefully planned and executed—forgive the pun. The killer is unlikely to commit another. On our side, it is clear the murder was personal. Ronald pissed someone off. Revenge. I'm into that. But first, his parents must be informed. It is their right. It will be their misery.

I pull up in front of the Steevers house. Mrs. Steevers is waiting for me on the sidewalk.

"Well?"

"Can we go inside?" I say, getting out of the car.

"No. Right here. Right now."

Mr. Steevers comes out of the front door and watches us.

"You tell me. I'll tell my husband," she says.

"Ronald is dead, Mrs. Steevers."

Mrs. Steevers turns around to face her husband.

"See? I was right."

Later, sitting at the Steeverses' kitchen table, before I can say how *sorry I am for your loss*, or ask if Ronald had any enemies, or if Ronald ever discussed being threatened by anyone, Mrs. Steevers says, "That evil bitch killed him."

It is possible I may agree with her, for sometimes, when *evil bitch* wives who have been slapped, punched, thrown down flights of stairs while hearing their children scream in panic (if it's the first time they've seen Daddy beat on Mommy) or watch in sullen silence, yes, sometimes those *evil bitches* do kill their husbands. It is, in my experience, very rare. I will admit in my own *evilest bitch* moment the husband may have had it coming.

"Tell me why you think so, Mrs. Steevers."

"Ronald was afraid of her. Said she was crazy, said she was violent."

"He feared for his life," Mr. Steevers added, swallowing his third shot of vodka, which is no comfort to the numbness that comes and goes in waves until he must retreat to their bathroom and throw up.

"She poured boiling water on him while he was asleep," Mrs. Steevers says.

I take out my notebook. For the moment, we are done with grief. "Ronald told you this?"

"He showed us his arms. They were all red from where she did it."

"When was this?"

"Back when he was working at Farmingdale. Two years ago."

"Did he report this? Did he file charges?" I know this is specious—cops usually don't call cops—but I'm interested in Mrs. Steevers's answer.

"No. He said it wouldn't look good on his record. He was thinking of quitting Farmingdale, getting a job closer to the city."

Not close to interesting.

"So he quit Farmingdale?"

"Yes."

"Home Depot was just temporary?"

"He was waiting to hear from the NYPD," said Mr. Steevers, sitting down. There are wet spots on his shirt from his cold face rinse. We all look at one another. I want to leave, but I have to ask more questions.

"As much as you can tell me about Ronald's wife, anything that will help me find her."

"Try Alaska," Mr. Steevers says. "She's from there."

I know this. Her lousy lover Brian Robbins at Sunny Gardens told me. "Does she have any family here? Do you know of any friends?"

Mrs. Steevers is shaking her head. I wait for more information. She gets up and puts her arms around her husband. It is a signal for me to leave.

"You've helped me a lot. We'll start looking for Susan. I might have some more questions. They can wait."

I walk down the path to my car, knowing I have left behind sadness and despair. In a way, I was just a diversion, a distraction; now that I am gone, the Steeverses will be left alone with their loss. I have to find Susan, find out if she killed Ronald, and if she didn't, then find out who did and go back to the Steeverses, give them . . . what? Justice? I'm looking for some myself.

I know a Punjab Indian restaurant in Jackson Heights on the way back to Long Island City. There is no way to eat Indian food and drive a car. When I eat Punjab, I want the side dishes spread out in front of me, moist garlicky naan, snow-white rice, flecks of green with cucumber floating in a choppy sea of *tomasalat*, a golden *dhal* to go with the chicken tandoori. As I am led to a table, I check my cell phone. I have three unimportant texts, five ignorable emails, and a request from Nancy Pelosi to send money.

I bury the phone in my purse. I give the waiter my order and wonder what is causing me to drift back to memories of Grahamsville and how my mother came to conduct the Rondout Valley Adult Education Orchestra. What is the point of this memory?

In the 1950s, in order to modernize their water supply, New York City built a series of dams and reservoirs in the Catskills. One of the rivers they needed to dam was on Grahamsville land. Our civic leaders drove a hard bargain. New York paid a huge sum for the water rights, and Grahamsville went from Podunk to Athens. Our enlightened mayor and town council turned the elementary schoolhouse into a museum of arts and crafts, tore down the high school, and built a new central school with science labs, a well-stocked library, athletic fields, and a gymnasium with an indoor swimming pool. There were music lessons with new instruments, free lunch, and for the parents, a continuing adult education program with courses in everything from *The Fall of Communism* to *What's New in Fertilizers*. There, in the middle of the Catskill mountains, in an agricultural community, was an academy—hardly Platonic, but every child received an education taught by carefully selected teachers that would get them into a New York state college—and, for my mother, a community orchestra.

When my father closed his medical office and began commuting to Albany, my mother was freed from her role as my father's nurse/assistant. A few credits short of an MA degree from New Paltz in music education, she applied for a position at the new central school. She was hired with the understanding that she commute to New Paltz and complete her degree. We would have to cook our own dinners, she would need time to study, write her master's thesis, and practice her cello for a required recital.

"I would like a vote taken, please. It can be a secret ballot," she said.

"Will we still have pie?" Sammy asked.

"Bought."

"I vote no," Sammy said.

I offered to learn how to make my mother's apple pie, and Sammy changed his vote to yes. She got her degree and taught string instruments to the children of dairy farmers. One night a week, she conducted the Rondout Valley Adult Education Orchestra. At the first meeting, she told her adult players they would play a Mozart symphony for their first concert, six months away. Vern Farquhar, who played his fiddle on his knees, asked how that would be possible. "We're mostly beginners."

My mother said, "We will learn it one note at a time."

At the memorial service for my father, the orchestra played Samuel Barber's *Adagio for Strings*. They had learned it one note at a time.

I hear the notes in my head, the steady sadness of the chords, and tears flow; I can see the waiter is concerned as he arranges the shiny tin bowls in front of me. I smile and dab my eyes with my napkin. I am back in the present. I will seek justice for the Steeverses. For them, it will be an arrest, a trial, a conviction, and a prison sentence. For my father, my way will be quicker.

CHAPTER 11

After three rings on his Sunny Gardens Apartments doorbell, Brian opens the door. The odor of burned marijuana mixed with a hasty burst of Febreze wafts out of his apartment. Brian doesn't ask me in.

"Brian, I need to find Susan."

"Have you tried her doorbell?"

Is he being a wiseass or just stoned?

"Sorry?"

"She's home. I saw her just a while ago," he says.

Brian gives me a frozen smile to show it's information, but coming from him it's also just a bit wiseass.

"Anything else?" he adds unwisely.

"Say thank you," I say.

"For what?"

"That I don't haul your ass back to the station with all your weed."

"Thank you."

I remember Susan's apartment is 216, the corner unit above the Indian family. I see a window curtain part. The woman is watching me. There are no secrets in Sunny Gardens Apartments. I ring the doorbell. A woman opens the door to the length of the chain. I show her my police ID.

"May I come in, Susan?"

She opens the door, so she must be Susan. I photograph her mentally, consider adjectives I might use later to describe her in my detective's log: *wispy, slender, fragile, flowery, lithe*. One thing is clear. I seriously doubt this *petite* woman standing at the door could overpower six-foot-two Ronald, shoot him, tie his body to a handcart, and move it to a deserted factory in Queens—unless she had help.

As Susan shuts the door, her hand goes to her mouth just a moment too late to hide the gap in the row of her bottom front teeth. There are the faintest bruise marks on her cheeks and around her eyes. I assume they are the marks of her marriage to Ronald. A halo of Orphan Annie–orange hair frames her face. She has a '60s Woodstock look. Should I also consider *cute, vulnerable, optimistic, folkie green vegan?* What does she listen to? Aimee Mann? Edie Brickell? None of this will appear in my detective's log. I will simply write: *Susan Steevers, female Caucasian, age thirties, height five two, weight 110 lbs. (estimated).*

"I know about Ronald," she says. "If that's why you're here."

I am relieved that I don't have to give her bad news, but I continue with the detective response. I know it by heart. My words are as scripted as the ones on the wall of a Calcutta call center.

"I'm sorry about your husband."

Susan doesn't look like a grieving widow, or any kind of widow at all.

The apartment is in better shape than when Brian first showed it to me. The kitchen is spotless, and the ants are gone. I peer into the bedroom through an open door. Bed made, floor waxed to shiny. It doesn't look abandoned; there is a feeling of optimism. I'd like to look in the closet.

Is Susan thinking now that Ronald's gone life can be lived in the way she likes? She doesn't have to argue with him about anything. It's understandable, so why does it piss me off? She doesn't look bereaved; she doesn't look like someone who lost a husband. She doesn't look like my mother. She looks like a woman whose neurotic roommate finally left. "How did you find out?"

"I saw it on television."

Susan goes to the window. A driver of a car squishing the wet concrete on Utopia Parkway might look up and catch a glimpse of a woman in a window caught between mourning and relief.

"I'd like to ask you a few questions."

She doesn't answer. She may be thinking that this is the part where she can tell me she wants to talk to a lawyer.

"I'm allowed," I say.

"Okay."

"We think Ronald was killed on the night of the twenty-fourth—that's two days ago, Tuesday afternoon or night. Can you tell me where you were?"

"At friends. I was with friends."

"Okay." I take out my notebook. "Please tell me the names of these friends." She is silent. I think she is reflecting about the answer to this question, which I suspect she has rehearsed. *You will be asked for names.*

"I can't."

I'll wait this one out. It doesn't take long.

"I would be betraying their trust."

"Mrs. Steevers, you know I am investigating the murder of your husband, Ronald."

"Yes."

"You know what an alibi is."

"Of course."

"I just want to be clear about this. Your husband was murdered. You could be considered a suspect. You are telling me you have an alibi, and you won't provide any information to confirm it. Correct?"

"Yes."

We look at each other. I decide to be Socratic.

"What conclusion should I draw?"

"Whatever you want."

"Susan, I can put you in handcuffs, take you to the Long Island City police station, where you will be booked, photographed, your fingerprints taken, your name released to the media, who will make you famous or notorious. You will embark on the long, expensive process of arriving at some kind of truth. And, believe me, not in a way you will enjoy."

Silence.

"Do you want to change your mind?"

"No."

I go to plan B.

"Look, I don't think you killed Ronald, but murder is number one on our list. Since Ronald was a policeman, solving his murder is a priority and outweighs whatever your reason for not 'violating someone's trust,' as you put it. At some point you will have to divulge that information. Unless your friends are involved in a serious criminal enterprise, we can make a promise to be discreet, use any information that clears you, and go after the real killer."

I am lying my ass off.

"Understand? I only want to find out who killed Ronald, that's all. So think about it."

I give her my card and leave.

CHAPTER 12

Driving to the police station, I try to imagine Susan's next move. On a hunch, I turn around and park across the street from Sunny Gardens Apartments. I turn on the radio and listen to sports talk until Susan drives Ronald's Mustang out of the underground parking garage. I pull out behind her, call in my location for anyone in an unmarked car to follow if I lose her. Detective Higgins answers.

"A minute, okay?"

"Sean?"

"Sorry, I had Linda on the other line."

"Are you busy, Sean? I need help on a tail."

"I'm staring at a potential drug deal."

"This is better, believe me."

I know he's bored out of his mind and relieved to be called away from a stakeout that could last for days.

"I'm going west, on Fifty-Seventh Avenue, toward Queens Boulevard." I hear his car start.

"I'm on my way. What am I looking for?"

"A pristine red Mustang convertible—you can't miss it."

"Pristine? Damn, Karim, no wonder nobody can stand you."

"Okay. Look for me in the crap Nissan."

"That's better."

"Sean, I'm heading into the Queens Center mall. The party is white female, red curly hair, thirties, short and thin. I think she's meeting someone. Try the food court."

"See you there."

Susan gets lucky and finds the only parking spot on level three.

There are no spaces for me until I get to the roof. I sprint down the stairs, hoping her elevator is slow. It is. I see her come out of the elevator, follow her to the food court, a collection of fast-food franchises. If I were hungry, it would be a toss-up between Mongolian Madness, Tacos El Torero, and Nellie's Neapolitan. Susan buys a coffee and a Cinnabon, takes a seat at a table, then does what every human being does when their butt hits plastic: she takes out her phone. I find an empty table behind hers. A few moments later, Higgins comes in from the opposite side. He sees me; I nod in Susan's direction. He buys a slice and a Diet Coke from Nellie's Neapolitan, finds a table near enough to Susan so he can overhear a conversation if there is one.

Ah, what the hell. At Mongolian Madness kitchen, a Hispanic chef in a Genghis Khan hat swirls noodles and vegetables on an iron grill the size of a manhole cover. Two minutes later, he hands me a Styrofoam box with the weight of pure lead. I look back into the food court. Susan and Detective Higgins are gone. There are no texts on my phone. I don't worry. Higgins is following her. I stop for extra napkins and notice a short, stocky woman in a vintage Tenacious Dames motorcycle club vest, with a one-percenter badge (it's not an economic statement. Faced with bad press because of criminal motorcycle gangs, the American Motorcyclist Association declared that only *one percent* of motorcycle riders are outlaws). She is, therefore, announcing that she might be *outlaw*. But badges are cheap, so she could also be a social worker on her day off. We'll see.

We enter an elevator together along with a mother-and-daughter shopping team. Mom rests her bulging Gap bag on the floor. Daughter is wearing a new shoulder purse and clutches a plastic Zara bag to her chest. Ms. One-Percenter Tenacious Dame is inscrutable behind her pink Choppers. We all make one another uncomfortable, no small talk, holding our individual breaths until we reach our floor. Tenacious Dame checks her phone, raises it, and takes a selfie. Or not. Could have been a picture of me. I won't know. The elevator door opens; we all exit. The doors close.

CHAPTER 13

My call to Higgins goes to voice mail. The smell of the Mongolian noodles on the passenger seat is making me nauseous; I need a coffee. On my way out of a McDonald's drive-through, I throw the noodles into the garbage. I pour out an inch of coffee so I don't scald myself and pull into traffic just as my phone rings. It's Higgins.

"We had a nice chat," he says. "Susan's from Alaska."

"I asked you to follow her, not get to know her."

"She needed help on buying a game for her nephew. Should it be *Grand Theft Auto V* or *Minecraft*? One thing led to another. I have her number."

"So do I. Big deal."

"And I met her lunch date."

"You get a name?"

"No. But she's in the picture I'm sending you. Am I done?"

"I'd like to know where she goes next."

"Okay. I'll give them another half hour, but then I have to resume the war on drugs."

"I'll be at the exit of the mall. Just let me know when they leave and I'll continue the tail."

"Fair enough."

I drink my coffee and wait for Higgins's call. So far, Susan is a person who will not account for her whereabouts on the evening her husband was murdered and shows little remorse. She is becoming more and more interesting. I get a text from Higgins with a picture of Susan and her lunch date, a woman in a wheelchair. Sunglasses, a knit cap, a Hermès neck-hiding scarf, and not enough skin showing for any kind of facial recognition software. A few minutes later, the red Mustang emerges, and I follow Susan back to her apartment in Sunnyside Gardens.

A waste of time. Police work.

At my desk, I enter an account of this into my detective's log, starting with my visit to Susan and her refusal to provide an alibi for the night Ronald was murdered. I call Dave Liebowitz, my favorite district attorney, and explain the situation to him. If he wants me to arrest her, I'll do it, but we don't have anything on her except her refusal to divulge her whereabouts. Those situations can be embarrassing for a suspect when she does decide to tell. No one wants the Long Island City version of the country song about a guy who gets hanged for murder rather than say he was in the arms of his best friend's wife. Liebowitz says not to arrest her, just keep the pressure on. Since I didn't arrest her, my fear credibility is compromised. Detective Tessa Harper would be useful. She isn't physically imposing, but she has the face and temperament of your worst high school teacher. Susan is used to physical punishment. She learned about it from her loving husband, Ronald. Frightening for Susan needs to be psychological, and Tessa knows how to do it.

I send another email to Lieutenant Hagen, suggesting Tessa question Susan. There is a text from Ernie: The guy in Hawaii is ready to talk. Come.

Easier said than done. My first reaction is to tell Ernie that I want more information before I get on a plane and fly five thousand miles to Honolulu. Wait a minute. Is this me, suddenly less desperate to find out who killed my father? Is my hate diminishing, the revenge fantasies fading? *Have I gotten on with my life?*

I close my eyes and picture my father. A moving image comes. First the smell of his Old Spice cologne, then the feel of his rough tweed jacket. His face doesn't come. It will. I need to experience him first. He lifts me up and snuggles me to his hip and carries me. I am warm and loved, and I look up and see him now, every pore of his dark skin, steady eyes behind tortoiseshell glasses, he coos, *Baby, baby*, and that's all it takes for my rage to return. My mind camera pans over to Sammy, his wet tears, my mother's slow decline, and it doesn't take long for the physical sensation of hatred to return. My temples throb, my fists clench, my eyes tear. Fuck Ronald. Fuck Susan. I click on to my Orbitz page and make a reservation for Honolulu. I text Lieutenant Hagen that I need three days for a family matter. I'm technically off duty for two days anyway. She gives me the third. That's better.

I'm alive.

CHAPTER 14

Artemis Shelter for Women

I wake up in pain; my body is sore in places where I wasn't hit. How does that happen? My feet hurt, my ankles are weak, my back is in knots, when I take a breath my ribs protest, I have a headache. I open my eyes. *Ow, ow, ow.* Why does opening my eyes hurt? I'm on a couch. I wriggle out of a sleeping bag, sit up facing a window. I see morning light outside, catch a glimpse of barren tree branches sneaking under intersecting power lines. Two pigeons balance on a wire arguing their next move over the sounds of buses, horns, and a distant siren. I'm in a living room, comfortable and anarchic—it can't reflect any one person's taste. There is another couch, smaller, facing mine, chairs of all styles, old lamps, modern lamps, Ikea meets thrift shop, a Warhol Campbell's Soup reproduction next to a poster of dogs playing poker. It all lives in peace somehow, side by side. I don't care.

An angel comes into focus before me—or is it Botticelli's Venus's daughter? Whoever she is, she seems to be about ten or twelve years old with a bouquet of braids and cornrows, olive skin, oval blue eyes; the miraculous offspring of an Asian and Nordic coupling. She holds a glass of water and two Tylenols in her palm.

"What's your name?"

I take the pills. My fingers hurt. The pills go down. *Act quickly, please.*

"I'm Lucy," I say.

"You look like shit."

So much for an angel.

"I guess I do."

"Who did it?"

"A man. More water, please." I hear a woman say, "Bye, sweetheart," and a door shutting.

"That was Gerri. She's allowed to go outside."

A floppy dog sneaks under the girl's arm and lays its head on my lap. A giant Labrador combined with something else—I don't know. It must weigh more than me. I'm too tired to lift its head out of my crotch.

"Does he bite?"

"*She*. Bobo. But only if you say the secret word. She's our guard dog."

Bobo nuzzles me, begging for an ear scratch or a nose rub. She doesn't look like she could guard anything. This dog is only looking for love. It's also drooling on my jeans.

"What's your name?"

"Amanda. Can't tell you my last name. But I have a different one at my school, St. Anne's. It's Catholic. If I make friends, I can't go to their homes or invite them to mine. Ha. Like I have one. But it's better than staying at the shelter all day and being homeschooled."

The woman who let me in last night comes into the room.

"School, Amanda. Run along."

"Her name is Lucy. I'm in the sixth grade," she adds.

Amanda skips out of the room. Bobo wriggles free from my lap and pads off after her. The woman pulls a chair to the couch. She leans in close to my face. I feel caked blood around my nose.

"I'm Phyllis."

"Yes, thank you for taking me in."

"Why didn't you go to an emergency room?"

It is a logical question. I get up, limp to the window. I stare out at the street.

"Did you call the police?"

I turn back to her. "My husband's a cop."

"Did he do this?"

"Yes."

"Children?"

I ignore the question. She doesn't press me.

"Is he looking for you?"

"Probably."

Phyllis thinks for a moment. "He can't know you are here. It puts us all in danger."

"I'll be careful. But I can't go back. He'll kill me. I know he will."

"I have to ask you for your cell phone. If you need to make calls, you use mine. It's encrypted. Use yours, you can give away your location."

I hand her my cell phone.

"We'll have a doctor check you out. You'll want to wash the blood off. There's a bathroom over there. Coffee's in the kitchen." She gives me a clipboard. "And fill this out."

"He drives a blue Camaro, if you see it."

She nods. "You're safe here, Lucy."

I sit back down on the couch. The clipboard holds a welcoming statement, five pages of questions, and a list of rules. I learn I will get breakfast and dinner. I am asked to sign a statement that I will not reveal the location of the shelter. If I came by car, I will have to disable its GPS. I will submit to a drug test, take no photographs, not smoke in the house, *blah blah blah*, until my mind fogs.

But I'm in.

And I like Amanda.

CHAPTER 15

I step out of the airplane in Honolulu, thank the pilot for getting me there safely. It's a short, steamy walk to the curb where Ernie is waiting, leaning against his rented car.

"I got a Honda for us, honey," he says.

"I like Hondas."

The ride takes six minutes. The federal detention center is across the street from the airport. On the way, Ernie invites me to come back with him to Maui for a few days.

"You look like you could use it."

Do I?

"Tell me about this guy," I say.

"His name is George Candler. He owns a condo behind the Royal Hawaiian. His plan was to retire here when he quit running guns into New York from Georgia and West Virginia. He had two misfortunes: one of his runners got busted; another ratted him out. He'll be extradited to New York, where he will spend his last days in Rikers Island prison hospital because his other bad news is that he has stage-four pancreatic cancer. George will tell us everything. He just wants to die with a view of the ocean."

"You're breaking my heart," I say.

Robin Stella, the US Attorney, meets us in the lobby of the detention center. "I was on your father's case team when I was in the FBI. I met you then; if you don't remember, it's understandable. I know Ernie is still looking for the shooter, so I called him about this."

She takes us up to the dayroom of the prison infirmary. It's a sunlit room, with a worn couch, plastic chairs. Three sickly prisoners in wheelchairs watch a game show on a flat-screen TV. One of them, it must be George, sees us, grabs his drip stand, and backs his wheelchair away from the TV set. George is a tanned, wiry little man, made frail by his cancer. His face is blotted with dark chemo scars. As he talks, he moves his jaw from side to side, searching for lesser pain. Before he found his true calling— buying guns in the South, moving them north—he wholesaled oxy, meth, weed, coke, and the occasional runaway. He was a transporter of misery. Guns turned out to be easier and more profitable. George bought them legally with cash in stores or at gun shows. He owned a clean late-model Chevrolet Malibu, hired an apple-cheeked mom with kids to play in the back seat so they looked like a family, observed speed limits, filled the bottom of the trunk with pistols and automatic weapons for criminals in New York, Philly, Boston, wherever it was difficult or tedious for those criminals to purchase hardware of human destruction. George sold them out of his car after dropping off the "wife and kids."

"In between, I surfed," George said, "I was good enough to earn respect on the North Shore. Pe'ahi, Lanaiakea, the Banzai Pipeline—I was the real thing."

In between selling guns, one of which may have killed my father. I will keep that in mind.

Robin Stella has a look of disgust on her face. Maybe she is also a surfer; the idea of George polluting the Pacific is offensive to her.

She says, "Okay, Mr. Candler, can we give these people the information we discussed?"

George adjusts his chair and faces me.

"It was a Remington M24. I had an ordnance sergeant at Fort Drum who boosted high-end stuff for me on demand—grenades, even rocket launchers, shit you can't get. I already gave up his name. He's in the stockade now. That counts. Am I right, Miss Attorney General?"

Robin nods.

"So, I meet a guy who tells me he wants something special, a sniper rifle, the Remington M24, if possible."

"Where did you meet him?" I say.

"A gun show in Scranton. I tell him the M24 ain't that hard to find, maybe even here at this show. Oh, no, he says, he wants something stolen, so if it got traced it would be plenty of distance from him."

"Who was he?"

"From the Midwest, a tall white guy, probably a vet. He knew what he wanted."

"Did he have a name?"

"Clyde."

"That's it?"

"He didn't write a check. I didn't ask. He said he was gonna save a lot of lives, do the Lord's work with it."

"We showed George some pictures of people of interest in the Ohio area. I brought them," Ms. Stella says.

Ms. Stella opens her briefcase and shows me the pictures of possible suspects.

George wants to be helpful. "I have a bad memory, and it was a long time ago, but these three come close."

I study their faces. I imagine them as children with fathers who loved them, beat them, toughened them, or deserted them. *Now my son James has a tufty chin beard, a shaved head, a closed mouth to hide missing teeth. What's with the face tattoo, Dee? Sig, your Mom wishes you would call.* They are three hardscrabble working-class white guys. They've fixed your car, tarred your roof, broken into your store if your locks were easy. Maybe one of them killed my father. It's a start."

"Who's your favorite, George?" I ask.

George shrugs. His look says, *Kill them all, makes no difference. They are meaningless.* Likely, all three alibied out, and George doesn't give a shit.

"How did the sale go down?" I ask.

"Same as always. We meet. I say where. I usually pick the quiet end of an empty Walmart parking lot. I bring a backup. I open the trunk and show you the guns. You like. You buy, you take it to your car, come back for the ammunition."

"The buyer arrived in a vehicle. What was it?"

"I dunno. Shit Toyota. White."

Robin Stella shakes her head. I am collecting useless information. I look at the mug shot faces. James, Donald, and Sig.

"Clyde. That's the name he gave you?"

"That's what he said."

"Can I have a minute alone with George?" I ask Ms. Stella. She shrugs and leaves the room with Ernie. George is handcuffed to the armrest of his wheelchair. He isn't a threat. I lean in a bit closer. I can speak softly, sympathetically.

"How long do the doctors say you have, George?"

"Five, six months."

I take his hand.

"Is there anything I can do for you? Are you getting enough painkillers?"

George cocks his head to the side, contemplates a sarcastic reply, and changes his mind. He doesn't have the energy. Instead, he sags into a real feeling.

"I got no one. Something, eh? A whole life, nobody." He starts to cry. "You'd think . . . Nah, fuck 'em."

"Kids?"

"My son lives in Boston. He says he can't get away."

"I'm sorry."

"It is what it is."

"George, tell me some more about surfing. Where did you start?"

"I grew up in Ventura, so I started there, moved down to LA. I was a regular in Malibu. In those days, there was a direct line to Oahu. We all knew one another. It was a fraternity. We had our beaches; they had theirs. We hassled kids from the valley when they came to Malibu; they did the same to the haole kids from Kahala. But if we came to Hawaii to surf, they were cool with us, and vice versa. Before long I was bringing back weed to finance the trips."

I laughed. "I like that. Did you hollow out your surfboard?"

"Nah. I never carried anything. I had a girlfriend Alice, looked like a schoolteacher. She was my mule. She went first class, never got searched. Me, I had dogs sniffing my ankles the minute I got off the plane."

I'm not behaving like a cop. I'm a reporter. We are having a conversation. We could be on 60 Minutes.

"That's funny."

"You know what's funny? She really was a schoolteacher. Taught second grade at Horace Mann in Beverly Hills."

"You still in touch?"

George thinks, searches for a memory—or is he thinking I am full of shit?

"In touch? No, we're not in touch."

Yes, you are, asshole. She's your wife. She was your accomplice on your little West Virginia and Georgia gun-buying journeys. Of course I'm full of shit—I'm a smart cop. You don't think I came armed with more information? You wouldn't give her up, but there are enough lovely photos of Mrs. Schoolteacher Candler in her Chevy Malibu taken at various tollbooths on the New Jersey and North Carolina Turnpikes, on the G. P. Coleman Bridge, on the Dulles Greenway, and at a 7-Eleven in Durham. It's not called the surveillance state for nothing, dope.

"Perhaps we can find her for you."

"Don't bother. It was too long ago."

"George, I'm a desperate woman. I'm living with something that causes me a lot of pain. I'm not comparing it to yours, I'm looking to solve it, come to a resolution. You can understand that, right? It's the kind of thing that's hard to live with. I know you have something; you have a key to open a door. You have knowledge that would help me a lot. I know you do."

George is quick to reply. "What are you going to do for me? You got a cure for cancer? I told you what I know."

He turns away in his wheelchair. I am still sweetness and sympathy. I still *care*.

"George, here's what I can do. I can make you comfortable. I can get you into a hospice in Hana. It overlooks the ocean. It's clean, and you can hear the waves. You'll wake up out of your chemo nightmare, hear birds, smell jasmine and pineapple. You will be medicated and leave this earth with a smile on your face dreaming of curls, tunnels, and dolphins as the pain eases out of your body and your soul floats into the ocean. Or you can spend your last days in a damp basement cell at Halawa Correctional. You know it? It makes Rikers Island, where I know you spent some time, look like the Four Seasons in Maui. That's what I can do for you. I am looking for Clyde something. You have to do better than a tall guy with a white Toyota van and no last name."

George swings his jaw into a smile. This will be a minor victory for him. It turns out he is a big fan of *CSI*.

"I have his fingerprints."

Ah.

"I gave him a can of beer. Heineken. It's all I drink. He crushed the can and tossed it. After he left, I picked it up. You want it? It's in the back seat of my car."

That means Clyde's fingerprints and possible DNA on the beer can.

Later, Robin Stella, the US Attorney, says, "We still have the car."

I buy Ernie an oceanfront room at the Royal Hawaiian. Dinner is on me at Alan Wong's.

"We'll get the bastard now," Ernie says.

We both know better, but why spoil the meal with *ifs*. *If* the beer can is in the car, *if* we get prints off the beer can, *if* Clyde has been in the military, used a VA hospital, or been arrested in the last five years. *Then*, we might have a match.

"How long will it take?" I ask.

"A week. That's pretty fast with professional courtesy."

"Fine. You did swell, Ernie."

"Yeah, sure, but you know all those promises you made to George? Like the hospice in Hana. I don't think I have the kind of juice to get him in there."

"Neither do I, Ernie. Fuck him."

I book a late-afternoon flight to New York, which means Waikiki beach time, a long swim, and a farewell lunch with Ernie before he flies back to Maui. I wake up to a gray, lousy day with just enough rain to dampen the sand. I don't care. I grab a towel and my snorkel mask.

The beach is empty except for a few high school kids ditching, smoking weed under a ratty umbrella, and a man with a metal detector scraping the sand for buried treasure. A few surfers bob in the ocean, hoping for bigger waves. Sun or not, I spent good money to get here, so I am not going to let bad weather get in the way. The water is warm; the rain is of no consequence. I wade out until the water is waist high, adjust my goggles, and swim.

In high school, I swam the two- and four-hundred-yard free-style. I held a couple of school records that might still stand. My father drove me to practices and meets. There is no worse sport for a parent. A swim meet can last six hours, and you wait around for your kid to dive in the water and climb out two minutes later. Our team practiced from six to seven every morning. He was proud of me, meticulously keeping track of my times, waiting outside the car, handing me a cup of hot chocolate from a thermos. He liked to look up famous swimmers who had lesser times.

"See, Nina, your one hundred is now faster than Alice Nathan, who won the bronze in Paris in 1946. You are only a few seconds behind the great Johnny Weissmuller."

"Johnny who?"

"You never heard of Johnny Weissmuller? He was Tarzan!"

The memories came fast and delicious; they kept me swimming, head down, breathing through the snorkel tube, a tickling drizzle of rain pinging on my back. I was into the groove now, my arms moving mechanically, the subtle rise and fall of a wave carrying me to the next.

"What do you think of when you swim the long distance,

Nina? Do you go over the day's activities, do you review your French verbs, do you think about what you will have for breakfast?"

"No, Papa, I don't think of anything. I leave my mind on the pool deck."

"I was a wrestler in high school. I had to stay sharp, decide on strategies."

"It's different. When I swim, my mind forgets my body can't go on forever. I could swim forever. When I swim long distance in the pool, I zone out to the point that my mind doesn't take notice of how tired I'm getting. It only reminds me when the bigger markers pop up—like my stroke is getting sloppy or the flips are becoming harder. I could swim and not really know how tired I am until my body finally collapses, and I can't even stay afloat." I swim. I swim.

And then I realize I've reached that point. My arms are close to dead. I stop. I am in a fog bank. I tread water, spin around. I can't see the shore. I am blind. I try to sense a current. I feel one. It moves me. But where? Where is it taking me? Back to Honolulu? Or to China? I don't know, but I will surely drown if I make the wrong decision. The fog can last for hours. I am a fast swimmer, how far have I come? Two miles? Even if I knew the direction, I would barely make it. Who will save me? A kind dolphin, Poseidon with fat cheeks blowing me to shore? It won't be a sunset cruise sailboat, or a fisherman. I am alone. I feel a hand on my waist. My father is treading water next to me.

"Papa."

"That way, Nina."

He turns me, aims me into the current. I am six years old; I can feel his hand on my stomach, he is teaching me to swim. We are in a pool. My father walks beside me, holding me up.

"Just relax, Nina. Let the water hold you, breathe in, blow bubbles out in the water. I have you, I am with you. You are doing so well, darling. You will be a wonderful swimmer."

I can see the spires of the Royal Hawaiian hotel. The sun has come out, and the white beach is dotted with umbrellas. I am on my way home.

CHAPTER 16

It never fails. I click my seat belt and raise my window shade as the plane begins its descent to JFK. I see the thin strip of a deserted Fire Island beach, green waves breaking over what must be frozen sand. Queens will be freezing-ass cold, and I instantly regret my decision to leave Hawaii.

I'm politely turning down whispered limo offers by gypsy drivers when I get a text from Tessa Harper that says she's waiting for me at curbside. Tessa and I get along just fine. Especially since her husband tore up his knee skiing in Vermont and I sent him to my ex-fiancé. Darren did a brilliant partial replacement, gave him his best physical therapist, and kept the bill within their insurance. Tessa wants to tell me about her interview with Susan. A drive back to my apartment would be a good time to do that. I'm ecstatic. I just saved forty dollars.

"Can we turn up the heat, Tess? My body's still in Hawaii."

"Sure. You have a fun trip?"

"Rested and ready." She doesn't need to know about George Candler.

"Where's your tan?"

"In my luggage. Tell me about Susan."

"She didn't kill him. I know you don't think so, either."

"Then where was she the night of the murder?"

"I'll show you."

Five minutes later, we are on Thirty-Second Avenue, in Jackson Heights. Rows of narrow two-story postwar houses with shingle roofs, aluminum siding, various heights of chain-link fence, a car in every driveway, and a chicken in every pot. The neighborhood has had its ups and downs, but the people who bought houses from one another in a succession of ethnic convolutions, from white GIs returning from WWII to black families who sold them to East Indians who sold them to Jamaicans. Where there were once Koreans, there are now Pakistanis. The only people who haven't discovered the neighborhood are millennials, who will arrive later, when they realize they can't afford Brooklyn. There is something about these houses that makes people responsible to them. They are always in fresh paint with tidy front gardens, and satellite dishes on the roof.

"Here," Tessa says, pulling to a stop across the street from 12988, a house that looks just like all the rest except the four CCTV cameras discreetly placed under the eaves of the roof, the iron bars on the front door and windows. I'm willing to bet the windows are one-way and bulletproof. Tessa hands me a pair of binoculars.

I raise the glasses. You can learn a lot about a house from the roof. I notice 12988 and 12990 next to it have identical new air-conditioning units. It is an interesting coincidence. The two houses also have the same doormat. There is a high wall connecting the two properties so there is no view of the yard between them.

"Guess," Tessa says.

I can just make out the top of a swing set rising over the wall between the houses. "It's a day-care center, a foster home, a re-hab, or a women's shelter," I say.

"You got it." Tessa consults her notebook. "I was in domestic violence. I know every women's shelter in Queens, but I never heard of this place. Mrs. Steevers was in residence from December thirtieth to March fifth. That's her alibi for the night her husband was killed. She may know who did it."

"Let's get out of here," I say.

We drive in silence for a few blocks.

"Did you go inside?"

"No. I called Susan and made an appointment to see her. When I got to her apartment, she had a lawyer who showed me a video on her iPad. It was of Susan in the shelter, with plenty of time codes. They have CCTVs up the wazoo, plus a list of people who would swear she was there that night. I asked her where *there* was. That, she said, would require a court order. I left and waited in my car. An hour later, Susan drove out, and I followed her here."

Tessa loves detail; the rest of my questions might as well be over coffee. "There's a Starbucks on the corner. I'm buying." We order lattes and settle into a quiet corner. Tessa takes out her notebook.

"I checked the property records. It's registered under the name Artemis—that's the name of a Greek goddess."

I know this. In Greek mythology, Artemis is the goddess of the hunt, but she is also known as the protector of young women. The latter makes an appropriate name for a women's shelter.

"It opened in 1998 as a residence for women. Fire, health, and safety permits are up-to-date, but here's the weird thing: it could easily qualify for a 501(c)(3) nonprofit status. It means anyone who donates money to it would get a tax deduction. Of course, you would need to have a board of directors, list your donors, and make your tax returns available. It all has to be completely transparent. Artemis isn't a nonprofit."

"What is it?" I ask.

"A corporation. It's a business."

"Who pays for running it? The women?"

"I doubt it. They're running from their husbands. They have kids, nowhere to go. They don't have any money."

"What do you know about the corporation?"

Tessa looks at her notes. "It's registered in Delaware, so lots of luck in getting their tax returns. Corporate tax returns are not public record. All we know is there is a president of the corporation, named Phyllis Berke. She is also listed as the sole employee."

"So either Berke is wealthy, or somebody funded it and keeps it going. Who handles the business? Pays the bills, does the taxes?"

"There's a CPA in Merrick. Her name is Vali Lopez. I talked to her on the phone. She says she doesn't know Ms. Berke, never met her. She does the books, pays the bills. She said if I wanted any information, I would have to come back with a search warrant. Talk about under the radar."

"I get that part," I say. "If I were hiding women whose husbands are looking for them, I wouldn't want a sign out front."

"But we never heard of it." She scrapes the last bit of foam out of her paper cup. "Isn't that strange?"

"Not really. They don't want police to know where they are. Especially if they are sheltering women whose husbands are cops. Like Susan."

"So, what next?" Tessa says.

"Let's go back to Ronald. Assume he was fired for beating Susan when they were in Farmingdale. It was either because they had an enlightened chief of police, or his abuse was too over-the-top."

"I think it's more complicated. By the way, what's your definition of *over-the-top*?" Tessa asks.

"For me, touching any part of my body without permission is over-the-top. Was Ronald going to kill Susan? He may have been getting ready to."

"That's not what was scaring Susan."

"What was?"

"It's in the interview. She's a talker. I only asked a few questions."

She taps the voice recording icon on her phone. I recognize Susan's voice.

"We had a deal—he works days, I work nights, he keeps his car and clothes here, we don't sleep together, we don't eat together, until he finds a place he can afford once he starts working again in law enforcement. If he hits me again, then all bets are off. He has to move out. It was a crazy arrangement, but it was working. Until I made the mistake of saying hello. When did this begin? In group at the shelter, I was asked to create a diary of the past."

"Could you tell me what that looks like?"

"Imagine you wrote it in the present. You start with how you met, how you fell in love, how you decided to get married—you tell the diary about your wedding, your honeymoon, and the first time he hit you."

"When was the first time?"

"In Farmingdale. It was an argument about money. I said he spends too much on his car, his Islanders seats, his bike, his video games; he said I spent too much money on groceries. I showed him the credit card bills; he ripped them up and mashed them into my face. I pushed him away, and the next thing I knew I was on the floor, and I couldn't feel my jaw. I ran into the bathroom, locked the door, and called 911. The police came, but they were friends of Ronald's, and they talked me out of pressing charges. That was the first time."

"And the beatings, did they continue?"

"Yes."

"Did you call the police again?"

"Two more times. But by then he had convinced them that I was the aggressor. He grabbed my hand and scratched his face with it, so that he had the marks. And then he decided that I needed a different punishment when I was bad, and bad was a lot of things."

"What was the punishment?"

"He would throw boiling water at me."

"Ronald's mother said that Susan did that to Ronald," I say. Tessa pauses the recording. "She showed me the burn scars on her back."

Tessa hits play. Susan continues,

"Ronald was trained to be obeyed, to always be in command of a situation; his authority is not to be questioned. He was trained to use force, and he liked using it on the job, so I guess he liked using it at home."

Tessa and I look at each other. We both know she's right. If you are married to a male policeman, your chances of being abused go to 70 percent.

"It turns out I wasn't Ronald's only punching bag. We went to the movies one night and some kids in front of us were pretty rowdy, making noise. Ronald yanked one of them out of his seat and dragged him up the aisle and threw him out of the theater. The kid came back with his father and a couple of patrolmen. There was a lawsuit, and I was deposed. I admitted that Ronald was violent with me, too. They settled, but Farmingdale police fired Ronald. He blamed my testimony for losing him his job."

"What prevented you from leaving?" Tessa asks.

"At first because I guess I loved him. And we had a life plan. He would advance in his police career, we would save my nursing salary for a house, have kids, you know, a regular life. And after Ronald hit me, he would apologize, promise to change, swear he loved me, all the other bullshit, which I bought into. We moved here, he got his job at Home Depot, he had applications out to other police forces and a buddy who said he could get him into the NYPD, so things were looking up. But it wasn't right. I told him I wanted a divorce. That's when he showed me the bottle."

"The bottle?"

"Acid. It would go in my face when he found me. He showed me pictures of women who had had acid thrown at them. He poured out one drop on his own arm. You want to know what happens when a drop of acid hits skin? No, you don't. But I believed him. The boiling water was just a preview of things to come. Someone, don't ask me who, told me about a women's shelter where I would be safe. The next day, Ronald went to Home Depot and I went to the shelter. I didn't come out until I saw on TV that he was dead. I have no idea who killed Ronald, but you know what? I'm grateful."

"Can you tell me about the shelter?"

"No."

There was a pause. I was about to say something, but Tessa cut me off.

"Wait. There's one more part."

"Once, when he was slapping me back and forth, one hand holding my neck, the other whipping across my cheeks, I caught *a glimpse of a picture of him on the mantel—ten years old in a Cub Scout uniform. He looked proud, and his grin was so sweet. A permanent tooth not yet arrived, making him cuter. Freckles, bright eyes, combed hair still wet. Adorable. I wanted to ask him:* How did you grow up to be who you are? Who taught you to hit?"

CHAPTER 17

Bobby B is more optimistic than I am about my trip to Hawaii.

"If you get the shooter's identity from his DNA or fingerprints, all kinds of things fall into place. He'll have to explain travel, receipts, cell phone locations—we know who we're looking for on CCTV shots at gas stations, rental cars, 7-Elevens, McDonald's. The guy has to eat, right? If all else fails in terms of evidence, you can go back to plan B and shoot him."

"That's plan A, not B."

The sushi chef interrupts us with the next item in the *omakase*, an endless tasting menu he is creating: two porcelain teaspoons with a single clam floating in pink broth. We have worked our way through eight tiny, elegantly presented pieces of raw fish that could fit on a microscope slide. Bobby is a regular customer and is therefore allowed to say, "Hido, stop when you get to two hundred bucks, okay?"

"No prob."

"I'm done," I say.

We toss two credit cards on the counter. In the car, Bobby B says what he always says after a $200 *omakase*, "Burger King or Wendy's?"

I wake up in the middle of the night playing questions. Here's one: What came first, the chicken or the egg? Aristotle says *actuality* precedes *potentiality*. An egg is a potential chicken, and a chicken is a chicken; therefore the idea of a chicken must precede the egg. And why doesn't Mr. McDermott know whom he has killed? And where's Artie Crews's son's cat? Bobby wakes up and puts his hand under my T-shirt.

"Bobby, don't do anything. Just lie there." He knows what I like to do before he gets to do what I like.

The next morning, I drive by the women's shelter where Susan was staying when Ronald was killed. I just wanted another look on my way to work. Later, in the detective's room, Lieutenant Hagen stops at my desk, carrying an armful of thick folders. I know what they are: cold cases.

"Have a good time in Hawaii?"

"Yes. I needed some rest, warm sun, and pineapple juice. It's in the brochure."

"We got the guy who killed the girl in the car."

"The boyfriend?"

She shrugs. "He walked in yesterday. He read her cell phone. Saw texts to her other boyfriend."

Police work: luck, guilt, and a confession.

"You ready for some fun?"

I nod. She drops five of the folders on my desk. Cold cases, unsolved homicides. I am not expected to solve them in an hour as they do on television, I am merely required to go through them, look for clues, check out the suspects once again, see what crimes they have committed since, see if any of them resemble the original ones, and see what might be gleaned from evidence using more recent technologies, spectrum analysis, powder tests, murder weapon genealogy, and DNA. Then I am expected to write an evaluation statement, one that recommends the case be reopened or sent back as being impossible to solve: deaths of all witnesses, lack of any worthwhile evidence, and realistic chances of ever solving the crime, and use of police resources. We all know that occasionally, the process works, a detective notices a clue overlooked, a connection to another killing with the same method, and someone is arrested for a crime they committed twenty years ago and the victim's family gets justice and closure.

My cousin Aline works at a Wall Street law firm. She calls herself Rumpelstiltskin—a clerk or intern with a shopping cart loaded with merger documents arrives and places them on her desk. A minute later, she gets a call from a senior partner saying he needs these documents edited, prepared for signatures, and they had better be perfect—by tomorrow. "Turn straw into gold," Aline says.

In front of me is that stack of straw. They are only five on my desk, but there are more in cardboard file boxes in the basement of the building. I will consider these five, and there will be five more, and it will never end as long as people continue to do bad things to each other.

My first one is as thick as a suburban phone book, if they still have them. Everything one needs to know about an unsolved murder case is in them: photographs of the victim, the murder scene, the murder weapon, the mug shots or party pictures of the suspects, the family, friends. There are timelines, forensic reports, medical examiner reports, coroner reports, blood tests, fingerprint analysis, sputum, stool, and urine samples. Witness statements from the last person to see her/him alive, lists of people—using the means-motive-opportunity test—who might be suspects and deserve to be questioned again. Some cops see cold case files as containing *nothing* you need to know about an unsolved murder case; it's unsolved for a good reason—nobody solved it. Is the glass half-empty, or half-full? I'm an optimist, so I open the first file and look for inspiration, an overlooked possible killer. If it's a young girl, I will check out all the family members again.

The first case is a man shot to death, found in the trunk of his car. If it had not been for the smell emanating from the trunk of his decomposing body and the attempts of the restaurant to provide a pleasant outdoor dining experience, the corpse would have lasted for at least another month and into winter. Although the premise of the cold case project is that every murder leaves behind other victims—the family, the friends, the fiancé, the parents—this man in the trunk of his car seems to have died a singular lonely death. His biography begins in Tulsa, where he was fostered out of an orphanage to an older couple who are both dead. There was a serious attempt to find his birth parents; they, too, are deceased. No siblings, uncles, aunts; he died alone. Hopeless. Why he was killed and by whom would have to wait for a confession. I have no faith in that. It could have been a debt unpaid, an argument turned violent, or a revenge killing like the one I have planned for myself.

The next one has a yellow Post-it note attached to the inside of the file: *My advice: don't spend a whole lot of time looking for whoever killed this piece of shit.* The first document is a faded wanted poster with a mug shot of the victim: Nelson Gooding, taken at the prime of his career as a serial rapist and murderer. Nelson was a white male in his thirties, five eight, 175 pounds, arms covered with tattoos from wrist to shoulder. *He is considered armed and dangerous; call the following number if you should see him, and under no circumstances approach him.* No kidding. There are copies of his fingerprints at the bottom of the page. I visualize the rural post office in Grahamsville and can't remember WANTED posters on the walls. I wonder if this one is old enough to be appraised on *Antiques Roadshow.* I continue to read through the file containing the list of his rapes and murders, and how he tortured his victims, all of whom were under fifteen. Nelson was found under a bench in Forest Park, his throat slit and his penis stuffed in his mouth. Maybe Nelson got off easy, but I doubt if anyone will, as the Post-it said, "spend a whole lot of time looking for whoever killed this piece of shit."

My next file concerns the hit-and-run death of a Daniel Huang, sixteen-year-old high school student who worked nights stuffing takeout menus in mailboxes. His wallet was missing, which means the driver hit him, stopped, got out of his vehicle, and robbed him. I notice the original CSI homicide team didn't examine his clothing for paint fibers. The case is five years old, but the science is better now, so if they find any traces of paint, we can identify the make and model of the vehicle that hit Daniel. I compose a brief memo of why I want this case reopened. That's three down, two to go.

Cold case four is Sean Brody, an Irish immigrant who had overstayed his tourist visa—by ten years—and was employed as a medical aide at Queens General Center Hospital. He was found floating in the Eleventh Street Basin with bruised eyes, a broken nose, loose lower teeth, and a blood alcohol level that was off the charts. There were two theories—one: he was in a bar fight, stumbled away, fell drunk into the water, and drowned. The other was that he was beaten and purposely thrown into the basin. It was either a homicide or an accident. All the neighborhood bars were canvassed, and there were no reports of fights that night. Or of Sean's presence in any of them. Mystery of mysteries, and there wasn't enough information to justify further investigation. Noted. Cold case five is Juanita Castro Gooding, age twenty-eight, bludgeoned to death in her apartment in Rego Park. Prime suspect is Nelson Gooding, her husband, and aforementioned *piece of shit* whose case I just read. I went back and opened Nelson's file. There it was: a restraining order from the Queens municipal court forbidding Nelson from all contact with his wife, Juanita Castro Gooding, whether it be in person or by telephone, notes, mail, fax, email, or delivery of flowers or gifts. Nelson was a suspect in the murder of Juanita. He was questioned by police and released. A year later, he was murdered.

It was clear that the detectives in Juanita's case assumed Nelson was the killer, and since he was himself murdered less than a year later, there was no need to continue any investigation into either death. Technically, they were two unsolved cold cases, but for all practical purposes in the minds of the detectives, they were solved. Nelson killed Juanita, and someone killed him. I opened Juanita's file. There was a copy of the official restraining order, including her application. It was a sad and depressing litany of Nelson's beatings, harassment, stalking, and on two occasions, raping her. Juanita's domestic violence restraining order specifically included sexual relations so Nelson couldn't claim he was merely exercising his marital rights. It's the problem with restraining orders; the majority of people served ignore them, the victims have a false sense of security, and some experts maintain they tend to enrage the stalkers.

Something occurs to me, raises a flag, but the idea is too vague for me to consult Lieutenant Hagen. I make the rounds of the detectives who have cold case files on their desks and ask if they will let me know if any of their files contain domestic violence restraining orders. I add that they can give them to me and I'll do the evaluations for them. They all agree; it's less work for them, more for me.

Detective Mel Harden is first. He hands me a folder. "Two restraining orders on a victim. The guy was from around here and a local hero, if you are into football."

My last file: Derrick Matthews. His mother reported him

missing on December 3, 2003. Long Island City Police questioned his ex-wife, Janet Matthews. She had an airtight alibi. Janet was in a women's shelter for two months prior to Derrick's last known appearance, one year after he became a missing person.

Derrick, thirty-two at the time of his disappearance, was the father of Derrick Jr., four, and Deidra Matthews, two. Derrick and Janet met and married while they were students at Fordham, where Derrick was a star wide receiver. After graduation, the Jacksonville Jaguars drafted him. *Newsday* published photos of Derrick signing his contract wearing a Jaguars cap, holding his bonus check (two million dollars) and a copy of the signing bonus contract. A Jaguars team press release introduced Derrick to the Jaguars fans. It included a biography, which related how he met Janet, how they were inseparable in college, married in their sophomore year, and welcomed Derrick Jr. a year later. They bought a penthouse condominium in the Marina San Pablo Tower ($1.5 million) with an intracoastal view. I learned about Derrick's taste in music, his sterling work for the Dream Foundation, Janet's taste in music, her own sterling work for the United Way, their affection for the Jacksonville lifestyle, their plans to visit Disney World in Orlando.

It was more than I wanted to know, as the poor guy never made it to his rookie season. He tore his Achilles tendon in a spring training practice game. There was no hope of Derrick regaining his amazing speed, which had made him a two-million-dollar wide receiver rookie. He was out of the hospital and football. Things were not all bad. There was money left from the bonus, Derrick had bought his parents a comfortable home in Queens for cash, and there were new cars for him and Janet, plus the beginnings of college funds for Derrick Jr. and Deidra. The Florida condo sold at a loss, but it was a modest one, and they were able to return the furniture. All in all, the Matthewses were left with two hundred thousand dollars.

Piecing together detectives' interviews and affidavits from Janet, I got the rest of the sad history of the Matthewses.

Derrick's cousin Kevin managed a Ford dealership in Bayside, Queens. He gave Derrick a job in sales. Derrick still had a lot of residual fame from his Fordham years, not to mention his truncated Jaguars career. Kevin exploited the hell out of Derrick; he made him decorate his office with memorabilia: his trophies, autographed balls, his Fordham and Jaguars jerseys in Lucite frames. Kevin advertised autograph signing days; he got Derrick to bring his former teammates into the dealership with promises of big discounts. At first, Derrick went along with it. He posed for a lot of pictures, signed a lot of autographs. After a while, he got tired of posing for pictures for people who weren't interested in buying cars. About the time that Derrick was thinking of quitting, the dealership closed in the 2008 financial meltdown. Derrick and Janet both swore to live within their means while he looked for work, but the means were diminishing. Finally, he landed a job in a trendy Manhattan club, to hang out, be seen, greet people; it came with the promise of a management position. Before long, he was working the rope, deciding who got in and who didn't. Janet claimed there were late nights, drugs, other women. Derrick got a couple of DUIs and had his license suspended, followed by the inevitable crime of driving without one. Janet said, "He's working nights and complaining that I'm not, but I have Derrick Jr. and Deidre to look after."

There are pages of divorce documents that chronicle the unraveling of the marriage as Derrick loses his job, then gets another as a bouncer at a strip club with the same predictable results. Janet notices a different Derrick. He's got a quick temper, he's complaining of headaches, he's depressed and doing a lot of drugs, whatever he can get his hands on—oxy, coke, weed, painkillers—then in the middle of one of their arguments he punches Janet. She calls 911, the police come, she refuses to press charges.

"The cops told me they are big fans of his. They will let it go this time, but the next time they will arrest Derrick even if I don't press charges. There it is. I know what his violence will cost. I suppose deep down I am as afraid of the consequences as he is. Truce. Until the next time."

The "next time," the police arrest him. Derrick gets probation, agrees to attend anger management sessions. They attend couples' therapy, which doesn't work out. Janet files for divorce and moves in with her parents. Derrick can't make child support. There is no more money left; it went to the lawyers. Derrick moves into his parents' house, gets kicked out, sells his car, steals Janet's, and is jailed for another DUI. This time he serves six months. Janet gets a domestic restraining order forbidding Derrick from any contact with her. Derrick ignores it.

"He comes to my mother's house and demands money from me. He tries to take Derrick Jr. He beats me, really bad. When I get out of the hospital, I know I have to go somewhere he can't find me."

CHAPTER 18

Janet Matthews teaches seventh-grade mathematics at Albert Leonard Middle School in New Rochelle. I meet her in the teachers' lounge. She's got three inches on me, more if you count her Angela Davis Afro. She laughs between sentences and smells of chalk. I like her immediately.

"It's eighth period; we're supposed to have clubs. Remember clubs? I volunteered to teach chess, and no one showed up, so I have a free period. I love it. You want to know about Derrick? Why would you want to do that?" A male teacher at the end of the table grading papers looks up.

Janet says, "Phil, this is none of your beeswax."

Phil returns to his work.

"It's a cold case," I say. "We're always trying to solve them. Derrick disappeared. We suspect foul play. Sorry, I hate that term—it sounds like an English movie."

"Derrick doesn't need any solving. His life was tragic, and if he's not dead I hope he is okay, but I doubt it. Truth is, his life was over before it was over."

I think there is something hard about this. Janet catches my expression. "Look, for my children, he's not a memory. They have a new dad who loves them, adopted them. I do not want Derrick brought back into their lives. We are over him. It's sad what happened to Derrick, and I hate to say this, but it was a relief to a lot of people. The man caused a lot of pain. I don't see the point of finding him."

I tend to agree with her, but it's not why I'm here. "You were in a shelter when Derrick went missing."

"That's right."

"How did you get there?"

"There was a nurse at the emergency room. She wrote down the address on my cast. Yes, Derrick broke my arm. I went home, grabbed the kids from my mom's, and got a cab to take us over there right away."

Phil keeps his head down, but I know he is listening.

"Can you tell me about the shelter?"

"If you want the name, address, no. We're not supposed to tell the police. I can tell you I felt safe—that's the first thing. And so did my kids."

"How long were you there?"

"About six months. I left once to get some stuff out of the apartment. We moved in with nothing but the clothes on our backs. They advised against going back, and they were right. Derrick had a friend crashing in the apartment who told him I was there. Derrick came by. He was nice—at first—told me he was getting his life together, wanted to see the kids, wasn't using, wanted to go back to counseling. For a minute, I almost bought it. Then, I said that wasn't possible, there was no way I was going back to him."

She leans in closer to me so Phil can't hear.

"Then he took out a gun and put it to my head. I saw it in his eyes. He was crazy. I had been reading about concussions, brain damage, CTI, all the stuff that happens to men who have played football since they were six years old. Derrick was a wide receiver. Getting hit was his lifestyle. That could have been the cause, but I knew no matter what he said, the man was out to kill me. So I told him I would get the kids and meet him back at the apartment. He told me he knew where I was living, he knew about the shelter, and if I didn't show up, he would come there and kill me."

"And?"

"I went back to the shelter, told them what had happened. They said to just stay put, and they would deal with it."

I wait.

"I never left the place. I felt safe there for the first time. I home-schooled the kids, found out I liked teaching, got my teacher's certificate through courses online. Then they said I could leave."

"Who are *they*?"

"Somebody at the shelter. Oh, you want a name. Ummm. Don't think so. It was a long time ago."

A school bell rings. It reverberates through the building. It is the sound that brings relief to bored students and anxiety to the unprepared, and ends all conversations with people who don't want to provide any more information. Janet gets up, collects her papers, and walks over to Phil. She gives him a little shoulder rub.

"Time to go home, sweetheart."

Phil collects his papers and stuffs them into his backpack. Janet looks at me.

"My husband."

We leave the teachers' lounge together. In the hallway, lined with lockers, crowded with adolescent boys and girls hurrying back into their homerooms, I ask, "Was the name of the shelter Artemis?"

"Don't recall."

"Do you remember what you were told when you left? Exactly."

Janet stops. She lets the last students brush by her. A bell rings. Doors close. The hallway is empty, save for three adults.

"'You can go home now.'"

CHAPTER 19

Lieutenant Hagen wants to know who killed Ronald Steevers.

"For whatever his sins, he was police, and he is deserving of our extra efforts to find his killer."

"I agree, but I have two cases of women being in the same shelter when their husbands were killed. And they both took out domestic violence restraining orders."

"Is one of them Ronald's wife?"

"Yes."

"And the other?"

"Derrick Matthews's wife, Janet. He played for Fordham."

"The football player. I remember that one."

"His wife was in the shelter when he disappeared. Never found his body."

Lieutenant Hagen takes a bite of her cheese Danish. "Could be a coincidence."

"I don't believe in coincidences."

"Your theory is that there is a connection between the male victims and this women's shelter?"

"Yes."

I wait. She gets it.

"You will need to go over the rest of the cold cases. See if there are any others."

"I've already asked detectives to give me the files that contain domestic abuse or restraining orders."

"Okay."

"I should have asked you first."

"It's fine."

"I'd also like to see some of our recent closed homicide cases where the victims took out restraining orders."

"Why? They're solved."

"Curious."

"You know where they are. Help yourself."

It's what I like about Lieutenant Hagen. She is reasonable.

During the next week, detectives continue to give me their cold cases that deal with domestic violence or contain restraining orders. Of the seventeen remaining unsolved cases there are three male homicides related to domestic abuse histories. None of the women connected to them (two wives and a live-in girl-friend) ever mentioned being in a women's shelter when asked to provide alibis. One was out of state and proved it, one was in jail, the other died in an automobile accident six months before her husband was found in a dumpster behind Al & Eddie's Tire Emporium on Queens Boulevard. I am still left with Susan and Janet. They are not enough. Lieutenant Hagen will say two cases are coincidental. At the same time, I revisit murders of women, most of them killed by their husbands, lovers, and in a few cases, bar hookups. Apart from the latter, they all had restraining orders on the men who killed them. Jesus.

I hear a cough. Detective Claude Ito is standing at my desk holding a thick file.

Even when I was falling in love with Bobby B, I kept my crush on Claude. Maybe it was because he saved my life. After I passed the detective exam, I was assigned a rookie desk in homicide. A scruffy Dell monitor separated me from a beautiful Japanese American man with flawless light brown skin and smoky almond eyes. He was always polite; he never teased or used sarcasm.

I was attracted to Claude's gentleness, a rare quality in a cop, much less a veteran homicide detective. I knew Asian American cops who were just as hard-assed as anyone on the force, but Claude never raised his voice; he was always polite, patient; his inquisitive yet sympathetic expression said he was interested in what you had to say whether you were a witness, a victim, or a suspect. Claude always got answers in interrogations. We joked that Claude could calm a perp on PCP and extract a confession from a lawyer. My theory about Claude's gentleness was that behind it was his formidable strength. I saw it the day he saved my life when a suspect who was sitting along a wall waiting to be interviewed took out a pistol from an ankle holster (the cops who'd brought him in had forgotten to search him—they were fired) and yelled that he was going to kill some cops and aimed his gun at me. Like everyone else in the room, I had stowed my weapon in a desk drawer—sitting at a desk for hours with a two-pound loaded gun on your belt is uncomfortable—the man aimed his pistol at me just as Claude walked through the door behind him. In one fluid motion, the man was on his stomach on the floor, the gun was in Claude's hand, and Claude's foot was planted on his back. We all saw it. None of us could exactly describe what we had seen—it was that fast.

"Can you teach me that move, Claude?"

"Easy. Do you have a couple of years?"

Now he was standing at my desk.

"Hey, Claude, what can I do for you?" I would do *anything* for him.

"I sort of messed up. You're looking for male homicide victims who had restraining orders, so I didn't send this to you. I found a homicide named Joey Savone. Turns out Joey is a woman."

"And?"

108 | MICHAEL ELIAS

"I remembered you were questioning a suspect who alibied she was in a women's shelter. Or I heard it from Tessa. Anyway, Joey's wife was, is—damn, this is confusing. Joey's *partner* was a woman. Her name is Karen Marschner."

He hands me the file.

"It's all in there. She says she was in a women's shelter around the time of the murder."

"Claude? You are one smart dude."

"I know," he says. I have three cases. That's not a coincidence.

Joey (Jolene) Savone, white female, twenty-four years old, was found on the shore of the Flushing Meadows Corona Park lake. Her hands were tied behind her back, and a cement block was tied to her chest. She had been shot in the heart, so she didn't get to experience being drowned alive. Joey worked as a diagnostic medical sonographer in a Forest Hills gynecology group practice. Photographs show an attractive, serious-looking woman, unwilling to crack a smile, even when she tells you it's a boy/girl/twins and healthy. For Joey, posing for a picture, whether it's a high school yearbook, a driver's license, or with her spouse at a birthday party, seems to be a solemn occasion. *Come on, girl, smile.* Ah, here's one: a selfie of Joey and Karen. I look at the two women, I try to get around what I know is a cliché. Joey is the femme partner, slight, girlish behind Warby Parkers, while Karen is clearly butch, thick and menacing. So why is Joey dead and Karen alive? Pick out the violent one, pick out the scary one, pick out the one who wouldn't be afraid of a woman half her size—it is Karen, not Joey. Karen would check in at five four, around 225 pounds, dressed in black studded leather from her boots to her cap. Joey is half her size in every direction. They are standing in front of a stripped Harley that must belong to

Karen, who reminds me of the Tenacious Dame femme I spent thirty seconds with in an elevator in the Queens Center mall. I might ask her if she recognizes me. If she doesn't, my disguise was successful.

Putting these two women side by side, I would say Joey should be scared of Karen, not the other way around. Karen is the one who claimed she was in the women's shelter around the time that Joey was murdered. The file says Karen Marschner works as a bartender at the Bum Bum Bar, a lesbian joint on Roosevelt Avenue in Queens. I get there around six, figuring Karen will be taking advantage of the staff meal. I am correct. She's sitting in a booth along the wall, a red plastic basket of fried food in front of her. Under a top pomp with a side buzz cut, there is a round friendly face. I can see edge ends of tattoos trailing out of her white T-shirt under a blue work shirt. She's got a nose ring, a row of earrings on each lobe, and more jewelry in places I can't or don't want to see.

"Fish and chips look good," I say.

Karen looks up, pauses the journey of a skinny fry on the way to her mouth.

"I know you?"

I show her my badge.

"I'm with the Long Island City Police."

"We have video of the guy throwing the first punch."

"Sorry?"

"You're here about the fight last night?"

"No. What fight?"

She relaxes; my natural smile disarms her. Karen gestures for me to slide into the booth.

"I eighty-sixed a customer; he was drunk, homophobic. He called me a lot of names before he tried to hit me."

"You defended yourself."

"Had to, with some help from my manager. You're kind of cute for a cop. On or off duty?"

"On. I know you."

"You know me?"

"We were in an elevator at the Queens Center mall. You're a one-percenter, right?"

"So what? It isn't against the law, last time I looked."

"No, but I remember because you were wearing a very cool jacket."

Karen shrugs, smiles. "I still don't know you."

I have a notion that she finds this conversation borderline funny, and I do, too, in a surreal way. I'll keep it going until she tells the truth.

"Can I ask what you were doing there?"

"At the mall?"

"Yes."

"Shopping," she says.

"I see. Shopping," I say.

"Makes sense. It's a freakin' mall."

I nod my head. It may be a coincidence and I only remember her face because I am a cop, and she doesn't remember mine. I let it go. Then I say, "I'm working on a cold case."

"Like the TV show."

"Joey Savone."

Karen drops her fork into the red plastic basket.

"That is so fucked." Her face scrunches up, the tears flow. She makes no attempt to wipe them away, and I believe her.

"Three years, it still doesn't make any difference. Who said time heals all wounds?"

"I'm sorry," I say.

"Yeah."

She spears another piece of fish. "What do you want?"

There is a waitress standing at our booth. I order a Stella and some fries. When she leaves, Karen says, "I meant what do you want with me?"

"Everything about her so I can find out who killed her," I say.

Karen talks to me until she has to go to work. I take notes, drink two more Stellas, and split another order of fries with Karen.

"Joey was messed up. She got beat up by her father. She never knew any better."

"You broke up with her? Why?"

"We were going in different directions—new friends—I didn't want to be tied down."

"How did she take the news?"

Karen smiles wide, flashes rows of white teeth, top and bottom. "Do you like them?"

"I'm blinded by the light."

"The back ones are mine. Joey left the rest on the floor of our bathroom. It's what happens when you bang somebody's face on a toilet."

"Will you tell me the story?"

At the end, I have no questions. She is thorough and honest. I record it. I have enough to go back to Lieutenant Hagen.

Statement of Karen Marschner

Recorded by Detective Nina Karim, LICPD

"I sometimes think Joey was a punishment for something I did but can't remember what it was. God made me fall in love with her, like I was never in love with anyone like her. She told me she loved me, too, but at the same time she was one mean person. I once said, 'I have enemies who treat me better than you do.' She laughed. I made excuses. She couldn't handle being gay, so she took it out on me. It happens.

"My shrink said we were in a classic sadomasochist relationship. You know the expression, 'Sometimes paranoids have real enemies'? I have another one: 'Sometimes sadists kill the ones they say they love.' I know how I look. I'm as butch as they come. I attract a certain kind of femme, looking for strong, tough partners. Sometimes they were abused or bullied as kids. Joey wanted to feel secure. I give off that aura. The truth is I'm scared shitless like everybody else. What am I scared of? Using the women's bathroom, going to a gynecologist, having a waiter call me *sir*, for starters.

"We met at a lounge in Manhattan, flirted on Facebook, and finally went out. In three months, we were living together in my apartment. Joey took over, paid all the bills, redecorated, decided what stayed—mostly hers; what went was mostly mine. Then she got to work on my friends. Cut them out. That happens in the beginning of any love affair—you don't need anybody else—but she made it permanent. I didn't care. I was in love; Joey was enough for me. Then she got critical. Okay, I'm not the neatest person. I assumed Joey had an anal personality, so I tried. I made a real effort at crap like hanging up clothes, folding towels, not leaving dishes in the sink, making sure the toilet bowl was spotless. I was easy. When she complained, I laughed and said, 'Yes, ma'am, I will do better.'

"It became serious intense verbal abuse, comments about me, my hygiene, looks, weight, body odor, then it turned into a state of permanent pissed off—she wasn't happy with anything. I started to feel like everything was my fault. I lost my self-esteem, what little I had left. One day she got really angry at something—I can't remember what—yes, I can. I was in bed, and she came out of the bathroom saying there was an awful smell. I laughed. It was kind of funny, you know. Since when does shit not smell? The next thing I know she's on my stomach, punching me, pulling my hair, scratching with her nails; it was like having a hundred-fifty-pound rabid cat on me. I protected myself as best I could, grabbed her wrists and talked her down. She apologized, said it wouldn't happen again. I told her I was going to leave. She cried, begged me to stay, told me she loved me, and things were okay for a while.

"But the line had been crossed. I let her get away with physically assaulting me; it was like I gave her permission. If we argued and it got to the point where there was screaming, she would freak, go for me, then say she was sorry. She became more jealous, demanded to see my phone, check my texts, emails. She threatened me, said she would out me to my parents, go to my boss, get me fired. By then she had control of my money. The bank account was in her name. I was dependent on her. I felt trapped: I still loved her; I was in her power. I felt I had no place to go. Then she started talking about suicide. How we should do it together. Joey worked in a doctor's office. She could get pills. She joked, 'You go first, I'll follow. Trust me?' She said she knew lots of ways to kill a person. She could do it so it would look like a heart attack or stroke. 'Why,' she said, 'do you never hear of doctors in old age homes? They know how to kill themselves.'

"Then she took the abuse to another level. She started harping on how I was a bad person who needed to be punished. Of course, she was the one who wanted to be punished. For being gay. It happens. Yeah, there are homophobic gay people. They hate who they are; they can't deal with it, so they take it out on their partners. I'm aware of this now, but you should have seen me then. I was her accomplice in my own destruction. When she thought I would leave, she turned on the love; when she was sure I would stay, she turned on the hate. I started doing coke, which gave her another threat about my job. I started to hide money for a place to rent when I left, she found it, and I got a beating that night. There was no escape, no hope, no safety. She always apologized, swore she would change, I bought it; I had no choice.

"Then one day I knew she was going to kill me. It was clear she would do it, probably get away with it. I didn't know what to do except fill a backpack and leave. You know, I could have been the one. I could have been the abuser. I could have hit her. I was stronger. The trouble was I loved her beyond belief. If I love somebody, I will never put my hands on them. When Joey understood that, when she felt safe, then she went to work on me. I came to this realization in the shelter. I was getting my own life back. I went back to work, started doing counseling with other gay women victims of abuse. There is plenty of domestic violence in the LGBT community. I learned gay couples experience domestic violence at the same frequency as heterosexual couples; some research says it might be because gay individuals are less likely to report domestic violence. About a year ago, Joey showed up at the shelter with the husband of one of the wives inside—she wanted to kill me and he wanted to kill his wife. I never heard from her after that. I guess it was the last straw."

For whom? I wonder.

CHAPTER 20

I text Lieutenant Hagen: I have another person whose partner/ husband was murdered. Three women.

I check my own texts. Bobby B suggests a home-cooked meal. That's code for *my* home. Lieutenant Hagen's comes in: See me tomorrow. That's good news. In my car, I wonder if Bobby can tell the difference between store-bought and homemade pesto. Not in a million years. I have a plan. But there is a voice mail to play back.

"Artie Crews here, the weatherman. I just wanted to tell you we found the cat. My son hid it. He won't tell me why."

I should tell Artie that his son likely wanted some attention from his father. Looking for a cat together would have been just that. Artie's solution was to hire someone, demonstrating once again his indifference to his son. Another thing to do. Instead, I shop for dinner.

I leave the front door unlocked so Bobby can find me in the shower. It is better than cocktails before dinner. He takes off his jeans and T-shirt, climbs in, turns me sideways, soaps me with both hands. I close my eyes. I feel one hand trace a path down my back and the other down my breasts and between my legs. One stops in my butt crack, and the other thumbs against my clitoris with exactly the right pressure—how does he know how to do this? But that is a rational question and I am coming now, so the answer will have to wait. His cock is folded up hard against the side of my thigh, does he lower or push me to the edge of the tub—it doesn't matter, it was where I wanted to go anyway, so all I have to do is lean forward and take him in my mouth while he clasps my hair. I hold his two hard ass cheeks with skin like a baby's until he steps back, pulls me up to standing, turns me around, and enters me from the rear. I swear one of these days I will surely pull the pipes out of the wall. We dry each other and wear bathrobes to the table.

As much as he likes the melon and prosciutto, pasta with pesto, and veal scaloppine, Bobby B doesn't care for my plan. He refuses my request for him to beat the crap out of me.

"It's not like putting on makeup. Yeah, I could give you black eyes, but I might also break your orbital rim, do damage to the eye itself, tear the optic nerve, fuck up your eye muscles, the sinuses around the eye, and your tear ducts."

I wince. How could I not?

"You want a punch on the nose? I can break it, but if I don't hit it exactly right, I could also give you a nasal septal hematoma."

"How do you know this stuff?" I say.

"How come you don't?" Bobby replies. He is right.

"What else?"

"You can't fake the effects of a beating. You will need cuts, scrapes, bruises on your arms, your chest. You fought back, right? He pulled some hair out, you will need some lumps on the back of your head where he slammed you against a wall, a broken rib where he kicked you—when you were down, of course, a couple of punches to the mouth, which means a bloody lip, some missing teeth, usually the front ones. You think I'm going to do that? Get real."

He takes another helping of pasta.

"This is delicious. Did I ever tell you the story of my only bar fight? I was in a cozy little cocktail lounge on Eighth Avenue after a Knicks game, happy to watch the postgame on TV, have a beer, and . . ."

"And get lucky?"

"I never get lucky in bars. Let me tell the story. Two young guys are at a table drinking martinis, minding their own business. At the bar, there are three guys looking for trouble. Their dumb-ass backward caps say they are Nets fans, pissed their team lost. It wouldn't surprise me to learn they'd bet heavily on the game. They are in their twenties, a volatile age. The two guys at the table look gay—ah, fuck it, they are gay and Ivy League, wearing Ralph Lauren, slight of build, like I said, minding their own business. For some tribal or economic reason, this is infuriating to the three Nets fans. It starts like high school. They toss peanuts at them, each one accompanied by a little taunt. I can't remember exactly—it was in the neighborhood of *What are you gonna do about it, faggot?* The two guys are prudent, put some money on the table and leave. The three assholes decide to follow them outside and make shit happen. So I go outside, too. Now we are all standing on the street. There is going to be a fight. I hate these motherfuckers, and it's three of them against me."

"Wait. What about the couple?"

"They're smarter than me. They saw a cab and jumped in. So I say to the Jersey boys, 'See you later.' Or something like that.

"'No way. You're next, asshole,' one of the Jersey boys says.

"I back up against the side of the building so I can't be jumped from behind.

"'You sure? You really want to fight me? On concrete?'

"They nod.

"'You guys have health insurance?' I ask.

"'Huh?'

"'Look, I have no doubt you guys can take me, but it won't be easy. I'm an ex-cop. I'm not armed, but I am fairly dangerous, and a really dirty fighter. So, if we get into this, at least one of you is going to lose an eye, maybe a lot of teeth. I know how to break an arm at the elbow before I go down. Last time I looked, a broken arm is about fifty thousand, an eye a hundred grand, and I don't have to tell you what a broken jaw costs, besides having to sip food through a straw for three months. So I just want to know if you are fully insured.'

"They look at each other, at me. I am frighteningly calm. They calculate their potential losses. I wait another moment and tell them we should say good-bye."

"And?"

"We said good-bye."

"I like that story. I get your point. Are you sleeping over?"

CHAPTER 21

Lieutenant Hagen swivels her chair around and turns on her coffee machine. She opens a flat box. Inside are rows of capsules.

"Would you like one?"

"I'm partial to the blue."

She starts the machine and says, "Do you know how many women were in the shelter over that ten-year period? A hundred? Two hundred? You do know most women leave shelters within the first month?"

She hands me the coffee. The thin cup is hot to my fingers.

"I would like to go undercover. Check in. Snoop around, see what's up."

"You'll have to find a way to get in."

"I have a couple of fake identities left over from my undercover drug days. I'll need an abusive spouse, a couple of restraining orders, some bruises, and my own ingenuity."

"What if they find out you're a cop?"

"Let them. The worst they can do is kick me out."

"You hope."

"I want to keep this between us. If anyone asks, I'm on special assignment from you, and it's nobody's business in the station."

CHAPTER 22

My "fictional husband" will be a detective in a nearby police department, in and out of AA for years, a poster child for failure of its Twelve Steps. He is convinced his drinking is under control. When it isn't, he blames it on me, usually followed by a violent rage that results in him beating me. We have a ten-year-old son who wets his bed and tells me to stop making Daddy mad. Lately my husband has been talking of taking his own life and assuring me he won't go alone. I am scared and move out with my son. He finds me, pleads for reconciliation and couples' therapy, demonstrates sobriety, introduces me to his AA sponsor, then waits for me, drunk, forces his way into my apartment, rapes me, or tries to and can't perform, which makes him angrier, and I get another beating for being a frigid, cock-shrinking bitch. My son is still living with his father, but I fear for his life—and mine. Bobby B has a cousin, a clerk in the municipal court, who will produce a restraining order and backdate it. The restraining order doesn't mean anything to my husband. He has been beating me off and on for two years now; it's getting worse, life-threatening.

Now all I have to do is get Detective Linda Fuentes on board. It isn't hard. We haven't liked each other for a long time. The animosity began when we were both working on a robbery homicide. The killer walked into a dry-cleaning store on Queens Boulevard with an armful of dirty shirts in which he had hidden a handgun. As the owner was counting out the shirts, the robber showed him the gun and told him to empty the cash register. The owner had his own gun under the cash register, but the guy with the shirts shot first and killed him. He ran out, leaving his shirts behind. Two of them had little green paper laundry tags, so it was just a question of tracing the tickets to another laundry, going through receipts. We had the name of this idiot in two days.

Higgins and I found him a week later. The problem was that the sole witness to the murder was a Salvadoran tailor working at his sewing machine who used to date Fuentes. She not only failed to tell Lieutenant Hagen she knew the witness, she started seeing him again. Possibly the trauma of the killing reignited their passion. This was a major conflict of interest, a cop sleeping with a witness. It could seriously jeopardize the prosecution. Somebody informed Hagen, and she went ballistic, assembled the three of us in her office, and took Fuentes off the case. Fuentes always thought I'd ratted her out, but it wasn't me. There was no convincing Fuentes otherwise.

Building on the foundation of her dislike, a fight won't be hard to incite. I start with sarcasm, the fool's wit: "Cute dress, Linda. You going undercover to a flea market?" In the locker room with some of the male cops in attendance, I get laughs. Linda responds with Spanish invective that gets *ooh*s from the same male cops. I descend to the personal: "Is your ass jealous of the amount of shit that just came out of your mouth?"

Fuentes says, "You are dangerously close to totally pissing me off. The consequence will be a trip to either HR or the gym, where we can put on gloves and you will learn I am not to be fucked with, *puta*."

"Gloves. HR is for humans, not assholes, like you."

Like everyone on the force, I learned the basics of martial arts for police, a mixture of judo, karate, Krav Maga, the use of the baton, and some boxing. I was okay at it, but I had no illusions my superficial knowledge was going to make me secure in a physical confrontation with a man twice my size. I had more confidence in my ability to defuse a potentially violent situation with calm, polite persuasion. On foot patrol, I always had a male partner. I was also never too proud to call for backup. And I carried two guns: my department Glock and my Nasty Little Fucker in its ankle holster.

I explain to Sergeant Freeman, the soon-to-be retired veteran who is in charge of the gym, that Fuentes and I need to settle a *personal thing*.

"Okay with me," he says.

It isn't the first time cops have come to the gym to resolve a grudge. But two women lacing up twenty-ounce sparring gloves and headgear is a new event for Freeman, and he will also have to referee the fight. He proposes three rounds, three minutes each. I realize unless I just stand there and put up no defense, at most I will come out of this with a black eye, some cheek bruises. We box our three rounds, neither of us does much damage, and when Freeman calls time at the end of the third round we are both breathing heavily and I still have my looks. Freeman tells us to bump gloves in friendship, we do, and he excuses himself to go to his Little League coaching job. As soon as he leaves, Linda spits on the floor, just missing my Keds, and we take off the headgear and toss it aside.

Halfway through Linda beating the crap out of me, I realize this might be a really bad idea. At first, I thought I was holding my own—she's having a hard time hitting me, her jabs aren't connecting, the body shots are weak. Then it occurs to me that Linda was just figuring me out; now that she knows my speed and my defenses, she can really go to work on me. She does. The punches come faster and faster; she slides under my raised arms, pounds my kidneys, and sweeps my feet out from under me. I hit the floor; she delivers a kick in my ribs. Oh, Linda Fuentes, you are a gift: definitely a much better street fighter than me.

"You done, bitch?"

"I think so."

"You're fucked up, Karim," she says, heading for the showers, leaving me, well, fucked up.

But I'm dressed for a stay in Artemis, a shelter for battered women.

My name will be Lucy.

CHAPTER 23

Artemis Shelter for Women

I roll up my sleeping bag and down another of Amanda's Tylenols. Phyllis told me I have to be out of the room by nine to make way for the younger kids, who use it for a makeshift school. A doctor arrives. She carries a leather bag.

"Ruth Iskin. I'm at Flushing Hospital," she says, then cups my chin in her hand, whistles at my bruises, and puts me through a quick exam: blood pressure, chest, eyes, feels around my rib cage, tweaks my nose back and forth. "It's not broken. Any loose teeth?"

"No." Mentioning my rubbery molar would just prolong the visit. She applies bandages over my facial cuts, assures me they aren't serious, tells me it's just a question of time before the bruises lose color and the scratches heal.

"You take meds?"

"Over the counter."

"You'll live."

"Yeah, right."

Dr. Iskin packs up and leaves. Sergeant Freeman will surely tell the tale of two women detectives settling scores in the gym, my fight with Fuentes will be public knowledge. I'd like to look like less of a loser when I do return. Phyllis comes back with another woman and introduces me to my first adult resident of the shelter.

"Lucy, meet Sofia. We don't do last names," Phyllis says. That's fine with me. I don't want her to know mine, either.

"Hello and welcome to our safe home." Sofia has a soft Slavic accent that suggests she could be anywhere from Slovenia to Ukraine. She owns fashion model beauty, straight blonde hair that frames her face with luminous skin, high cheekbones, and perfect teeth. I feel small and beefy in her presence.

"Sofia is our resident teacher."

"Just the little ones," Sofia says. She gets a better look at me and my injuries, shakes her head. "You are lucky to be here. Excuse me, but I have to get the room ready for the children." She parts a curtain on one wall, revealing a blackboard, and for the first time I notice another wall is covered with maps, children's artwork, pop-star posters, and a bookcase with two old iMacs on the top shelf. Sofia empties a plastic carton with pencils, crayons, sketch pads, and books onto the table. A moment later, three children come in from the kitchen: two boys and a girl.

"Everybody say hi to Lucy, our new arrival," Phyllis says.

I get a disjointed "Hi, Lucy." The older boy gives me a handshake. "Ben. I'm nine." The younger one mumbles, "Frankie," and walks past me. The girl says, "My name is Tiffany and I'm seven."

Sofia says, "Frankie?" Frankie, buried in a book, doesn't look up. Phyllis leads me into the kitchen, where we pour coffee. "Frankie is Amanda's brother. He's quiet, withdrawn. He could go to school with Amanda, but he won't leave the shelter, won't really talk to anyone. Can't blame him. We all try to bring him out, but he's tough. Sometimes I wish we could get an abused wife who is also a trained child therapist. If you see an opportunity to talk to him, feel free."

"Sure." I don't tell her I have a lot of experience with traumatized nine-year-olds. I failed with one: Sammy, my brother.

"We do homeschooling here. The older kids sometimes go to local schools if we feel secure about them leaving. Sofia and I teach; the other mothers pitch in according to their skills. When you get settled, we can always use help."

"I was a teacher for a while. Math and English, junior high."

"Perfect."

I have value to Phyllis. That's good. And like all effective lies, it contains some truth.

There was a waiting period after my written and physical tests for the Long Island City Police to complete my background checks, interview my references, confirm my financial disclosures. I was told it might take a couple of months. While I was in this limbo, I ran into a high school friend at a Peet's. We grabbed our coffees, found a table, and *caught up*. I went first. I don't remember what I told Nancy—certainly not that I was waiting to become a cop, I must have said I was between jobs, not in a relationship, and yes, I was okay. Nancy told me she was vice principal at Better Beginnings Charter School.

"Would you be interested in doing some teaching? We're always looking for people. You could substitute. The teacher leaves a lesson plan; just follow it. Pays a hundred dollars a day."

"Sounds tempting. But I don't have any experience."

"It's a charter school, Nina, you don't need experience. Fill out some paperwork, leave your phone number, and when one of our teachers is sick, you come in. The kids are well behaved. It's easy."

She was right. It was that easy. I taught off and on for six months, and when I got my acceptance into the Police Academy I resigned.

Phyllis says,"You can also help kids one-on-one." She looks back at the three children at the table. "Our classes tend to be small."

"Can I get some stuff out of my car? Clothes, toilet articles."

"There's a protocol for anybody leaving the shelter. We need to be careful about maintaining our own security. We are wary of husbands or boyfriends waiting outside."

She leads me out of the kitchen door into the yard between the two houses. "First rule, we never use our front doors." She steps up to the side door of the adjacent house and punches a code into a lock. We enter into a kitchen. "There's a gaggle of locks. Same code, but we change the code every week. It's a pain, but you'll get used to it. We make it a game for the children—'Who knows the code?'—so they can remember. We try to keep the single women here; the women with kids live in the bigger house. A friend owns the house behind this one. She lets us use it as a conduit to the street outside. We'll go through her backyard, into her house, then you can go out her front door into the street. You come back the same way. It's not foolproof, but if anybody is watching the front door of the shelter, they won't see anybody entering or leaving."

Phyllis unlocks the neighbor's back door. "Same code." We enter into a kitchen. A woman's voice calls out, "I'm in the living room."

"Say hello to Myra Eisenson," Phyllis says.

Myra, a fortyish woman in a housecoat, waves to me from her desk, barely taking her eyes off the two large computer monitors that display stock charts, graphs, and real-time market quotes.

"She's a day trader," Phyllis says.

"I never go out," Myra says.

Myra's front door leads to Eightieth Street. There is a small video monitor on the wall displaying rotating views of the doorstep and the street. Phyllis studies the monitor, opens the door.

"Where's your car?"

"It's around the corner on Northern Boulevard."

"I'll wait here for you."

I walk to my Prius, checking to see if I am being followed, look at messages on my other phone, send texts to Bobby and Lieutenant Hagen: I'm in. I collect my bag and return to Myra's house. Phyllis lets me back in, and we retrace our steps back to the Artemis compound. Lieutenant Hagen and I have devised a cover story that will get me out of the shelter during the day. Before we go into the main house, I spin the tale to Phyllis.

"I have a job. My husband doesn't know about it. I'd like to keep it."

"Is it safe?" Phyllis asks.

"I do freelance editing for a woman who takes on more work than she can handle. I'm like a ghost. I work out of her apartment on one of her computers. She pays me cash. She knows I'm hiding, but she doesn't know where. I park in an underground lot and always make sure no one is following me. I take an elevator to a higher floor and walk down two flights."

Phyllis nods. "Smart."

"I saw it in a movie."

"Okay. Just be careful coming back. I've been thinking," Phyllis says. "There's a cot in the basement you could use. You'll be more comfortable there. It's kind of dark, but you'll have privacy; you won't be in the way when the kids are around."

She takes me down through a door in the kitchen. It wouldn't qualify as a finished basement, but it's clean. There are faded rugs on the floor, the walls are whitewashed, a metal Ikea single cot for sleeping. There is a lingering smell of cleaning chemicals, heating oil, and the coal that preceded the oil. A small toilet closet has a yellowed sink basin. If I were who I pretended to be, a battered woman on the run, it would be just fine, but I am playacting, and I already miss my own bed with Bobby B in it. Upstairs is activity, life: I hear footsteps, chair legs scraping, dulled voices of women and children, TV, doors slamming. It's familiar. I realize I am back in my own house, living in my own space, in my father's old medical suite, in the house but not part of it.

"I'll take it."

CHAPTER 24

In the basement room of the shelter, I imagine life upstairs re-sembling a college sorority: a comfortable house, a flag with Greek letters unfurled from its second-story balcony, home to women living together, dedicated to sisterhood, companionship, and study groups. Phyllis is the housemother with an apartment on the ground floor: a sitting room office and a small bedroom.

"My door is always open," she tells me.

The women in this sorority don't go to classes, football games, have sex, drink alcohol, and smoke weed at parties with boys becoming men. Here in the shelter are women who, in differ-ent ways, have experienced men as people who abuse, beat, and sometimes try to kill them. In this sorority, I sleep in the base-ment. I wake up, climb the stairs, and emerge into another life: I have coffee with the women who have just seen their children off to school, or are assembling the ones who are being home-schooled because their lives are at risk from homicidal fathers or vulnerable to kidnapping by less-than-homicidal fathers. I learn that *daddy* and *husband* are often not terms of endearment. In this ordered and tremulous environment, we go over kitchen and housekeeping duties. There are schedules and timetables posted for whose turn it is to buy food, cook, or clean.

On some mornings, I help Sofia teach. Frankie allows me to correct his math problems but refuses to engage in any conversa-tion. Then I leave, having memorized the present code, making sure to go out the side door across the yard, into the adjacent house, into Myra's house, and out her front door. I walk to my car, unfollowed and safe, drive to police headquarters, and resume my work as a homicide detective. Linda Fuentes and I maintain a correct professional relationship. The other detectives are indifferent to my fading bruises; a gym fight between cops is not a big deal. Fuentes and I are just two of the boys. And no one, so far, no one seems to care about my erratic coming and going. If anyone wants any further information, I'll tell them to ask Lieutenant Hagen. No one does. I spend the morning dropping off hit-and-run victim Daniel Huang's clothes to Libby Murphy at the NYPD Crime Lab in Jamaica. I ask her to search for paint fragments in the fibers. Libby promises me results, possibly that afternoon. She is outraged about the son of a bitch who not only hit Daniel, but robbed him, too. On my return to HQ, I find another three cases on my desk in which the victims obtained restraining orders from their abusers. Two were married, one had a boyfriend, and none of them were anywhere near a women's shelter when they were killed. Which, I suppose, is one of the reasons they were easy to kill. Lunch is a takeout pho bowl from Tuk Tuk, a Vietnamese cafe. At four o'clock, Libby Murphy calls.

"I found paint fragments on Daniel's hoodie."

"Make and model?"

"White Toyota—a delivery van, I'd say. There were also traces of red exterior paint. A flake contained part of a number that means the van was pimped out with logos or ads. So look for a new Toyota that delivers something. Like flowers or booze."

"Thanks, Libby. We'll find it." I download the list of licensed auto body repair shops in Queens. Unfortunately, there are also a lot of unlicensed shops. The Iron Triangle, bordered by 126th Street and Willets Point Boulevard, contains more than two hundred independent body shops. It will be a long and arduous search, but we'll find the van and its vile driver. I will be obsessive.

When I return, I park my car in Myra's driveway and wind my way back into Artemis.

I'm in my basement room, trying to scrub yellow stains out of the sink, when Phyllis knocks and calls out from the top of the stairs, "May I come down?"

"Sure."

She descends the stairs, a coffee mug in each hand. She hands me one and sits on the bottom stair. "Can you stand a few more questions?"

"Like what?"

"Your name. Your real one."

"Look, I told you I'm married to a policeman. My trust level is pretty low, so for now my name is Lucy. You can kick me out or let me be anonymous."

"You're not the first woman who has been here escaping an abusive cop husband. I don't trust them, either. In my experience, cops are the most dangerous abusers; they know how to get away with it. If your husband is a cop, you are high risk, not only to yourself, but also to us, so you have to be doubly careful. Understand?"

"You don't have to tell me. The last time he beat me, I called 911. Two of his buddies showed up. We know them socially. I know their wives; our kids play together. You know what? He said we got into an argument. I was violent and attacked him. He had to restrain me. That's coded language. Cops know what it means. They refused to arrest him, said we should go to marriage counseling. If I filed a report, I would ruin his career. I told them he was going to kill me. They told me to calm down; they would talk to him. I'm finished with the police."

"I don't blame you for your reluctance to open up right now. I'd still like to ask you a few questions."

"Okay."

"Who knows you're here? Have you told anyone?"

"No."

"Do you have outside support? Family?"

"I have a sister in Rochester. She'll call me when her husband isn't around. I'm not welcome there thanks to mine. He was awful to them, too. They couldn't stand him."

"What about friends?"

"I've crashed, hid out, slept on couches. My husband knows who they are and where they live. If I go to any of them, I put them in danger. I won't do that."

Phyllis looks at me, her eyes steady behind the delicate octagonal granny glasses, her head slightly cocked, her good ear aimed waiting for more. I know the stare. I've used it in interrogations to make the suspect talk. I'm not playing the game. But I want to keep it friendly, so I sneeze.

"Bless you," Phyllis says.

I got her to speak first.

"Our mission is to create a safe, supportive environment for women in danger. Safety, outside and in. You can't tell anyone where you are. You have to respect our rules inside. We are all responsible for one another. That means rules, too many, so we aim to strike a balance between ones that keep us safe and those that create another oppressive environment."

It makes sense. Phyllis says, "One more thing. I need to know if you think you are in a life-threatening situation."

"Do I believe my husband when he says he's going to kill me? I do."

"When is he violent?"

"When he's drunk, depressed, or can't get an erection."

"Have you talked about divorce?"

"Let's see. He says he can't stop me from getting a divorce, but I won't live to sign the papers. Then he tells me he loves me, promises to change, begs forgiveness, cries, tells me about his own brutal childhood, how his father beat him, says he will go to anger management, AA, we can go to therapy."

"Couples' therapy is useless if he's hitting you. It isn't about making you change, it's about him stopping."

"We tried it, but it only made it worse. We would have these calm, honest conversations with the therapist, and then when we got in the car, he would smack me around for dissing him in front of a stranger. Can you suggest anything I haven't tried, other than poisoning him?"

"It's always an option."

There is no irony in Phyllis's speech. She reminds me of Mr. McDermott, who can't remember who he killed but said, "It does sound like something I could have done."

"You're serious."

"No. You'll go to prison. Jails are filled with women who thought they could kill in self-defense."

"Then nothing will change. Until he kills me, right?"

"What about your children? You said you—"

"A boy. He's ten. Lucas. He lives with my husband." Of all my lies, my rehearsed fabrications, this one is the most depressing. It will be convincing, as it is closest to the truth. Lucas the son I have created to deceive Phyllis to make my marriage authentic is based on Sammy, my brother.

"My parents divorced when I was his age. It was devastating. I swore I would never put my son through that. The strange thing is my husband is a terrific dad."

"Except when he beats you."

"Still, Lucas idolizes him. What ten-year-old wouldn't? He's a cop, an ex-marine who went after the bad guys in Iraq. He talks about honor, patriotism, and the flag. He volunteers—Little League coach, Cub Scout leader—he can play video games, play guitar, go camping, and make his son hate his mother."

"Has he threatened you with his gun?"

"Often."

Phyllis stands up, puts her hand under my chin, gently tilts my face up to hers.

"When you are ready, I want to know your real name, and I want the name of your husband. In the meantime, we will keep you safe."

In the meantime?

CHAPTER 25

I've been in the shelter long enough for my bruises to begin to fade. My ribs don't ache when I turn over in my sleep, and I've been weaned off Amanda's painkillers. My assignment as an undercover cop obliges me to look for information that might implicate one or more people in three murders. I need to listen, snoop around, find a roll of duct tape, see if it matches the one used on Ronald, a new handcart in case a corpse needs moving, but most important, make friends, get people to trust me, and then if they are legitimate suspects, betray them. Normal police work. I'm getting to know the women in the shelter; my notes mention April—Amanda and Frankie's mother. She's in her early thirties, overweight, always in sweats, brown hair with a tiny and unnecessary rubber-banded ponytail. I know the look; she does not want anyone to be attracted to her. She is wearing her wounds. There is Sofia, the former teacher: tall, slender, twenties. Paula, black Jamaican, early thirties, holds her one-year-old boy, Byron, in a baby wrap so she will always know where he is: close to her body. Gerri, thirties, she has a lined, weary face; her front upper teeth are missing, making her look older than her years. I learn later they are missing because her husband punched them out of her mouth. There is Haneen, Middle Eastern—it's an easy guess from the name. She's in her twenties with a flawless cocoa complexion and black hair, perfect except for her gnawed fingernails. She wears Ralph Lauren and designer jeans. What the hell is she doing here? She looks too young and well placed to be a victim. I'll get her story. Last, Janice, Tiffany's mother. She told me over coffee that her husband is in full-time therapy, completing anger management classes, and they have met outside the shelter. He pleads with her to come home; he claims to be a different man.

"Truth is, I'm terrified," she says.

"Of what?" I ask.

"That I'll believe him."

Lieutenant Hagen has given me flexible duty hours that allow me to spend time on my other cases and then return to the shelter in time for dinner. It's like being under house arrest without the ankle bracelet. Phyllis is used to me leaving for work and has stopped asking questions.

On this Friday morning, I walk with Amanda and Ben to school. They take different routes in case their fathers are stalking them. Ben walks slightly ahead of us, never joins in our conversation. As we walk, I get bits and pieces of Amanda's life.

"My mother was a bookkeeper in a wholesale flower business. The owner, Mrs. Bartolini, taught me how to make rose bouquets. When I got good at it, she paid me twenty-five cents a bouquet. My father was a chef at the Waldorf Astoria—it's, like, a big hotel in the city. Then he quit and he and another chef opened their own restaurant in SoHo. But it went out of business and he lost a lot of money, so he had to go back to hotel cooking, which he hated. He was working all the time and he got into coke and stuff turned bad between him and Mom. He was always blaming her for things. Mom says he started hitting her when they got into arguments. One night he banged her head against the wall so hard she had to go to the hospital. He was supposed to go to jail for six months, but he got time off for good behavior, did community service teaching disadvantaged children how to cook, and got his job back. But he's looking for us, and my mom says he is not well. He could kidnap us, so we have to be really careful. My mom has double vision—she can't use the computer or concentrate on numbers, so she can't work."

"Your brother, Frankie?"

"He likes to stay in the bathroom, where he reads and does his homework. Why? Because he can lock the door. But we're lucky: we could be on the street, or in a homeless shelter, where we were before we came here, or back in our own home. If you asked me, I would say the homeless shelter is bad, street worse, home with Mom and Dad the worst."

"Do you cry?"

Amanda stops. "That's the first interesting question you've asked me. I know babies cry for lots of reasons—they are tired, hungry, maybe something hurts them, like a strap is too tight, or their diaper is full—but you won't ever know because they can't talk. It's always a mom who hears the crying and knows what to do. They get a hug, kiss, bounce, loosen a strap, change a diaper. But what about when she's crying? All of us . . . let's see, that's me, Frankie, Ben, Tiffany, Byron—not Byron, he's only one year old; he was too young to understand what it meant when his daddy punched his mommy—we all have to deal with mommy crying. We grew up with it. We used to cry when she cried, but we stopped doing that. It didn't seem fair. We learned to stop crying and try to take care of her after daddy hit her, or yelled at her, or like Ben's daddy, who liked to throw food at her if he didn't like it—he thought it was funny, so he laughed while she cried. No, I don't cry."

"The future?"

"Mom says my dad might get a job in Miami, which would be a solution. He would get out of New York, and we could move out of the shelter, take charge of our lives again. Mom says he can take out his craziness on somebody else. Best of all, we'll always know where he is."

"What's the worst part?"

"It's when Daddy promises. Promises never to hit Mommy again, or promises not to do drugs anymore, and Mommy promises us that Daddy is going to be nice to her, starting right now, and she won't make him angry because he has such a bad temper. Then we all hug and laugh, and we go to Chili's or even a fancy place where Daddy knows the chef. Mommy says Daddy loves her and she loves him and Daddy loves Frankie and me, so from now on we are going to be a happy family and we feel good. It's the same for all of us here. I know. I asked Ben, Tiffany, and they said the same thing: under feeling good, we feel real bad. We know it's all going to happen again. Mommy and Daddy are fucking liars."

"You sound older than twelve."

"I listen in on group. There are a lot of messed-up people in this world, wouldn't you say?"

"I would say."

"Most of them are men, wouldn't you say?"

"I would say."

Ben waits for us to catch up to him.

We take turns cooking dinner; it's mine tonight. There are recipes in the shelter cookbook, a loose-leaf binder. My co-chef will be Amanda. Before she left for school, we went through the recipes, decided on roast pork with brown rice and creamed spinach. Normally, groceries are delivered to the shelter via Myra's house, but I can leave the shelter, so I'll shop for this meal. For the women who can't leave the shelter because of the danger, cooking is a diversion from boredom. The result is meals that verge on gourmet, the kids rebel, and extravagant French food is tossed and replaced with mac and cheese. The instructions say the chef is supposed to prepare a vegetarian alternative, but Amanda tells me there aren't any at the shelter.

While the pork is roasting, we cook the spinach, turn on the rice cooker. Meals are sometimes served buffet-style since there are too many different schedules to allow for a regular sit-down meal. Amanda makes extra money babysitting when any of the three mothers must leave the shelter to visit various social agencies, welfare offices, or meet with lawyers or doctors.

I notice simmering tension between the women regarding rooms, their proximity to bathrooms, size of closets, and windows. The walls are thin; conversations, babies crying, children arguing with mothers, and mothers losing it with children—all this is shared. People are living under incredible strain. Women are worried about their children, their lives, money. They are angry, away from their homes, powerless, and it all tends to put people in bad moods. The kids pick up on it. Feeling safe is important. So is missing Daddy when he's being a nice daddy. Not having your own room, not having your toys, your dolls, your books, and sharing a TV and a bathroom with five other kids isn't fun, either.

As a result, a lot of Phyllis's time is spent keeping everybody calm.

"We didn't escape a prison to create one of our own. We need to cooperate, act collectively in the interest of one another by making the best of a bad situation. We're all stressed, but we have to live together, and the friendlier we can make it, the better it is for us and the children."

She leads meditation sessions, yoga, exercises in the yard, whatever helps to keep tempers, frustrations, and despair on a low flame. And tonight, after dinner, when the children are asleep, will be our group discussion, or "group"—my first one since I came to Artemis.

"Friday nights there's a kind of group discussion after dinner," Phyllis said.

"Attendance required?"

"I'm afraid so. But talking isn't. See how you feel."

After dinner, we assemble at the dining room table in front of a teapot, mugs, and a plate of cookies.

Phyllis says, "We can call it 'group' but not group therapy. I'm not a trained psychologist. I haven't had any shrink training. Most of what I know, I learned from watching Dr. Phil." She gets a few smiles; the joke is for me. I'm the only one who hasn't heard it. I am being observed by the women in the shelter, even as I observe them. No one knows my story except Phyllis. I am simply the "new arrival"; wounded, frightened, and guarded. The women are kind and don't press me for information; they know it will all eventually come out.

"I know we can learn a lot from each other. You may think you are the only one struggling—but you're not. It helps to know you're not alone. So. There are two rules: April?"

"No bullshit."

"Why?"

"Because we've heard enough from our husbands."

The women nod.

"You got that right, girl," Paula says.

"The other rule?"

"No interrupting," April says.

"Good. Who'd like to begin?"

Silence. Phyllis looks at me; she's inviting me to speak. I lower my eyes, avoid hers. I'm not jumping in. I'm the new arrival. My bruises have faded, but I feel uneasy in this place. I have nothing about me to share yet.

I observe the women around the table: on my right is Haneen. Then Amanda and Frankie's mother, April, sitting ramrod straight in her chair. I see her daughter, Amanda, in her face, but the eyes are different. Amanda's eyes are always searching, exploring; she's a bumblebee. Her mother's eyes find a place, her neatly folded hands on the table, and they will rest there, uncurious and safe. I remember April's husband liked to grab her by the back of the neck and bang her head against the wall.

Next to her is Gerri, Ben's mother. She leans forward to Phyllis.

"Can I talk about my family first?"

"You can talk about anything you want," Phyllis says.

Gerri speaks quickly, anxious to get it out before someone tells her to *shut the fuck up*. No one will, of course. But she has been well trained by her husband. "Yeah, well, I've been remembering how he made me separate from my family. He said I had to choose; it was either him or them. They hated him, so it was a question of my loyalty. He was right: my parents got it about him; they saw through the charm and thought he was a phony. I wish I had listened. I was young. I was still rebelling."

"Making you sever ties with your family is a typical abusive technique," Phyllis says. "You become dependent on him. He's got you where he wants you."

"It was crazy. I rejected my family for him and he accused them of rejecting me. *They don't love you like I do. They abandoned you. I'm all you have. I'm the one who loves you.* He kept saying that. *I'm the one who loves you.* He said it when he hit me, when he choked me until I passed out, when he accused me of having affairs, when he showed up at work, when he accused me of dressing sexy for other men. It went on for three years. The beatings got worse. I felt I had nowhere to turn; I couldn't face my parents.

"I took out a restraining order on him, like, he couldn't come within four hundred feet of me, then he started harassing my parents, telling them I had become a prostitute, calling my boss, telling him I was dealing drugs, until I lost my job. Then my father had a heart attack and died. I felt it was my fault. I was afraid to go to the funeral. My brother helped me move out, and my husband was afraid of him, so he didn't try to stop me. I was starting to get my life back, but he found out where I was living. I came home one night, there was a note on the bed: *I'm the one who loves you.* He told me he could always find me, and the next time he would kill me. The police said they couldn't do anything unless they could catch him in my presence. I finally called my mother. She wouldn't see me; she said I'd caused my father's death. I write to her every week, Phyllis—a real letter, not an email."

Haneen says, "She'll come around. I'm sure. Just give her time. The thing is you're safe here until then."

Janice, Tiffany's mother, raises her hand, then lowers it as she remembers it's not a classroom, it's a group of women sitting around a table swapping stories about men who beat them.

"Motormouth. That's what he called me just before the slap. Not a hard one. Just on the wrong side of affectionate. Wait. Is there such a thing? An affectionate slap? A love tap? A punch on the shoulder to get my attention? A slap on the back of my head as he walks by while I am at the computer?

"*Sit up straight, motormouth. You'll hurt your back.* My head is still ringing. So it got to be a thing, him slapping me on the head.

Then, like it was something he discovered, it gave him pleasure. Slaps became punches, at first on the shoulder, then to the stomach, like he was seeing how far he could go and how much I would take. Obviously, a lot."

"Why?" Phyllis asks.

"Why did I stay?" Janice says. "Where was I supposed to go? I had no money. I had nowhere to live. He had control of the credit cards, the bank accounts, everything."

Gerri waits a moment and says, "My husband did the same thing. He transferred all the bank accounts to his name. He owned the house, the business, the cars. The credit cards were in his name. He gave me cash for shopping and demanded receipts. I had to account for everything."

Phyllis says, "I know that game. You've got nowhere to go and no way to pay for it if you did."

Gerri nods and continues, "Before I married Tom, I built an online business making personalized picture frames of deceased pets. The bereaved owner would send in a picture of their dog or cat, then I'd make a carved wooden picture frame with the pet's name and dates engraved on it. I did it out of my home on a small laser-engraving machine. I met Tom on a Christian dating site. He had recently retired from the military with a disability pension. At first, he wasn't involved in my work. He was developing his own Internet business, but that didn't go anywhere, so he started working with me. I liked the idea of us working together. He was smart, had lots of ideas. We expanded the business into other kinds of pet mementos: charm bracelets, pendants, statuary. After a while, it was like he was making all the decisions, taking over, and before long I was feeling like we weren't working together, I was working *for* him. When we needed capital to expand, buy better laser engravers, advertise, I was the one who borrowed the money. At the same time, we owned the business together. I was taking on debt while he was keeping the assets. It wasn't fair. He said he had lousy credit and it would be ours in the end. I loved him, trusted him, I wanted to keep everybody happy.

"Tom liked to 'fake fight' with our son, Ben. That's what he called it, 'fake fight.' They would shadow box, you know, not hitting him hard, Tom was faster, stronger. He was an adult, and Ben was just a kid. Tom said it was good to teach him how to fight, said he never really hurt him—he did. A slap, a punch, a mistake. Tom always said, 'Oops, sorry, kid, got too close, you okay?' Ben said he was okay, but I knew he was on the verge of tears. He didn't like 'fake fighting.' I told Tom he should stop. His reply was 'I will tell you this once: You never criticize me in front of my son, you understand? I want Ben to learn how to fight, to learn how to defend himself.'

"I said, 'You know what he's learning, Tom? He's learning when it's his turn to fight, he'll find someone smaller. You're teaching him how to be a bully, for God's sake.' I saw Ben turning into his father. I knew we had to get out."

"What did you do?" Sofia asks.

"I signed over the business to Tom so he wouldn't fight me on custody of Ben and left. Tom drove the business into the ground. He lost everything, blamed it all on me. Meanwhile I got my life back, started another business, dating a nice guy. Tom started threatening him, and we broke up. He stalked me, demanded money, beat me a few times. He drives a mini-camper, sleeps in it. He's always moving. The police can't seem to find him, but he can always find me. He's out there."

Paula holds her one-year-old son, Byron, in her lap. She speaks softly in a lilting Jamaican accent, as not to wake the child.

"My husband's a lawyer. The first time he hit me, I told him if he ever did it again I would . . . He said, 'Yeah, what? What? What are you going to do, leave? You want to see Byron? I'm a lawyer; you won't have a chance.'

"I said, 'If you hit me again, I will get scissors and cut off your dick in your sleep, I will put rat poison in your coffee, and I will tell my brothers you beat me and they will come after you.'"

We all nod. This seems like a reasonable solution.

"That night he raped me. He knew I was just talking. I knew his plan. He would divorce me, make me an unfit mother, get custody of Byron, and think of a thousand ways to fuck up—excuse me, ruin my life. He could do that. So I took Byron and came here. I'm figuring out my next move, but in the meantime . . ." She looks at Phyllis. "I'm safe."

Haneen speaks next. And I get the story. Of all the women in the shelter, I think she is in the most danger. There is no misogyny, sadism, sexual jealousy, or alcohol-fueled rage, just a perverted notion of honor for which women are murdered. Haneen's Pakistani father and brother are sworn to kill her, and Haneen's mother isn't on her side.

Haneen was five years old when her family came to America from Karachi. On her fourteenth birthday, her father promised her in marriage to a distant cousin. She was never informed of this. Haneen went on to become a thoroughly Americanized student at Astoria High School, then Queens College, where she majored in Middle Eastern languages with a minor in economics. In the summer of her junior year, she interned at Chase and met another intern, Teddy Wang, an econ/math/software triple major from Stanford. Because Haneen had a working knowledge of Urdu, Arabic, and Punjab, she was promised a job with the Chase private banking team specializing in Middle Eastern clients.

Chase was counting the days until Teddy graduated; when he did, he would start at two hundred thousand dollars a year, with million-dollar bonuses within five years. Haneen would earn about the same, minus the bonuses.

When Haneen told her parents she and Teddy were planning to marry after graduation, her father informed her that for all practical purposes she was already married. Haneen protested, refused, and said there was nothing they could do about it. She was a US citizen and she was going to marry Teddy. There were laws against what they were proposing. "He got a knife from the kitchen, placed it at my throat, and told me there was a higher law. He would kill me rather than dishonor and shame our family. My brother was sent to Teddy and told him I didn't want to see him again, and not to call me. So what were my choices? Obey, go to Pakistan, marry someone I had never met? Go to the police? Have my father and brother arrested? What happens to my mother, my two younger sisters, my young brother if they go to jail? I came here. Teddy and I made a plan. I'm working on a new identity, Teddy will get a banking job in Singapore, and I'll join him. We just want to move as far away as possible and hope and pray they never find me."

Phyllis says, "Anybody else want to say something?"

She means me. Phyllis smiles. "Okay. Same time next week."

I want a cigarette. Something for me. I'm exhausted from the stories the women tell; I have been a homicide detective for five years and there isn't much I haven't seen in what people do to each other, but here I'm in an epicenter of crimes waiting to happen. Every one of the women have been beaten, and that's terrible, but the fact is that they are still in danger, they know who waits for them to emerge from the shelter and the risks they take in merely stepping outside. I go outside to the children's swing set, plonk down, kick my heels in the sand, and start to move, slowly. I put a cigarette in my mouth, search for a light. I don't have one. Fuck. I am too lazy to go back in the house and find my lighter. A flame flashes. Sofia holds a lit match.

"Thanks."

"You are welcome."

She mounts a seat next to me, lights her own, and we swing gently back and forth.

"I feel uneasy talking in group," Sofia says.

"I understand. I'm not ready, either."

"It's a long story."

"I'm not going anywhere."

"I feel I can tell you. The others, I am not sure they would even believe me."

"Does Phyllis?" I ask.

"She does. I was a teacher in Ljubljana. Chemistry. I also played flute and gave lessons on the side. I met an American boy. He was on an exchange program teaching English, and he wanted flute lessons. He found me, we played together, and—how romantic—we fell in love. He wanted me to come back to the US and marry him. I think I was the fantasy, but when I became the reality, he couldn't handle it—we broke up. I was alone and vulnerable in New York. What do they say, no support system? I ran into a guy I used to know in Ljubljana—we played in the same youth orchestra. Now he was living in Manhattan, doing business."

"What kind?"

"I didn't ask, never found out. Just business. He had an extra room, put me up, introduced me to his friends, bought me clothes. I was broke. He said I was beautiful, smart, and sexy. I spoke three languages, which made me perfect company for him and his friends. We partied, helicoptered to the Hamptons, and flew on private planes to the Caribbean, Las Vegas, and Aspen. The men on the plane got older and richer, and I realized I was part of the package. By the time I wanted out, I was who I was. Politely, an escort. Less politely, a whore. I was owned. I knew what was in store for me if I wanted out. My visa expired, I had no money of my own, and they had my passport.

"On one of the trips, I met a psychiatrist who worked for a security company that provided protection for some of the people on the plane, and also celebrities and movie stars. His job was to evaluate letters from fans—the crazy ones, who sent anything from death threats to marriage proposals. You'd be surprised how many letters these people get, and how many of them put their return address on the letter or sign their names. Put that together with the postmark and you can identify a lot of them. They were stalkers, crazies, paranoids, and extortionists. After he read the letters, he would write reports that began with "Take this person seriously" or not. I was a full-time escort by then. He didn't care. He liked my company; what I did on my own time was my business. We started out slow, and he took me to museums, art galleries, it was a friendship, though I kept waiting for it to change.

"One night he took me to a party—a surprise birthday for one of his clients, a New York City hedge fund guy. I was the surprise. He was married, but he went crazy for me and must have made a deal with the Russians. I became his full-time mistress. He was powerful and rich, and I don't even want to mention his name. He was also crazy. I was his escape, his other life. He was into voyeurism, made me have sex with his friends and took videos on his cell phone so he could watch them whenever he wanted. He was in them, too. One night I copied them from his phone, told him I had them and if he didn't let me go, I would post them. He said if I did, he would have me killed. I realized he would have me killed no matter what I did. I knew too much. One of the girls I knew told me about this place."

That night, after the rest of the women have gone upstairs, I read in the living room. I like to stay upstairs in the house until I feel tired enough to go down to my basement bed and fall asleep. Phyllis comes in and sits next to me on the couch.

"You seem to have settled in."

"It's a big adjustment."

"At some point, we need to know more about you, despite your obvious wounds."

"I'm not ready."

"What we really need to know is what kind of danger you are in. It's a matter of risk assessment. It impacts on the shelter and the people in it."

"Who makes that assessment?"

"You do. I can help. I have a lot of experience. I've been wrong sometimes. It's hard to live with."

"Okay. My husband? When he gets bad, yeah, I think he could kill me."

"You said he's a cop, right?"

"Yes."

"Then he could."

"You want to know all about me?"

"Yes."

I tell Phyllis I'm not ready to tell my story.

"We could help," she says.

CHAPTER 26

I want to know more about Haneen. On my way to HQ, I stop at Astoria High School, where I look at old yearbooks. Haneen's last name is Lakhani. Her yearbook profile says her nickname is "Nee Nee," she will be going to Queens College, made Honor Society, played on the girls' volleyball team, was a member of the French Club, Chess Club, and Peer Tutoring, and wrote for the student newspaper. Back at headquarters, I log into the INS secure site, where I learn her father, Amar Lakhani, was naturalized in 1999. He has been a steady employee of Mammoth Security Services, moving around to banks, museums, department stores—I will check to see if he is licensed to carry a gun. I scan Amar's citizenship application, apartment lease, driver's license, and telephone records. Haneen's mother is Rameesha. She has two younger daughters: Rida, aged nine, and Tamsila, aged eleven. The older brother, Isar, is twenty-two and works for an air conditioner repair company in Manhattan. The younger brother, Azfar, fourteen, is a sophomore at the MDQ Academy, an Islamic school. From the New York Police Department/NSA database on all Mideast immigrants in New York City (compiled after 9/11), I learn the Lakhani males worship at the Masjid El-Ber mosque in Long Island City. I know everything about them. They are a law-abiding, hardworking, typical New York immigrant family. I need some advice. I find Detective Akram Danai in the coffee shop on the first floor.

"I need a favor. Can you help me with a Muslim family situation?"

Detective Danai laughs. "It's my specialty."

I hand him my notes on the Lakhani family. He takes his time, reading carefully.

"Very interesting. May I ask why you are showing me this?"

"The oldest daughter is being threatened into an arranged marriage in Pakistan."

"That's pretty rare these days. It's more of a problem in the UK. Can you define *threatened*?"

"As in death."

"The rest of the family?"

"The older son is on board, the mother is passive at best, the other kids are too young to count."

"The father may have a big debt back in Pakistan. This might be how he's repaying it."

"With his daughter?"

"It's a win-win: he marries off a daughter and settles the debt. Since he has also given his word to this man, he knows if the marriage doesn't happen it will bring dishonor to the family name. He's not a bad guy, he's just locked into a system, and he doesn't know any other."

"Yes, he does. It's called Queens County, New York State. He put a knife to her throat; he'll kill her if he finds her. His idiot son will help."

"I know the imam of his mosque. He won't countenance this. Do you want me to talk to him?"

"Yes."

"Where's the daughter?"

"Hiding."

"I can get Dr. Kahn to talk to him, the most he can do is threaten to expel him from the mosque."

"Is that meaningful?"

"Maybe."

"Thanks."

I have done my good deed for the day. I drop in on Lieutenant Hagen and give her a report of life at Artemis. "It's like an Airbnb for battered women. Everybody who's in it is a victim. There are children who have seen their mothers beaten . . ."

Lieutenant Hagen holds up her hand, stopping me. "I've been doing this for thirty years, Nina. You're not telling me anything I haven't seen. I want you to get back and find out if these people had anything to do with your cold cases." She pauses for effect. "And the murder of Ronald Steevers."

After dinner at the shelter, I am on wash-up detail with Sofia. Phyllis went to Ikea for new towels and came back with two bags of frozen meatballs. She heated them up in a thick commercial tomato sauce with frozen peas. They weren't bad.

Phyllis tells Sofia she will take over the cleanup. Sofia quickly hands Phyllis her yellow rubber gloves and goes out to the back porch, where she will smoke and bite her nails. We load the dishwasher, I swab the counter with the sponge, and Phyllis starts the machine and says, "I would like to talk to you in my office, if you don't mind."

It is my first time in Phyllis's office. In this house's prior life, it was most likely the breakfast nook. Now it barely has room for a battered couch loaded with pillows against the wall. The shelter dog, Bobo, has taken up most of the space on the couch. She sees me and beats her tail against a pillow in greeting but is too lazy or comfortable to get up. There is no desk. I like that. Two straight-backed wooden chairs with thick cushions face a coffee table. There is a vase of yellow lilies. On one wall, there are four framed prints of the same thatched cottage, one for each season.

The cottage is set in a slightly mysterious Victorian forest at the end of a country lane. Bulbous rosebushes and fecund apple trees line the lane. Smoke rises out of the cottage chimney, soft light glows through the windows. It is home idealized, surely inhabited by kind, welcoming people. In a bar, it would make drunks weep. Somewhat to my surprise, I find it pleasing.

"Have a seat," Phyllis says.

I obey. Tea is not offered. Phyllis sits opposite me, holds up her iPad, where there is a photo of me in an elevator in the Queens Center mall that I remember was taken by a Tenacious Dame.

"It's time to come clean, dear. I know you're a cop. What I don't know is what you're doing here."

Busted. But I'm still ahead of her.

CHAPTER 27

Phyllis knows I'm a cop; she has that part right. The rest of her information is wrong. Lieutenant Hagen is an expert at placing people in undercover situations.

"I have a graduate degree from the FBI in undercover. I could put a cop in your family and have you believe he's a long-lost relative."

She knew Phyllis would copy my license plate. Tracing a license plate isn't hard. Phyllis would then have my identity. Or think she did. The license plates were false. They would lead her to me, but it wouldn't be me. It would be a made-up person. It's my history that matters: it has to be convincing. Here's how I got mine.

When my doctor fiancé and I separated, I wanted a bar in Manhattan where I would not run into any of my off-duty colleagues from my Long Island precinct. Not that I didn't like them, I just wanted to meet people with whom I could start fresh, or if I wanted, be anonymous, or pose as someone else: a student, a lawyer, a techie, anyone but a policewoman. I had read about the White Horse Tavern in Greenwich Village; one visit and it became my nights-off drinking headquarters. The White Horse is a famous literary watering hole, having served Dylan Thomas, Brendan Behan, Jack Kerouac, and later, generations of novelists, journalists, and aspiring writers. At the bar I met and fell under the spell of a semifamous novelist, James X, who won me over with his wit, erudition, and interest in my current bullshit identity as a salesperson at the Museum of Modern Art gift shop, and sealed the deal with a promise of bagels and lox with the *Sunday Times* crossword in bed the next morning. There was sex—I remember it as something we did, but it happened so we could have earnest conversations afterward. He was a real writer, my first, so I asked the obvious: I asked him what was the most important thing to know if you wanted to be a writer.

He said, "There are two. In fiction, your life comes in handy, so write about it. And if your life isn't interesting, steal someone else's."

What applies to writers of fiction also applies to cops who go undercover. It's what Lieutenant Hagen said to me when I told her I wanted to go into the women's shelter.

"You'll need a story, a convincing one. You need to pretend to be a cop married to a nasty, abusive cop. I know one. Use hers."

The story of my fake past belonged to Marlene Davis, formerly with the Merrick, Long Island, police force.

We met in a McDonald's near LaGuardia at four in the afternoon. Slow time, not many customers—Marlene was easy to pick out: a middle-aged, grim woman in a police uniform, sitting in a chair with her back to the wall. As she talked, she kept her eyes focused on the doors, not on me. Her paranoia was infectious, and it didn't take long for me to want a seat against the wall, too. She sipped a black coffee and skipped the small talk.

"Lily said you wanted a story for undercover work."

"A cop married to a cop."

Marlene took a deep breath. "That's me. I have twenty minutes."

I nodded.

"Okay. He told me how he would kill me. He knew lots of ways to do it; he said he could make it look like an accident or suicide. If he was drunk enough, I knew he would also kill my son and then himself. You could start with that."

Marlene is calm. She's not asking for sympathy, or even understanding.

"Could you tell me why you went into law enforcement?"

"Sure. I became a policewoman for the same reason men become policemen. I wanted to be useful. I wanted to help people,
protect the people in my community from criminals. Then
there were the not-for-publication reasons. I dug the uniform,
the car, the action; I was a jock in high school. I like physical
stuff, sweat and bruising. In high school, I rock climbed, ran mar-
athons, played soccer. I was a gym rat; endorphins were my best
friends. Conversely, my homemaking skills sucked—I couldn't
boil an egg or use a vacuum cleaner—I learned, of course. To be
honest, there was also the money. New York State Police start
around fifty thousand dollars a year, and I could get to the low
seventies pretty fast. Good health insurance, paid vacations, ma-
ternity leave, a secure pension plan; with overtime, promotions,
I could end up at one hundred K by the time I retired after
twenty years, and I would still be in my forties. Not bad. How
about you?"

"Pretty much for the same reasons. And I had something to
prove, but I can't remember what it was."

*I went into police work so I could better find a murderer and kill
him. Do we have something in common? Or will we?*

"Can you tell me about your husband? Lieutenant Hagen says
he's also a cop."

"Was. No, is. He's on suspension. I don't know if he'll get his
job back, and he's going to have a hard time finding another in
New York. He's a big guy who swaggers up to you at a bar, gets
right in your face. He knows how to make other men fear him.
No one on the street questions his authority; no one asks why
they are being stopped, pulled over, frisked, or pushed against

a wall. He has a hundred ways to hurt you that won't show; he can inflict pain and not leave a trace. He does it to black teenagers, kids on skateboards at the 7-Eleven, minority drivers passing through the wrong neighborhood, and his wife."

She glances at the time on her phone and takes a last sip of her coffee. "But there's another side to him: at the YMCA where he swims and teaches, at church, at Scouts—he's a *role model*. Little boys want to grow up to be like him."

"And the violence?"

"He likes to hit me when he wants to improve my memory about his likes and dislikes. The thing is, he's discreet. We could be on the couch after dinner watching television, nice and cozy, and he'll turn to me and punch me on the arm, hard—he knows exactly where, so that it numbs down to my wrist—to remind me that he doesn't like *fucking, fucking, fucking, steak well done*. But it usually depends on how much he has had to drink. If it's a lot, it means I'm on the floor, his hand around my throat, and he's slapping my face. I don't scream so I won't wake up our son. Anyway, I'm learning my lesson. And I can't breathe because his knees are on my chest and he weighs two-twenty. When he goes to the bathroom to throw up, I call the cops. When they come, he goes outside and talks to them. They try to 'calm me down.' I have a reputation for being hysterical. I lose control and hit him. He has to protect himself and the children. He can show them scratches, a bruise. They tell me the 'blue line' stuff about 'keeping it in the family' and urge me not to ruin his career and mine. 'Come on, Marlene, you guys can work this out.'

"I filed for divorce, and hired a lawyer to sue him and the department. I was taken off active duty and assigned to the evidence room. A few weeks later, cocaine was found in my locker. It was from the evidence room, of course. I had a choice: withdraw the lawsuits, or lose my job, maybe go to jail, but for sure ending up a single mother with no money. Fight? I remember my lawyer asking me, 'How much justice can you afford?' So I'm back. Life is fine. I see my kids, I have my job, and I try to behave. And I read a lot. Mostly about ways to kill him."

She shrugs and crunches her paper cup in her fist.

"Thanks. You've been a big help."

"Yeah."

Now, at Artemis, as I sit under the prints of the seasonal cottages, Bobo resting her head on my lap, I make a restrained and tearful confession to Phyllis. "I *was* a cop."

"Are you still working?"

"I was. I have this other job."

"Editor?"

"Yes."

"But your husband is a cop?"

"Yes." Bobby B will portray my abusive and dangerous husband. If Phyllis finds out that I am lying, I have a backup story, better bullshit. My life is lies layered on lies, one is exposed, there is another to cover it. I slip into Marlene's story; it is now my own. I tell her about Bobby's (Robert's) threats to me, my parents, his talk about suicide. Phyllis listens. She doesn't interrupt; she absorbs my information and processes it as it arrives.

"He's on temporary suspension. He stalks me. The last time he found me, he beat me so hard (*Thank you very much, Linda Fuentes*) that I went to the emergency room and a nurse suggested I come here."

"Do you think you're in mortal danger?"

Mortal danger? It's a quaint way to question my situation; it is a question that would never be asked in the thatched cottage on her wall.

"He's out there," I say. "He's convinced I'm responsible for his suspension, and he has friends on the force who think so, too. I have a job. I had a place to stay—a friend's spare room—but he found me. So far, he hasn't found where I work, or that I'm here. My boss lets me sleep on the couch when I work late, but I'm safer here. He's out there, looking for me. One of these days, Robert will find me and kill me. Sometimes I think it would be better to kill him first, go to jail."

Phyllis nods slowly, deliberately. "I don't want to frighten you, but the really crazy ones, they kill their children, too." She pauses, gazes up at the winter cottage print on the wall, snug, cozy, inviting. "Then they kill themselves. Why can't the bastards go straight to suicide?"

She says this last sentence so calmly, so coldly, so much as a logical conclusion that it strikes me as coming from her own experience.

"I don't want to see my women in danger. You, my dear, are in danger. I think you understand."

I nod. Yes, I am in mortal danger. *Are you going to kill him for me?*

"What should I do?"

"For now, you are safe here. I'll think about it. It would be best to get you out of the East Coast, far away. We don't do witness protection, and it's a bad solution, anyway. You have to really change your life, start over again, and what's harder, teach your children to do the same. He's a cop, so he knows how to find you. He has at his disposal software you don't even know about. He can source bank accounts, credit cards, licenses, IRS, Social Security. He can tap your parents' phone, access their computers—it's not legal without a warrant, but he'll do it any-way. So it's not just about disappearing; you have to re-create yourself. About your family? You don't get to see them again. Ever. So it's possible, but it's difficult. Then you also get to live your life looking over your shoulder. What if you meet someone, you remarry, you have children together? It will just make your ex-husband crazier. Do you tell your new husband the truth? If your ex is out there looking for you, insane and jealous, you are putting your new family at risk. Welcome to a life of paranoia."

I think about Marlene sitting with her back to the wall, staring at the McDonald's door.

"I want to go home," I say.

"I'll tell you when you can go home. When I do, you will be safe."

Amanda bursts into Phyllis's office. She takes my hand and pulls me off of the couch.

"You have to talk to Haneen. Now!"

Phyllis is right behind me as we go into the living room. Haneen is descending the stairs. She's wearing her padded parka.

"Haneen, what's going on?" I say.

"She's leaving," Amanda says.

"Haneen?"

"My mother had a heart attack. She's in the hospital."

"Where?"

"Mount Sinai. Astoria."

Phyllis reflexively steps in front of the door, blocking her path. "Don't go, Haneen. Not yet. We can check this out. It may not be true."

"My sister called. I believe her."

"Call the hospital. Make sure. It could be a trick to get you out of the shelter. Where's your father?"

"He's at work."

Phyllis has no real authority over Haneen, and everybody knows it. Phyllis only has the voice. "It's not safe, Haneen. Until then, you stay here. Upstairs."

I heard the unsaid *young lady*, as in, *Upstairs, young lady*.

Haneen is fighting tears. Phyllis is still blocking the door.

"Let us check it out, Haneen," I say.

Haneen takes out her cell, calls, speaks in Pashto. I hear *Mama*.

"That was my sister," Haneen says. "She's at the hospital with Mom. Okay? I'm going."

She reaches behind Phyllis for the doorknob. Haneen's *get out of my way* trumps Phyllis's *I can't let you do this*. Phyllis steps aside, looks at me, cocks her head. *Can't you do something?*

"I'll come with you," I say. Haneen shrugs, steps outside, walks and texts. I catch up.

"My car is around the corner."

"I already Ubered."

The Uber driver consults his dashboard GPS, takes the Grand Central Parkway west, toward the Triborough Bridge. In the distance is the skyline of the Manhattan island, flat against the pale yellowish sky. I want to be there. But we are on the opposite side, traveling parallel to the East River. Manhattan is a backdrop. We will soon be heading away from the glass towers packed against one another with their permutations of bars, restaurants, museums, galleries, theaters—all out of reach for me. I have to find a way to prevent Haneen from walking into someone else's lethal trap. Our journey is replicated on the driver's GPS. The thick red line says exit at Hoyt Avenue. We travel under the elevated train tracks.

Haneen stares ahead. "She has heart disease. It's not the first time. When she gets chest pains, she goes to the ER. The doctors tell her she is having small heart attacks. They tell her she needs bypass surgery; she refuses and goes home. The next attack may not be small, it might be big, it could be her last."

At Thirtieth Avenue, the hospital comes into view. I tell the driver to stop at the emergency entrance. Leaning against a parked ambulance, a driver furtively smokes a cigarette. Aside from him, there are no adult males in the vicinity.

We get out. I let Haneen walk ahead of me for a few steps so I can discreetly reach into my purse, where I am carrying my second gun, the little .38. We enter the ER receiving room. Normal. A bored security guard on duty, a nurse's station, a couple of doctors filling out paperwork, indifferent to the three rows of people sitting in interlocking plastic chairs. Mothers with feverish children, a leathered motorcyclist cradling what might be a broken wrist, an old woman sitting next to her husband, who's leaning forward, his folded hands a pillow for his chin resting on his cane. They are citizens in various stages of pain waiting to see a doctor.

"I'm here to see Lakhani Ramesha. She was admitted into the cardiac unit today."

"There's my brother," Haneen says, as if he is the proof their mother is in the hospital.

Haneen goes to a teenage boy, sits in the empty seat beside him. I watch them embrace. I see tears on the cheeks of the boy as he puts one arm around his sister, and with the other he takes out a small revolver and shoots Haneen in the head. She falls backward off the chair. People scream, run for exits. The boy drops the gun to the floor. He puts his hands on his head.

I kick the pistol away and handcuff the boy. He is sobbing

now, his chest heaving, gulping for air. A security guard appears, followed by two ER paramedics pushing a gurney. They look at Haneen. They know there is nothing to be done.

A man walks up to the teenage boy. He kneels and puts his arm around him. I recognize him—Haneen's father. Mr. Lakhani looks up at me.

"It was necessary," he says.

There will be wailing tonight.

CHAPTER 28

I find Bobby at Ducky's, a hipster diner that serves as his office. He can't really like the food, but Ducky's is convenient and discreet for his business meetings when his clients come to borrow money or pay back their loans. Bobby has a deal with the owner; when he accumulates too much cash, the manager on duty will put it in the restaurant safe. The food is '50s nostalgia—it tastes just as bad now as it did then. The cashier points me to the rear. Bobby is sitting in a booth; his tabletop jukebox is playing the Shirelles.

"You don't look well," he says.

I tell him about Haneen.

"I made a big mistake, Bobby. I left her alone. It's my fault."

Bobby takes my hands in his and squeezes gently.

"Don't let go, Bobby. I feel so bad."

"I got you."

"I'm so fucking stupid. I was looking for her father. I never imagined it would be her brother . . . Ah, fuck, I can't even say the words."

"Her brother?"

"He's a teenager; he gets a lesser sentence than the father would. The family survives."

A young waiter with a carpet of tattoos up his arm tries to decide where to place Bobby's order, a gooey tuna melt with chili fries. I slip out of Bobby's hand embrace. The waiter offers me a menu. I shake my head. Bobby picks up a fry, considers it, then drops it back into the chili mush.

My phone vibrates on the table. It's an 808 area code: Maui.

"Hi, Ernie."

"Hi, doll. Can you talk?"

"I'm with Bobby."

"Put it on speaker."

I tap the phone, place it on the table.

"We're here."

"Hey, Bobby," Ernie says, like they are old friends.

"Hey, Ernie," Bobby says.

"They found him."

Bobby and I know who *him* is. The *cowardly bastard* who killed my father. The air is out of me. I sit up straight, close my eyes. Find my breath. Catch it, ride it until I can open my eyes. "What's his name?"

"Clyde Fairbrother."

My heart beats with the prospect of revenge. I have to lose Haneen for now. Revenge trumps tragedy.

"Tell me about Fairbrother."

"I'm sending you a picture—it'll be on your phone. I overnighted a file on him, long as your arm. I don't know who's going to jump on an old connection to a beer can from a dying con looking for a deal—the FBI, the local police? It's also ten years old."

"Where is he?"

"Malone. It's upstate New York. Near the Canadian border."

"I know Malone. It's where those two guys escaped from the state prison. Dannemora, correct?"

"Correct."

"What's he doing in Malone?"

"He's a prison guard."

I wanted to hear that Clyde is a minister in a queasy storefront church (*horribly shot in front of his congregation*), a truck driver (*his bloody head slumped against the steering wheel*), a short-order cook (*crumpled on the floorboards under the coffee urns*), or unemployed and homeless (*half-frozen corpse under a blue tarp*). I want him exposed, reachable, mine for the taking, mine for the killing. I don't want *him* to be a civil servant working for the New York State Department of Corrections.

"What I told you is what I got from a buddy still in the Bureau."

"Was it the DNA?"

"And his prints. Big-time. He left traces all over the place: Marine Corps, state corrections agency, a DUI arrest in Albany. He got off with a warning."

"What are the chances of charging him with the murder?" Bobby asks.

Ernie has the information ready.

"Encouraging. Three reasons. One: the US Attorney has an affidavit from George saying he sold Clyde a sniper rifle; the DNA and the prints on the beer can in George's car puts them together. Two: there was a theft of weapons from the army base before the shooting; it may be one of them. Three: if they find the rifle, or his little homemade bullet workshop, it would be enough to hold him and take it to the local DA. I can be on a plane tomorrow, Nina."

"Not yet."

"I want to see the bastard hanged. Or whatever they do today," Ernie says.

"They don't do anything. New York doesn't have the death penalty. Best hope is he dies in jail," Bobby says.

"Let me know," Ernie says.

"I will. I will."

"By the way, I got George into the hospice. He doesn't have long."

The call ends. My cell phone face reverts to the picture of Sammy, my brother, smiling in his soccer uniform. I linger on the picture. *I found him, Sammy. I found him. It won't be long now.* A beep. A message with a photo file appears in my mailbox from Ernie. I download the picture; it's a military portrait of a marine recruit, his head shaved. A trace of a smile. The man is proud to be photographed in his marine dress blues.

It all comes back to me. Not his name, but his face, his eyes. There are pictures of Clyde Fairbrother in my files of anti-abortion activists. He appears in my collection of taped newsreels of demonstrations in front of women's clinics, hospitals, Planned Parenthood, and doctors' offices. I have videos, newspaper clippings of Clyde's interviews. In them, he is a voice of moderation, talks about his concern for the health of the women who are about to have abortions, the threat of cancer, depression, heart attacks, and always, his love of the unborn child. He is, as he says over and over again, in every interview, against violence. His message is that protests must always be prayerful, peaceful, and law-abiding. Clyde argues for counseling women before they go into the clinic. He will argue that the life of the woman is not as important as the life of the child who has not yet lived. He never gives his name. "I am an unnamed servant of the Lord. I am doing his work with modesty." The man in my files who had no name now has one. I reach for my purse.

Bobby says, "Do you want me to go with you?"

He means to Malone. Bobby and I have no misunderstandings even when we speak in shorthand. It's one of the reasons we love each other. He knows I want to make sure that Clyde will *not* spend the rest of his life in the safety of a jail, one with comforts for former prison guards. I don't have much time before police question or arrest him. Bobby walks me to my car. We don't talk.

I am imagining the movie of me in a courthouse; I am my own moving camera. It begins with an establishing shot of the exterior of the courthouse, then a tracking shot of me climbing the stairs to the entrance. Cut: I enter the lobby. Another angle. I am waving to the security guards, who by now are my buds, especially Danielle, with whom I have had a beer or two at the River Tavern. She wants to move to Brooklyn. When she does, I promise to help her get a job in my police force. This one time, because the line is long and Danielle knows I am in a hurry (I'm a witness), she waves me around the metal detector. That is how I will bring a gun into the courtroom. Cut to me sitting in the witness chair, cross-examined by the defense attorney. When he is finished challenging my memory of the evening Clyde *allegedly* shot Dr. Karim, this attorney will turn to the judge. "No more questions, Your Honor."

The judge will respond, "The witness is excused." I rise from my hard-backed wooden chair, walk to the defense table, take out my .38 Ruger LCR, pause for a second before I pull the trigger so Clyde knows what to expect, dash any hopes he has for an acquittal, a hung jury, a long or short sentence with the possibility of parole. I put a .38 slug into Clyde's brain, then another to his heart. He falls over dead, just dead. Like Haneen's brother, I drop the gun to the floor, put my hands on my head, wait for my close-up. I will say, "It was necessary."

There will be no wailing from me.

Bobby reads my mind. "Once they have him, you'll never get within ten feet of him. They are not stupid."

He is right. I delete the courtroom shooting scene from my movie.

"I have to go home."

"Are you sure you don't want me to go with you?"

"Yes."

"Tell me, how you plan to get away with this?"

"I don't plan to."

"That's a dumb-ass mistake."

"I know."

Have I just become a lost cause to the man I love who loves me? If I kill Clyde and admit it, I will be arrested, fired from the Long Island City Police. Returning to college becomes problematic unless I can do an online course from the prison where I will be spending a large part of the rest of my life. A talented defense lawyer might be able to convince a jury that I acted out of diminished capacity, the insanity defense, but I would never agree to that. I am not insane. I am perfectly sane. I was seeking justice. Bobby calculates. Does he want to wait for me to finish my sentence, then come out of prison, be his wife, mother to his children? Bobby is a realist; he plays the odds. I imagine him crunching the numbers of our future. Bobby's expression says maybe, maybe not. We realize we've both been living in a fantasy world. Mine is my obsessive revenge. Bobby's been humoring me, going along with it by helping me find Clyde, trying to keep me sane while we do, also not facing what the consequences of finding him will be.

I think neither of us really believed it would happen. Now it has. The *cowardly bastard*, the murderer, is within range. If I make good on my promise to kill Clyde, then this present delusional life might be over. I can see Bobby pull out the receipt from the life calculator. Does it say his investment in me is a bad one, write it off? In the movie of Bobby and me, there are quick close-ups of two people who realize life has just caught up with them. Am I selfish? What is the point of this act of revenge? My own logic says since Clyde killed my father, I will kill him. My act will be illegal, a violation of due process, my role as a police officer. I will take responsibility for it. Once again, the circles created by the stone of my father's murder spread outward, and Bobby B is brought in. Who else?

"Do you want me to come with you?" Bobby asks again.

"No."

"Then you will need an alibi when you get back."

It's what I love about him.

CHAPTER 29

I leave the shelter early the next morning and drive to my apartment, where a thick FedEx envelope leans against my door. I make coffee and read the file Ernie Saldana sent to me.

The first document is a photocopied history of the Army of God compiled by the Southern Poverty Law Center. The center tracks domestic hate groups like the Ku Klux Klan, the Aryan Brotherhood, neo-Nazi groups, racist biker gangs, the Jewish Defense League, and the Army of God. The next item is a two-page FBI biography of Clyde Fairbrother. He was born to Anne and Dennis Fairbrother in Nantahala, North Carolina. When Clyde was ten, Anne divorced Dennis and took Clyde to Missouri, where she joined her sister in a compound known as the Church of Israel. The Southern Poverty Law Center lists it as a Christian Identity hate group. Clyde spent four years at the compound, homeschooled; worked part-time as a carpenter's helper; and got his high school diploma at the same time he was certified as a junior minister in the Church of Israel.

Clyde married Shirley Ruiz, a member of the church. They had a daughter, Glory. When she was three years old, Glory died of meningitis despite the efforts of Dr. Robert Matthews, the founder of the church, to cure her through prayer. There was an unsuccessful attempt by the Missouri Department of Health to prosecute Clyde, Shirley, and Dr. Matthews on charges of child endangerment for refusing to take the child to a hospital or physician. A year later, Clyde and Shirley divorced.

Clyde joined the marines, took basic training at Quantico in Virginia. Following a tour in the first Gulf War, he was assigned to embassy duty in Moscow, Helsinki, and last, Cologne. In 2009, the year before his discharge, Clyde was sent to Afghanistan to serve in an outpost in Kandahar province. Its mission was to expand protection to the nearby villages and provide basic training to local army units, some of which were infiltrated by the same people they were supposed to fight.

The unit spent a year doing cursory patrols, making sure the army cadets they were training did not have live ammunition that could be turned against them, and constantly strengthening the defensive position of their base from attack by Al-Qaeda. Detective Higgins, who also did a tour in Afghanistan, told me a similar story. He put it succinctly. "The training and protection mission was bullshit; we changed it to ensuring our own survival."

In a night attack, Clyde was wounded by shrapnel from a mortar round and flown out, recuperated at Walter Reed and enrolled in a dodgy for-profit college that took his GI Bill money and promised him a career in respiratory technology. Halfway through the course, it went out of business. Clyde returned to the compound, married Bea Turner. The next year, the Church of Israel became a familiar presence on the anti-abortion road show, with Clyde Fairbrother as its star. It is more than I need to know, but there is something vaguely familiar about this. It will come to me, as all things do; perhaps on my drive to Malone to kill Clyde. I leave a voice mail with Phyllis that I have a job emergency and will be away from the shelter for one or two nights.

According to Google Maps, the town of Malone is a five-hour-and-twenty-seven-minute drive northward on the Governor Thomas E. Dewey Thruway, also known as I-87. Governor Dewey is less remembered for his governing accomplishments than for the picture of a grinning Harry Truman holding the

Chicago Tribune with its blazing headline "Dewey Defeats Truman!" that wrongly proclaimed Dewey winner of the 1948 presidential election. It is a lesson about getting it right. I have been preparing for this moment for a long time. I will get it right. There are CCTV cameras at bridges crossing the Hudson and at every thruway tollbooth, so I will take a route that is longer, complicated, and not recorded.

I take a bus to Penn Station, then another to Newark Airport, and get on a shuttle to the Avis rental office. At the counter, a woman takes my fake New Jersey driver's license with a photo of someone who looks like me but isn't. I give her a prepaid debit card I bought in a Walgreens, emerge from the parking lot in a rented gray Ford Escape that smells of tobacco and lemon oil. My driving outfit will be a black parka with a high collar, a knitted cap, sunglasses, and a thick scarf; there isn't much of my face that is visible to any CCTV cameras, anywhere. I am on the west bank of the Hudson River; there are no bridges to cross all the way north. When I get to Malone, the Ford will be unremarkable, harder to remember than my red Prius.

I zig and zag through New Jersey suburbs until I hit Route 9W in New York. It runs north, parallel to the thruway. It will cost me an hour going through towns, but I will leave no tracks. I obey speed limits, don't tempt yellow lights, make one bathroom coffee break at Kingston, refill the gas tank and pay cash. North of Kingston, the traffic thins out. The scenery is monotonous; orderly green pine trees line the road. Except for the occasional DEER CROSSING warnings, there are no road signs, billboards, or other distractions. The only obligation is not to fall asleep at the wheel. There is no chance of that. I will not listen to music, news, or talk radio. I will spend the time figuring out the best way to kill Clyde Fairbrother. In the trunk of my car is the backpack I prepared for this mission. It contains dark clothes, Bausch + Lomb night-vision binoculars, a loaded Walther P22 pistol, its serial number filed off, with a Finnish SAK noise suppressor. I discovered the Walther behind a toilet in a drug dealer's abandoned apartment and kept it. The noise suppressor went missing from the Long Island City Police evidence locker a long time ago. No one noticed.

I stay on 9W for another three hours, passing the lakes: Lake George, Lake Placid, and Lake Saranac. At Plattsburgh, I switch over to I-90, drive due west for fifty miles until I enter Malone. Signs inform me the Lions Club meets on Thursday, the Knights of Columbus Tuesday, the Moose on Monday. Malone's population is 12,500; elevation is 790 feet above sea level. At a stoplight, I read a historical marker. I am glad to learn the husband of Laura Ingalls Wilder, the author of *Little House on the Prairie*, was a native of Malone.

When I have done what I set out to do, I write a letter.

Dear Mom and Sammy,

    Greetings from Malone in way upstate New York—just below the Canadian border. I drove up from Long Island City. It took almost six hours but, in the end, it was worth the trip. Or, as they say in the Michelin Guide, "worth a detour." I'm sure you guys are wondering, why Malone? Here's why: him. The one who shot Daddy. I found him. I had lots of help from Ernie Saldana. He heard about a man who sold a sniper rifle to the killer. He got the FBI to trace the DNA on a beer can the killer left in the man's car, and he was traced to Malone, where he was working as a prison guard. I drove up as quickly as I could to get to him before the police did. His name is (was) Clyde Fairbrother. About the past tense, you can have no doubt.

In the end, killing Clyde was simple. Easy simple. I stopped at a diner in Malone, ordered some food at the counter, went to the bathroom. There was a pay phone on the wall with a local phone book on a chain. Can you believe it? When was the last time you saw a phone book? You guessed it—Clyde Fairbrother was listed, with his address. The house was ten minutes out of town. It was a typical upstate two-story wood frame, probably built in the '40s like ours. It had a porch, a fireplace, a detached garage, where there must be tools, a workbench, a boat on a trailer, and a chest freezer. It abutted a woodsy area. Best of all, the porch faced the trees.

I parked at the end of the street and waited until he came home from work. When it got dark, I drove farther down the road. Then, using night-vision binoculars, I found a spot in the woods under a pine tree where I could see the house. I watched him eat his dinner with a woman who must be his wife. When they finished, he put the dishes in the washer. Then he went outside on the side porch and lit a cigarette. I walked right up to him. I was wearing a black jacket, black jeans, and a black knit cap. Oh, I had a pair of hospital booties over my shoes—no footprints. I had a sign hanging from my neck with the words I AM THE DAUGHTER OF DR. MARTIN KARIM.

He said, "Please don't."

They were his last words. I put a bullet in his head, then one in his heart. I used the Walther P22 with the SAK noise suppressor. Sammy, the sound isn't like in your video games, that pumf-pumf; it's more like a sharp door knock. He went down on his knees (the P22 doesn't have a lot of punch), then I repeated the process; four rounds in all. As I walked back into the woods, I heard a woman's voice call out from the kitchen, "Clyde, you okay?"

I went back to the car and drove home. I stopped at a gas station. In the bathroom I burned the paper booties and the sign I had hung around my neck, and flushed the ashes down the toilet. I broke down the Walther. I threw its parts, one at a time, separately, into the woods along the forest road at ten-mile intervals. In a few years, it will be just random rusted junk. There will be no murder weapon. I tossed the shell casings and the noise suppressor into the Hudson River south of Poughkeepsie. I'd left my phone with Bobby in my apartment. He checked my Facebook page a few times, sent some emails, looked at my bank balance. The phone will be additional supporting evidence that I never left Long Island.

For sure I'll stop at the cemetery next week to say hello, do some weeding around the stones. I'll bring some tulips—I know you like them, Mom. I'll leave some of Dad's favorite halvah. Sammy, two comic books for you: a Garth Ennis you will like called Preacher *and a new* Wolverine.

It's done. I'm sorry you both didn't live to see it happen. I hope you can all rest easier. I know I will. Strangely, I will have to figure out the rest of my life now that this is done. I still have one more big case I want to solve, then I will decide if I want to be a cop or go back to school. I'm probably in a state of shock. Right now, it feels okay. I'll give it time. Maybe it'll be different later. I doubt it. I don't regret what I did. He deserved it. You know what I always said: "Forgiveness is overrated." If I feel badly for what I've done, I'll convert to Catholicism and go to confession.

Your loving daughter and sister,
Nina

CHAPTER 30

I return the Avis car at Newark Airport, leave the keys in their lockbox, and take a bus back to Penn Station and then another to Long Island City. On the way to my apartment, I stop at a newsstand and buy a *New York Post*. There's an article: "Prison Guard Murdered", and a photograph of Clyde. A State Police spokesperson theorizes Sergeant Clyde Fairbrother was killed by an ex-convict seeking revenge. This is good news for me. I walk into my apartment to the *bing* of a text from Ernie in Maui. I call him.

Ernie gives me another piece of news: while I was driving to Malone, the FBI questioned Clyde Fairbrother about where he was on the night my father was murdered. Clyde told them he was racing his Dodge Charger at the Airborne Speedway in Plattsburgh, two hundred miles away from our house in Grahamsville. He showed them a dated article from the *Albany Times*. There was a photograph of Clyde standing next to his Dodge in the winner's circle. It was proof, incontrovertible, unshakable—it was the truth. Clyde didn't shoot my father.

I killed the wrong person.

CHAPTER 31

Bobby is waiting at the apartment with white boxes of takeout from Mandarin Chef. A ninja killer's meal?

"Can I jump in the shower first?"

"The food will wait. Go ahead."

I sink to the floor, my favorite place in the shower, curl up, and let the hot water fall over my body in a Macbeth-like fantasy that I can wash the deed away. It doesn't help. I have done something irreparable. There is nothing I can do to change, adjust, or alter my action, no computer program that can retrieve the event, find it, or delete it. It's done. My life is changed forever. I killed an innocent man. Or did I? I remember a story about an IRA terrorist who set off a bomb in a London mailbox that killed an innocent bystander. Later, it was revealed the man had murdered his wife earlier that day.

I can justify what I did by saying I didn't kill an *innocent* man. I killed the *wrong* man. I know who Clyde Fairbrother was, what he stood for, who he served. I know he was a zealot in an organization that pickets abortion clinics, intimidates pregnant women, threatens physicians and their families. There are real victims: David Gunn, John Britton, George Tiller, and Barnett Stepian were doctors who provided legal medical procedures to women and were murdered for doing so. I killed the right man. I just didn't kill the one who shot my father. I'll sleep.

In my bathrobe, clean and righteous, I sit down next to Bobby at the kitchen table. "You saw the news?"

"I spoke to Ernie. How do you feel?"

"I don't know," I say. "No, I do. I feel exhausted. Do I have to start over?"

"Ernie insists Clyde got the rifle from George. But he may have bought it for someone else, another shooter in the Army of God. He's going to look into that. Try to get a list of their members, see who would know how to use it. Maybe someone Clyde knew in the military."

I don't have the energy. I stare at the row of white boxes, the packets of soy sauce and mustard. I crush open a fortune cookie: *Today you screwed up big-time.*

"Nina?"

"Sorry. Yes, that makes sense. Right now, I'm kind of numb."

Bobby starts unpacking the food.

"Eat something."

"Sure. I still have my appetite, don't I?"

I remember Truman Capote's *In Cold Blood*; there is a description of the meal Dick and Perry consumed in a Kansas diner after murdering the Clutter family. It went on for a page. Murder as an appetite stimulant. "Bobby, I think a drink makes more sense."

"No. We're not finished."

We eat quickly. We burn my killing clothes in the fireplace, scrape the ashes into a plastic bag he will later flush down a toilet in a public restroom. Bobby is now an accomplice to my murder.

I crush open a fortune cookie: *If at first you don't succeed try, try, again.*

"What's funny?" Bobby says.

"Was I laughing?"

"Yes."

"Jesus, Bobby, I have to do this again. Find him. Do it all again. Until I get it right."

"No, you don't. You can go back to work. Solve crimes."

He's right. I have three cold case murders. And I'm still undercover in the shelter.

"Should I ask for counseling? I'm a cop psychologically unfit, not ready for active duty?"

"Any way you cut it, killing someone, unless you are a complete sociopath is messy business. You know that. You are on the other end now. You've done all the right things so far to get away with it, but this thing isn't over yet. You took out a civil servant, a prison guard. It's lower than a cop, but they won't let it go. You'll be a suspect. You need to clear your head, be sharp. And be careful: they could put someone smart on this, someone like you."

Bobby's right. I run down the list of cops I know I don't want on my ass, starting with Lieutenant Hagen. Bobby knows I brought him into this, this shit in my life; he is my accomplice. If I go down, so will he. We are bound together now more than ever. I try to remember: Did I ask him to do this for me, or did it just happen?

"Bobby, I'm sorry."

"Sweetheart, we still need to come up with your alibi."

Of course. It is only a question of time before my name is added to the list of suspects and I am questioned by law enforcement. The US Attorney in Maui knows I was looking for Clyde. I have a motive: revenge. I need to be ready. I am going to have to account for where I was the night Clyde Fairbrother was shot. The days of *I went to the movies* or *I was home watching television* won't cut it. There are too many CCTV cameras to trace my movements, computers installed in cars; my phone is a vault of information—it's why I left it with Bobby. If any law enforcement agency decides to consider me seriously as a suspect, I will be put under a microscope, a forensic one.

Therefore, Bobby suggests, we will take a cue from Susan Steevers, Ronald's widow, who wouldn't give an explanation of her movements on the night he disappeared, even if she went to jail; that's how strongly she wanted to protect the women at Artemis—and that gave her eventual alibi more than a ring of truth. As for me, Bobby says I will begin by claiming I was home with him. He will corroborate this. The police will be reluctant to believe him. Bobby has a shady past, a dicey present; he is a loan shark. The police will demand more substantive proof from me. Bobby says I should hint there is an alibi but I can't give it to them. *I was home, I was home, I was home.* Be like Susan, Bobby says. To get me to give them an alibi, they will have to badger me, threaten me, until I break down and finally give them the thing that will absolve me, prove my innocence, and account for me being three hundred and forty-three miles from Malone on the night Clyde Fairbrother was shot to death.

The alibi Bobby proposes is a home video of us having sex.

"No."

"It'll work," Bobby says.

"We'll be like Pamela and Tommy, Kim and Ray J. No, no, no."

"You'll be in good company," he says.

"What about the time code?"

"A buddy gave me a program that can change it to when Clyde Fairbrother was killed. If the police want to prove that the time was altered, they can't. I'm not saying you hand it over—you fight not to show it, you will be humiliated when you do, but they will buy it and leave you alone. And me."

"It'll get out. Every male cop will have it on his phone. They'll be showing it in the locker room."

"It beats an arrest and a possible conviction. You can also make it clear if you discover the one who posted it (always possible now), you will sue his ass, own his house."

That is the future, and it's irrelevant.

"Then I will be free to resume the search for my father's killer. Nothing else matters."

"If you like."

"Bobby?"

"Yes?"

"Get the camera. I'll light some candles."

CHAPTER 32

Twelve hours ago, I killed a man. I covered my tracks, erased the murder weapon, destroyed the evidence, and prepared an alibi. On my way to the station, I worry it will show on my face, be revealed in my behavior. Will anyone at the police station notice anything different about me? *She's acting strange. Did she just kill someone? What's up, Karim? You look like you took somebody out.*

It is not completely fanciful. My fellow detectives are suspicious, observant; we study behavior; we are trained to read faces. On the other hand, we are also trained to deceive, role-play, hide our emotions, nod sympathetically when a child molester seeks our understanding, though we would like to rip out his throat. It is how we get information. The cops in my department consider me a bit weird anyway. My personality is mercurial; my little frozen smile confuses, I think I can appear *normal* despite the fact my stomach is gurgling like a broken pipe, and I feel like I am still wearing the sign that told Clyde who I was in the moment before I shot him.

When I enter the detectives' room, I am mostly ignored. No one seems to notice anything different about me except Emile Keller, a loathed member of the vice squad, standing at the water fountain. We call it Keller's "other office." He stares at me with his usual mixture of curiosity and contempt. Keller has never gotten over the fact there are female detectives. I could be a three-headed turtle. He always looks at me as if he is going to say, *Can I help you, miss?*

When I worked alongside Keller during my obligatory term

in vice, I came away feeling like I would rather be in the company of the felons we were looking for. Keller called himself *old-school*. I hate that expression. Was he nostalgic for the days when varying degrees of brutality, racism, and corruption were acceptable? Does he long for those days? Keller wasn't dumb, just lazy. He knew how to disappear, cover his tracks, yet find a way onto every overtime assignment. His size and gruff demeanor gave the impression he was a tough guy. He was the office bully; he enjoyed pushing new recruits around, loved practical jokes.

Cops get burned out in vice; they're dealing with drug dealers and their customers, prostitutes and their customers, the bottom rung of crimes—gambling, number running, alcohol abuse, loan sharking (sorry, Bobby). After a while you can't tell whom you are protecting, whom you are serving. There are too many people willing to pay you off in cash, drugs, or sex. Keller claims a stable marriage, is a devout Catholic. As for *corrupt*, there are rumors, but they mean nothing. He may just be better at covering his tracks. The only good thing about Keller is that he plans to retire soon. He's on the wrong side of history, the poster boy for cops that enlightened urban police are trying *not* to hire now. When Keller once bragged that his sons wanted to grow up to be cops just like him, people shuddered. I never underestimated Keller, I just will be glad to see him go.

When I graduated from the academy, Bobby gave me a lecture on what to expect. "Law enforcement is binary. There is a line. As a cop, you stand on one side or the other on a number of issues: the line between the brutal and the nonbrutal cop, the line between integrity and corruption—there is nothing in between. The line between assholes and nonassholes. Plus, you're a woman, a cop, and smart. The assholes will resent you, and try to fuck you up, and probably try to sleep with you, too. It's hard, Nina. People are offering you money to pretend you didn't see something, look the other way. You also got people hating you, and it's easy to hate them back, or hard not to. It is not a job for the immature, either. They make cops too young. You have kids in uniforms with guns. They're in their twenties, just past teenagers; you know what teenagers are like—they have to be right, they think they know it all, and worse, they have no introspection. By the time they grow up, they are fixed in those same personalities as when they were teenagers."

It was mostly true but Bobby was wrong about cops falling into one category or another: they were also on different sides of the line in certain areas. There was a detective who had the gentlest, most caring, sympathetic presence, polite to suspects, lawyers, and fellow officers. He ended up in jail for taking bribes, extorting businesses, and selling information to the mob.

But Bobby was right about Keller: he was a case of arrested development.

"Haven't seen you around much, Karim," Keller says.

"Busy, busy."

"You want to tell me about it?"

"No."

"Why not?" *Asshole won't let it go*.

"It's a secret."

Keller knows undercover work is confidential. There have been plenty of cases where undercover cops are betrayed by corrupt cops in the same department. To be exposed in narcotics or gang cases can be a death sentence. Lieutenant Hagen and I are the only people who know I am undercover in Artemis. On the other hand, I'm not undercover in a Colombian drug cartel. I'm in a women's shelter. But I don't like it.

"You want to know what I'm doing, ask Lieutenant Hagen; otherwise it's none of your fucking business."

Keller tosses his paper cup in the basket without looking. He doesn't need to aim; he's been doing it so long. He adjusts his pants, moves toward me slowly. He wants to make sure everyone in the detectives' room gets a good, long look. I know what he's doing. He's going to invade my space. In martial arts, it's called the *ma-ai* zone. If he crosses into it, I am supposed to attack. Of course, I can't or won't; he's twice my size. So he will get right up on me, tower over me, be a wall, one that might fall on me and crush my bones. I will back away, then he will mark me humiliated and it will give him pleasure. He won't be the first. I know how to deal with guys like him.

"It won't work, Keller, so back off. All you're going to do is inflict some of your bad breath on me. And I'll tell your mother."

That stopped him.

"My mother?"

"Yeah. You're being a bad boy."

The detectives watching this little drama laugh. I'm not humiliated. Keller is. Such is the workplace situation in Long Island City homicide. Before he can determine his next move, Lieutenant Hagen opens her door. "Karim, in here, please."

Keller gives me the finger. I enter Hagen's office. Lieutenant Hagen closes the door. She doesn't make it to her desk.

"Talk to me."

"Lieutenant?"

"Who the hell are you, Karim?"

I take my time with the question. I know it is not an existential one. It might be *Who do you think you are?* I play it safe. Polite.

"I'm not sure what you mean, Lieutenant. Have I done something wrong?"

"You're under suspicion of murder. I'm not supposed to tell you."

"By whom?"

"Take your pick. Let's just say I got a call asking about you. So again, who are you?"

There is a copy of the *New York Post* on her desk. *Aha.* She pushes the newspaper into my view. I glance at it.

"It's about this murder, right?"

"Right. The victim was active in the anti-abortion movement," Lieutenant Hagen says.

It is time to tell Lieutenant Hagen everything. On the other hand, she may already know what I am about to reveal concerning my past. It happens sometimes when a suspect finally confesses. He thinks you are going to be surprised, but you already know what he was going to say. Lieutenant Hagen will have her moment, then she will hear it from me. I tell my story wearily. It is not the first time I have had to explain; it's like being an ex-con. You are always a suspect.

"I assume you know about my father. He performed abortions at a Planned Parenthood clinic."

"Yes. He was assassinated by a pro-life zealot."

"He was *murdered* by a pro-life zealot," I correct her. "Whenever something bad happens to one of those cowardly bastards, my name comes up."

"This guy upstate, was he one of them? Ever hear of him?"

I can't deny indifference to my father's possible killer, or his opposition to abortion.

"I never knew his name, but I knew about him. He was always anonymous. Or was. If you want my personal opinion, he deserved it."

I remember Mr. McDermott. *It looks like something I could have done.*

"I tend to agree with you, Karim, but if you are asked, I wouldn't go there."

No shit.

"The ex-con angle makes sense," I say.

"Would you?"

"I'm sorry?"

"If you could?"

"Would I kill him?"

Can I pull off a convincing consideration of such an outrageous idea?

"It has occurred to me."

Pause for effect.

"No, I wouldn't."

Lieutenant Hagen shrugs. She is convinced. I am innocent in her mind. She has more pressing matters.

"How much longer do you need at the shelter?"

"I'm close. Phyllis is convinced my life is in danger. After Haneen got killed, she is not taking any chances. She doesn't want to lose another woman. If she is certain my husband is a real threat, I think she'll try to have him killed."

"She has accomplices, then."

"She must. I think we can find them, keep an eye on them, I can let you know when Phyllis goes out. She may ask me to help her set up Bobby, but not tell me too much so I am not involved. I think that's how she dealt with Susan and the other women. They know enough to be grateful, but not enough to turn her in. If we can run a sting for whoever is helping her, one of them will talk; we will clean up at least three murders. Who could ask for anything more, as the song goes."

"My favorite song," Lieutenant Hagen says.

She opens the door for me. As I leave, I hear her say in her most authoritative and unfriendly voice, "Keller, get in here."

Sisterhood.

CHAPTER 33

On my way to the shelter, I stop off at Cannelle's and buy two dozen cupcakes. I give one to Myra as I walk through her house to the shelter. Amanda and Bobo greet me at the door.

"Good thing you're back," Amanda says. "We're having a funeral for Haneen tonight."

"You mean a memorial service."

"What's the difference?"

"You need a body for a funeral."

Am I being flippant with a twelve-year-old?

"Okay," she says. "A memorial service."

"What about the rest of the kids? Do they know?"

"They think she just went home. I'm the only one who knows. Hey, where were you? You're supposed to call in. Phyllis was worried about you."

"Sorry."

Phyllis comes out of her office.

"I told her," Amanda says.

Phyllis nods. I hand her the box of cupcakes and retreat to my basement home.

The atmosphere at dinner is subdued. The children are sullen; they complain about the lasagna, and then argue over the size of the portions. Phyllis busts Ben and Frankie for playing games on their phones under the table.

"Next time, guys, I'm confiscating them," Phyllis says.

Byron begins to cry for no reason. Paula gets up, carries him into the living room, and walks him in circles until he calms down. The mothers are tense; everyone is in a bad mood. Phyllis raises the spirits of the children by telling them there are cupcakes for dessert and they can watch a movie after dinner.

Gerri and I clear the dishes. Phyllis places a bowl of fresh roses on the table next to a framed photograph of Haneen that she downloaded from the "Our People" page on the Chase website. It shows Haneen—*Human Capital Management New York* sandwiched between Dana—*Global Compliance London* and Matt—*Private Equity New York*. Haneen is wearing a hijab, smiling her infectious smile, confident, competent. She is someone you *want* to manage your money, your life. The message is clear. These young people who work at Chase have been raised to be vibrant, responsible, caring young adults. They aced their SATs and went on to excellent colleges, then into well-paying, fun jobs in the new economy. They are your children. Of course you would trust them with your money. I want to work there. I want to be a part of that family. I also want to experience *life away from the desk* at Chase, river raft with my fellow traders, do yoga, wear Chase team T-shirts when we plant vegetables in urban garden plots, take cooking classes, mentor inner-city children—it is a wonderful, satisfying life/job, or is it a job/life? Either way, I would do anything to be in the company of these people. They appear content, happy. They have meaningful lives. They are safe, and unlike me, they haven't killed anyone.

"Let's all hold hands, have a minute of silence for Haneen?"

Phyllis speaks softly, not wanting her voice to carry into the living room, where the children are watching *Frozen*. They know Haneen is gone. The older ones, Amanda and Ben know why; the younger ones have been told tales designed to reassure them, ranging from "Haneen went home" to "Haneen moved away to a safe place." It will only be a matter of time before the rumors are aired and exchanged, the adults overheard, the lies they told exposed; the children will learn Haneen was murdered. They will make their own adjustments. Added to their own number-less anxieties will be the worry that Haneen's murder will be the fate of their mothers. It will be the subject of their nightmares when they wake up at two in the morning. But that's for later. Now they are watching *Frozen*.

Phyllis sits. We all do. We release our hands from one another.

"This shouldn't have happened," Phyllis says. "We lost a young woman who came to us for safety. She was tricked out of here. We had no way to stop her. You are all here voluntarily—you can leave anytime, but this is a lesson of what can await you outside. I'm sorry to begin like this, but I can't say it enough. You have to be careful."

What are we supposed to do? There is nothing.

"April, would you like to go first?"

"I liked her. Ah, that's kind of dumb. We all did. She was great at helping the kids with their math. I told her she should get out of banking, become a teacher; she said she just might. She had a real gift. Ask my kids."

She pauses. Closes her eyes, takes a deep breath.

"So here's where I start to cry, which I haven't done in a long time. You know what she said? 'The one thing we have in com-mon, all of us, is the people we love and are supposed to love us back are the ones we're most afraid of.' Isn't that crazy?"

We all agree. Yes, it's crazy.

Byron is asleep on Paula's lap. She raises her hand and lowers it. It's not school, it's not group.

"Sorry. I'm just thinking how hard it is to be here. We're afraid to go out, afraid to let our kids go to school, afraid to have lives.

It's not fair. I want to say, and I know Haneen would agree with me, we are all grateful to be here. We have to take care of one another. Thank you, Phyllis, for this place. Really. Thank you for the love you all have shown me and Byron."

There is a silence. Do we applaud?

Janice says, "I guess it's my turn. I don't have anything to add except . . . yeah, I agree with Paula. We owe you, Phyllis."

Sofia is next. "You know what happened to Haneen was, like, baggage that should have been left behind in Pakistan. You come to America; you have to leave stuff behind. We all bring something, don't we? Sometimes we bring the best, sometimes the worst. It's too bad. It was an honor killing. I think the two words don't go together. There is no honor in killing. No honor at all."

I'm next. The one who also killed. Was there any honor in mine? I put that away. This is about Haneen, not me. My thoughts:

Yeah. I messed up. I believed her. I believed her about her mother having a heart attack. Where did I leave my police skills, my skepticism, my trained mistrust of anything people say to me? I wasn't doing anything, my friends and I are just lost, Officer. Is the subway that way, Officer? My son wouldn't do anything like that, Officer. He's been here all night watching television, Officer. I have been bullshitted by the best. Why I fell for the not-so-elaborate trap set by Haneen's father is my own mystery. All I can do as a homicide detective is solve crimes, not prevent them. I can't say this to the people around the table. All I can do is apologize.

Then my words:

"She was a beautiful, generous, sweet woman who obviously touched us all. I don't have much to say about her that you all haven't covered. I have to live with another reality. I shouldn't have let her go. I should have tied her to the chair; I should have locked her in the cellar. I let her go. But she was so convincing."

"Like there was something you could have done to stop her," Gerri says. "That girl was going, no matter what."

April takes my hand.

"You would have had to tie her down. You can't blame yourself. It's just awful. That's what it is. Awful."

Phyllis removes her glasses, places them on the table.

"I want to add something that's really important to us here. It's trust. I don't have to tell you we live in a dangerous world. I want to remind you about whom we trust and whom we don't. We need to learn *not* to trust. Men who threaten us, men who swear to kill us, men who are crazy, hopelessly jealous, sick, and damaged. Yes, there are laws to protect us from them. These men won't obey courts, they won't respect restraining orders; the police can put them in prison where they spend their time planning how to kill us when they get out. These men are sick. Mentally. Can they be cured? I doubt it.

"It is clear to me society is not interested in spending the money, the time, the resources —here I sound like someone who thinks that will be a solution to take these men and cure them. I have long ago given up hope it will happen. Instead, I see us in a war; we and our children are the innocent victims who are told we can call the cops *after* we are murdered. I'm sorry. I don't buy that anymore. If a man tells you he wants to kill you, or threatens to kill you, you'd better believe him. You trust him to do it. You must protect yourself and your children."

She scans the women at the table. She says what she knows we are all thinking.

"Easier said than done."

Done. We all silently repeat it, like *amen* in church. We get up from the table. April, Gerri, and Janice go into the living room. They plop on the couch and take their children into their arms in front of the television set. It is all they can do, to make them feel safe, make them feel loved as they sing along with Elsa's "Let It Go."

Sofia catches my eye and puts her fingers to her lips. Time to go outside for a cigarette. We sit on the swings, next to each other, kicking our legs out, stretching after the confinement of the dining room table.

"What will happen to the boy?"

"He'll plead guilty. He's underage, so he'll go to a juvenile facility and get out with good behavior in a few years."

"His father?"

"He could be named as a coconspirator; depends on the boy— if he testifies against him, if he says he told him to kill Haneen. He probably won't. It's why the father made him do it. The boy is another victim. He killed his sister; he'll have to live with that. The father, he's a cowardly bastard."

I'll add him to my list of *cowardly bastards*.

I decline Sofia's offer of another cigarette. I remember smoking in the winter after high school, cupping my hands around the lit end, feeling for warmth. Now we are two girls on swings. We don't talk about boys. Sofia and I talk about murder, personal safety, sex trafficking, and escape.

"I have a plan for my life," she says.

"Let's hear it."

"A friend told me to commit a crime and get caught. My visa is expired, so I will be deported back to Slovenia. Is this true?"

"Yes. Just make sure you steal something expensive, so it will be burglary, not just petty theft. Go to a high-end department store like Bloomingdale's. Put on a cashmere sweater in the changing room and walk out. You'll get as far as the front door. The police will deliver you to an INS detention center, where you'll spend a lot of dead time, but you'll be safe. If you can give them a false name, you might be able to come back someday under your real name."

"I don't think so. I like America, but I don't want to be looking over my shoulder."

Cigarettes done, like the children we once were, we take a few more swings and jump off onto the sand.

CHAPTER 34

At Ducky's, Bobby takes a last sip of his coffee and says, "Do you mind if I ask you how I'm supposed to be murdered? Like how she is planning to kill me?"

"We're not there yet, Bobby."

"In the interest of my own safety."

"She doesn't know where you live."

"And when you tell her?"

"I may not. The whole thing has gotten out of hand."

"Do I hear the sound of mixed feelings?"

"Yes. Surprised?"

"Hell, no. Way I see it, you're in a tough spot. If you don't go through with this sting, you will betray your—what shall we call it, your chosen profession? You're a cop. You're supposed to solve murders, find the people who committed them, see them off to jail. That's the way the system works. Excluding you, of course. On the other hand, if you follow through with this entrapment of some very good people, you will betray the women's shelter, the lady who fell for your line of undercover shit and took you in, and the poor women and children who depend on her to save their asses. Honey, I don't want to be in your sneakers. It's why I couldn't become a cop. I didn't like the idea of getting people to trust me so I could arrest them."

"I would be lying to you if I said these weren't my own thoughts," I say.

Bobby runs his hand across my cheek. It is so gentle and comforting and I want to cry. I wish I could.

"Honey, it's why I love you."

"What am I going to do?"

"The right thing."

"You know what that is?"

"I'm working on it."

I add up my life, I list my missteps, my failures. I failed to stop a crazed son who believed killing his sister would save the family honor. I am now bringing my lover into a sting operation that may cost him his life. I killed the wrong person. The *cowardly bastard* is on the street. I am unavenged. Is that a word? I am merely a bobcat in the snow with one paw in the air.

"I'll call it off," I say.

"You can't."

"Why not?"

"You think the police don't know what I do? Even though I have all kinds of fancy names for it, in the end I'm just a fucking loan shark. The DA can either not give a shit about me, or his office can find enough statutes to charge me so I will spend every dime I have on defense lawyers."

"Who told you this?"

"It doesn't matter. For me, going along with this deal is now a business decision."

"I'm sorry."

"And if it helps you, too, then it's a win-win."

"The shelter, the women in it?"

"Lose-lose."

"I'll need a threatening phone call."

"No problem," he says.

Then in unison we say, "I didn't know there was one."

And smile because we both hate it when people say, *No problem.*

But this time it isn't that funny.

CHAPTER 35

Phyllis is waiting for me. "I made tea. We can share that last cupcake."

I follow her into her office. A tea service sits ready on a tray, with a red velvet cupcake on a paper napkin, sliced into two equal parts. Phyllis hands me a cup, I look up at the country cottage pictures on the wall, where life is cuddly and warm.

"Sweet, aren't they?"

"Very."

"A friend and I saw them in a hospital thrift shop. We also discovered a beautiful Indian linen skirt. We fought nicely about who got what. In the end I took the pictures; she bought the skirt. She was wearing it in her car when she got into an argument with her husband. He liked to flick lit cigarettes at her for his own sick amusement. This time a cigarette bounced off her and dropped into her lap. The skirt burst into flames. She suffered third-degree burns from the waist down. She lives in a wheelchair now."

"Her husband?"

"He said it was an accident. Felt terrible about it. They got a divorce, and I don't know what happened to him. Or care."

I look at the pictures and imagine a cigarette-flicking husband buried under one of the cottages.

"The pictures are not exactly my taste in art," Phyllis says.

"I'll never look at them the same way."

"Yes, that's the point. There was her insurance money, a big settlement from the hospital store that sold the skirt—it was enough to start Artemis."

"How do you keep it going?"

"We have a couple of ex-residents who widowed well. We can survive."

"Widowed well?"

She laughs. "A joke. Two of them lost husbands who were rich. They give us a lot of support."

We drink our tea.

"You can move into Haneen's room, if you'd like."

Murder will wait. Lieutenant Hagen won't.

"I don't think so. Use it for the next person who comes in. I have a feeling I'm not going to be around much longer."

"Are you leaving us?"

"I don't see any alternative. My neighbor tells me my husband's been coming around looking for me. He's drinking. He leaves me scary messages."

"Can I hear one?"

I take out my phone, play my voice mail. *"Listen to me. I'm at the end. I'm feeling like I got nothing else. Just you and Lucas. Got to be a family again. I can't live like this—life isn't worth shit."* Then his voice modulates, settles into another timbre: lower, threatening: *"I'll find you. When I do, we will be together. In heaven if we can't be together here."*

Phyllis asks me to play it again. She cocks her head slightly to the phone and concentrates like a symphony conductor who has asked the violin section to replay the last three measures. Phyllis reaches for a pen and a file card. Bobby is convincing. His voice is a mixture of icy calm and maniacal rage. I would not want to be the real recipient of such a message. She makes some notes. I wonder if I get to search her office I will find others like it.

"I take this very seriously," she says.

Success. I have convinced Phyllis my husband is a danger not only to me but also to the other women in the shelter and the shelter itself.

"So do I. It's why I want to leave."

"Where will you go?"

"It's an interesting question. I could do a Google search for 'Ten Best Places to Escape From Men Who Want to Kill You': Pyongyang, North Korea? Aleppo, Syria? There's Israel. The law of return says any person of Jewish origin who comes there is automatically a citizen. I'm not Jewish. Can I convert?"

Phyllis smiles. "Seriously."

"I don't know. If I stay here, he'll find me. He'll kill me. I know he will."

"What about your son?"

"I'll take him with me."

"That's kidnapping. Abusers love when you do that. It puts you on the other side of the law. He's a cop; he can get cooperation from every law enforcement agency in the country to track you down. You know he will."

Silence. Tea. Fantasy cottages. Fiery dresses. A burned body.

"I'm a cop, too. I'm armed. I'll shoot him."

"You'll go to jail. You will not raise your son. A foster home will."

"If you have a better idea, I'd like to hear it," I say.

"Give me his address. Tell me where he lives."

"And then? Will I be able to go home?"

"Yes, dear. And you will be with your son."

"I think I know what you are talking about, Phyllis."

"No, you don't. You don't know anything except your life is in danger. And the less you know, the better. His existence, his craziness. He threatens the women and children in this shelter.

I won't allow that. You came here, we took you in, protected you, we made you safe. You have an obligation to us, to keep us safe. What you do with your life is your decision. But you can't jeopardize ours. You understand? We won't be victims. We will protect ourselves. If you want to leave the shelter, it's your decision. There are two ways you can leave. Your way or ours."

"Let me think about it," I say.

The cupcake remains untouched.

On my way out, Myra looks up from her computer terminal. "There's a couple I don't like, been sitting in a Lexus too long. The woman shooed away a parking ticket lady. Get my drift?"

"Thank you, Myra. How's the market?"

"Amazon up, Apple down."

"Good or bad for you?"

"Today it's good; tomorrow, who knows. Be careful."

I spot them in the late-model Lexus. The car doesn't belong to the Long Island City Police. I agree with Myra; they are cops. I'll make life easier for the driver; I continue walking in the direction he's parked, save him a U-turn. Their car glides out into the street and follows me. Fine. I also don't want to be seen talking to them by anyone in the shelter. I come to the corner, turn right. The Lexus does the same. I wait for it to pull up alongside me. The woman in the passenger seat lowers her window.

"Detective Karim?"

"Are you following me?"

"Yes. We'd like to talk to you," she says.

I stop at a red zone, and they pull in and brake to a halt.

The woman holds up a New York State Police badge. She and her partner are dressed in business suits; his is dark blue with a pin-striped shirt, a paisley tie. He has Ray-Bans pushed back on the top of his head, ready to be dropped as soon as they hit the road. I sense he's wearing his father's clothes or is bent on imitating his style. She's wearing the female detective's uniform: a navy-blue blazer and slacks, a white shirt. Carries a workingwoman's handbag that holds her weapon. She could be me, only instead of my smile she's got a permanent skeptical expression that says, *Make me believe you.*

These two can pass for a married couple on their way to dinner, the movies, or work. Who do they resemble in my recent memory? Of course, the happy workers on Haneen's Chase website. But they are civil servants working for New York State, not bond traders or fund managers. They will never receive six-figure bonuses, have family vacations in Tuscan villas, or fly to Paris for the weekend and eat in starred restaurants. These are my middle-class police colleagues; they must be treated with respect.

I get in the back seat.

"We're looking into a homicide that took place last night. Upstate."

"How can I help?"

"You're on a list of suspects," he says. "We'd like to get you off it."

"A suspect? Last night? Upstate?"

"Yes."

"I was home with my boyfriend watching television."

She gives me a condescending nod. She has heard this alibi many times.

As an informal interrogation, it resembles a conversation

between fellow police officers, polite, nonthreatening, fairly benign. We remain in the car. It must be uncomfortable for these two detectives; they have to twist around to talk to me sitting in the back seat. This was obviously planned; the headrests of the front seats had been removed. They are smart enough to dispense with the good cop/bad cop routine. The male cop takes notes; there are no outdated gender roles. Most likely, I am also being recorded.

"You should know I am on an undercover assignment and I need to be discreet. If you want to make inquiries about me, or find out what I'm doing, you'll have to coordinate with my boss, Lieutenant Hagen."

"We want to know about Clyde Fairbrother."

"He is?"

"Was. He's the victim. Clyde was active in the anti-abortion movement."

"I see. Then you know my history."

"Most of it," she says. "And unfortunately, that makes you a suspect."

I repeat my true story: that I am the daughter of an abortion provider who was murdered, likely by a pro-life assassin, possibly Clyde. I give them that. I admit I am looking for my father's murderer; in fact, it is close to a life-defining obsession. I tell them I promised my late mother and brother I would find that man and bring him to justice, so he could be tried by the State of New York, convicted by the people of New York, sent to prison to rot in the company of the most violent convicts in Attica. I also hope he will be brutally stabbed to death in a shower with a sharpened screwdriver by one or more of his fellow convicts. Failing that, I wish him abject misery for the rest of his life. If Clyde Fairbrother is dead, I don't take any satisfaction in him skipping a trial or naming any of his coconspirators. I didn't kill him. I'm a police officer; my duty is to capture criminals, not kill them. I take that seriously. *Whew.*

They understand, but I had a real motive, and they aren't impressed with my story that I was home watching television with my boyfriend of dubious character on the night of the murder. The male cop adds, "The dude's black, isn't he?"

He just made his first mistake.

"Would you like to tell me and your recording device what his race has to do with anything?" I say.

"Not much," he says. "Just asking."

"You want to know what show we watched? *Empire.* Nice talking to you both. This little chat was your freebie. Next time, I'm bringing a lawyer from my union."

"Sure. You're entitled," the male cop says.

Cards are exchanged, we say good-byes and I get out of the Lexus.

"Detective Karim?"

"Yes?"

I turn around and face the male cop—like the suspect does in every episode of *Columbo*—and he says, just like Peter Falk, "Just one more thing."

"Yes?"

"We know you were on the thruway."

Unlike the suspect in *Columbo*, I don't make a run for it, grab a gun and try to shoot my way out, or trade knowing glances with Peter Falk—mine: *You got me,* his: *All this time you thought you were smarter than me.*

I didn't ride the thruway, so I walk away. They just blew their whole interview. They have nothing. I am in the clear. I got away with murder. I'll cook a Persian dinner for Bobby and me: lamb kebabs, baghali rice, yogurt and cucumber salad. Afterward, we'll watch our sex tape and then repeat it for real just before we erase it. Yes, that would make a fun evening. Then I remember what I have to do first: betray the women in Artemis and find the *cowardly bastard*.

CHAPTER 36

Lieutenant Hagen listens to Bobby's voice mail as he pretends to be my crazy husband. *"Listen to me. I'm at the end. I'm feeling like I got nothing else. Just you and Lucas. Got to be a family again. I can't live like this—life isn't worth shit. I'll find you. When I do, we will be together. In heaven if we can't be together here."*

She purses her lips, approves. "Impressive. You played this for Phyllis?"

"She was convinced. She wants Bobby's address."

"She asked for it?"

"Yes."

Lieutenant Hagen feels she has enough information to get the DA to approve a sting on Phyllis and her unknown accomplices. The point of this drama will be to catch Phyllis or her friends about to kill Bobby, and get them to confess to the murders of Ronald, Derrick, and Joey, or possibly more. I'll be the spouse in jeopardy, Bobby the dangerous husband. It will be standard procedure.

I'll give Phyllis Bobby's address. I'll tell her about his routines, when he is alone, on duty, off duty, the bar where he drinks, the gym where he works out, the Food Bazaar market where he shops, and Rosario's Delicatessen, where he goes when he wants Italian takeout. These are the places where Bobby goes alone and can be snatched, kidnapped, or drive-by shot on the way home. I will give her the make and license plate of his car if they want to arrange a minor traffic accident on a deserted street that gets him out of his vehicle, then shoot, stab, or break his skull with a baseball bat. As an undercover police officer, I will be a part of the conspiracy to kill Bobby. I can also just give Phyllis the information she needs to arrange the murder herself or with her accomplices. For Phyllis, the less I know, the better. For me, the more information I give her, the better. What a dance. There will be other cops assigned to watch Bobby and protect him. If they don't, he will be a real victim.

Phyllis knows that planning to kill someone is a conspiracy to commit homicide, or attempted homicide. She will be smart enough to keep that out of the conversation or deny it. When I said, "I know what you are talking about," she didn't reply, *I am planning to kill your husband.*

At best, we want her to make an attempt to murder Bobby. If not, if we can produce a weapon, plus my testimony, my notes on our conversations, her proximity to Bobby—the closer the better—it will be enough. There is one last matter.

"Should we be worried this might be entrapment?"

"Entrapment?" Lieutenant Hagen says. "You bet. This woman is offering to kill your husband; it's something she may have done at least to three other people, including a police officer. God-damn right, it's entrapment. You are the one who will entrap her, Karim, and I will be the one to arrest her. Then we will get a confession from her for the other murders . . ."

She stops herself, looks at me, and not in a friendly way. "You're not suggesting we call this off, are you?"

"No."

"You have a problem with any of this, Detective?"

Detective is the reminder that I am a policewoman, she is my superior officer, and if I do doubt her, then I am untrustworthy, since doubt itself is untrustworthy, and she has a reason to demote or even fire me.

We both know entrapment is a perfectly legal police procedure. The jails are filled with husbands and wives who thought they were hiring "hit men" to kill their spouses and discovered they were making deals with undercover police. Cops joke it's always better to kill your husband yourself—don't outsource the job.

"I'm good with all of this, Lieutenant," I say.

CHAPTER 37

I find a parking spot on Steinway Street for the Prius and begin my walk to the shelter. On Thirtieth Avenue, I see him looking in the window of the Tea Plus Cafe. He sees me. I won't ask him if he is following me. Or has been.

"Hello, Higgins, what a coincidence."

"Not so much," he says. "It's only Astoria. I buy green tea for Danielle here. Cures her asthma. What about you?"

"Doctor. Checkup."

I'm lying. It doesn't mean Higgins is. Relax.

"Buy you a coffee, or an exotic tea?" he says.

"Sure."

Inside, we study the menu.

"I recommend the fresh mint. I don't think it cures anything, just tastes delicious."

"Sure."

We settle in. Cozy. Friendly. We are just two cops having tea.

Higgins sips his tea and says, "*Sure.* You said it twice. There's a poem by Delmore Schwartz, 'The Beautiful American Word, Sure.'"

"I don't know it."

"Do you like poetry?"

"Some."

"Here's a bit of it."

> "'*The beautiful American word, Sure,*
> *As I have come into a room, and touch*
> *The lamp's button, and the light blooms with such*
> *Certainty where the darkness loomed before,*

As I care for what I do not know, and care
Knowing for little she might not have been,
And for how little she would be unseen,
The intercourse of lives miraculous and dear.'"

Higgins recites it in a dry, undramatic manner. As I listen, my mind wanders. One line stays with me: "Knowing for little she might not have been."

"Lovely," I say.

"It's about how precious life is."

"I got it, but I don't need a poet to tell me that."

"No, of course not. I think our work demands we be reminded. We deal so much in needless death."

What's this about, Higgins? Poetry and tea, needless death?

I want out of here. I need to end this innocently, like we began, like we met coincidentally.

I ask him about his family, then if he watches *Game of Thrones*. He does. We are into Jon Snow rumors and close to the end of our tea. He insists on paying. I leave the tip.

Outside, we play *Who's going in what direction?*

"My car is around the corner."

"I'm just down the street," he says.

We say good-bye. I walk back to my car. Beautiful poetry aside, I drive away and remember I don't believe in coincidences.

CHAPTER 38

Amanda sits on the steps of the shelter, doing homework, listening to music. She looks up, removes her earbuds.

"Hey," I say.

I sit down next to her.

"Where's Bobo?"

"Sniffing out the new arrival." She shudders slightly. "Guess what? Phyllis gave her Haneen's room."

"When?"

"This morning."

"What's she like?"

"Scared, beat-up. The usual. She's not talking a lot. Most of the new ones don't. You didn't say that much either when you first came here."

"Does she have a name?"

"Sharon."

"I brought you a present."

I hand her a comic book: one of Sammy's graphic novels. After Sammy died, I went to Jericho Pines to collect his belongings. The staff prepared everything for me—his clothes lay neatly folded on the bed, a pair of jeans, a pile of underwear and socks, his T-shirts, his favorite, a yellow SpongeBob that I held to my face in search of him, his smell, but they'd washed everything, and my little brother was gone.

Sammy's gray Gap hoodie, Mets cap, flip-flops, and a pair of black Vans sat on the floor. His toilet articles, meds, computer, flip phone, and comic books were stacked on his desk. I went through the pile of comics—they were a fraction of his collection; he'd only brought his favorites with him to Jericho Pines. The rest are packed in boxes in a storage locker along with the material remains of our family. I am left to deal with it. *I will*, I tell myself, *I will*. *One day*. But what am I to do with everything my family owned? The precious and the useless, the sentimental and the utilitarian, it doesn't matter. It's all heart-breakingly sad. Storage is just another grave, and I don't have the stamina for another one.

Whatever money Sammy earned from odd jobs, his allowance, birthday presents, he spent on comics, or as he liked to remind me, *graphic novels*. My mother and I, his virtuous, academically proper sister, disapproved. My father didn't.

"I don't care what he reads; the important thing is that he reads. Today it's Batman—tomorrow, Tolstoy. You'll see."

He was wrong. Sammy didn't live long enough to read Tolstoy, but I came around to comics. I was the older sister who only read *good* books, *important* books dictated by my English teachers. Sammy read comics; I read literature. Until one day I accepted his *Oh, yeah? Try this* challenge and read *Preacher*, a baroque tale of a man born of the union of the devil and an angel, and his sidekick, an Irish vampire. The Irishman was hundreds of years old. He was fond of recounting stories about the IRA and the Easter rebellion, and quoting Irish writers: Behan, O'Casey, and Shaw.

The comic book got Sammy interested in Irish history and lit-erature. He read *The Hostage*, and we watched *The Informer* and *Michael Collins* together. It was all so much more relatable to him than *A Tree Grows in Brooklyn*, a novel Sammy was struggling with in his eighth-grade English class. I stopped bothering him about the Western Canon, encouraged him to read whatever the hell he wanted, and we traded comic books from then on.

Later, Sammy turned to another theme: a postapocalyptic world, a place he lived in his mind. There were two. The first was *Y: The Last Man*. In it, all males, human and animal, died as a result of a plague. Sammy knew the irony would hit my feminist sensibility. From the introduction of *The Last Man*:

> *Welcome to the Unmanned World:*
> *In the summer of 2002, a plague of unknown origin destroyed every last sperm, fetus, and fully developed mammal with a Y chromosome (with the exception of one young man and his male pet). The "gendercide" instantly exterminated 48% of the global population, or approximately 2.9 billion men, including 495 of the Fortune 500 CEOs.*

In the comic book, airplanes dropped out of the sky because ninety-nine percent of the pilots were male, suddenly there were only a handful of people in Congress, armed widows clamored for their husbands' seats, ninety-five percent of all truck drivers and ship captains died . . . as did ninety-two percent of violent felons. And my favorite: *"Worldwide, 85% of all government representatives are now dead . . . as are 100% of Catholic priests, Muslim imams, and Orthodox Jewish rabbis."*

It wasn't original—there have been other "last man" stories; but this one had tough women characters: one-breasted Amazon motorcycle gangs, widows of dead congressmen demanding their seats, the few remaining women combat soldiers.

Sammy lived vicariously through Marvel's extreme heroes: *Iron Man*, *Captain America*, and the *Hulk*. After our father's murder, he gravitated to the DC world for heroes whose pain mirrored his own: young Bruce Wayne, who saw his parents gunned down; Peter Parker's *Spider-Man* avenging his uncle Ben, who was murdered by a burglar; Frank Castle becoming *The Punisher* after his wife and two children were killed by mobsters in a cross-fire shoot-out in Central Park; Kal-El, exiled to earth to become Clark Kent. Sammy shared grief with these comic book characters. It was solace for Sammy to know there were characters like him, who also lived in a memory world of horror, loneliness, and loss. Unfortunately, his past didn't flash forward to acquiring bat wings or spider strings or discovering the strength to bend steel and fly faster than a speeding bullet. Sammy just remained sad, human, ordinary, and powerless. It was for me, his sister, to be the superhero.

"Did you find him?"

"Not yet, honey, but I will."

His other favorite comic book was Garth Ennis's *Rover Red Charlie*. The one I gave to Amanda.

"You should read it, sister," Sammy said to me. "It's about what it's like to be a dog."

"That's it? What's the story?"

"Hmmm. Okay, it's about three dogs who travel across the country after the apocalypse. Like a dog Odyssey."

"Is this another apocalypse story like The Last Man?*"*

"No, in this one all the humans are dead. Only animals are alive. The dogs want to go to the Pacific Ocean, which they call 'the big splash.' They have adventures along the way. There's a crazy German shepherd who won't stop guarding his dead master's truck, and an abused fighting bulldog, and they eat chickens." He laughed. "Chickens are really dumb, sister."

Amanda looks at the comic book, flips through the pages.

"My brother liked this one a lot, Amanda. It's about dogs."

She tosses it on the step next to her.

"I'll give it to Bobo."

I can hear traces of anger in her voice.

"You okay, Amanda?"

"No, I'm not. You're leaving us, aren't you?"

There it is. Pure Amanda. Total honesty, no passive aggression, sarcasm, sulking. The terms of commerce among teenagers and adolescents are unused by Amanda. I still haven't found the words to ask why she is so direct, so straightforward, without guile or manipulation. I decide it is time to ask.

"Why are you so honest?"

"It's a decision I made. I knew everybody around me was lying, and it didn't seem to make them any happier. I wanted to see what happened if I told the truth. See if it was a better way."

"Was it?"

"Sometimes. Mostly it didn't make much difference. I found if I kept the truth in me, then I had a better way of figuring out when people were lying to me. Does that make sense?"

"Sure. You didn't play their game. It takes people a long time to learn that."

"Have you?"

"That it's better to tell the truth? Not when my husband asks where I am."

"Duh."

"I guess so." I don't tell her I'm a cop and I lie for a living. "We're friends now, Amanda. I take friendship seriously. We'll always be in touch."

"Yeah?"

"Yeah. It's a promise."

She looks at me. Fixes a silent stare on me. I say it again. "I promise."

"Okay."

"Who's cooking tonight?"

"No one. It's pizza delivery night."

"Silverware or plastic?"

"We're on cleanup. Plastic."

We both sit silently for a moment. A big, wet, hairy face nuzzles itself between us and tries to push us apart.

"Hey, Bobo."

We each move a few inches. Bobo squeezes in between us. Her tail wags as we scratch and pet her. Hooray for the simple things: girlfriends on a stoop in Queens, comic books, and a goofy dog.

Our reverie is interrupted by a text from Lieutenant Hagen.

"I have to go, Amanda. See you at dinner."

CHAPTER 39

Detective Keller is at the water fountain. He gives me a chin up and points a finger.

"Hey, Karim, your pal is here. He wants to confess."

McDermott is seated at a table in the interrogation room facing me. The place stinks of coffee, sweat, and lies. I've asked Tessa to watch the interview on a CCTV camera in another room.

"Has someone read you your rights?"

"The Miranda warning? As in, I can call a lawyer, everything I say can be held against me?"

"Yes."

"Like on television. But I don't want a lawyer, or really need one."

"Why is that?"

"I think I know what I did. It's a relief, actually. It's been bothering me. I'm glad to know you have finally caught up with me."

"I didn't catch up with you. You walked in here and insisted on giving your confession to me. Why?"

"I consider us friends. I thought it would help your career."

"You think I need help?"

"Frankly, yes."

Tessa must be laughing. I am so tired of this jerk.

I turn on the voice recorder and the microphone attached to the table. It's not real; its purpose is to distract the suspect from the people who are watching him behind a two-way mirror. There is also a working recorder in the CCTV camera hidden in the lighting fixture above him.

"This is Detective Nina Karim. The time is five fifteen p.m.

I am about to take the statement of Mr. Lawrence McDermott.
Mr. McDermott, do you waive the reading of your rights?"

"Yes."

"Then you can begin."

I settle back in my chair, not for comfort, but distance. Mc-
Dermott clears his throat and adjusts his tie.

"Well, where shall I start?"

"Wherever you want."

"All right, I followed her home."

"Who?"

"I don't know her name. A woman. I followed her home from
her job. Twice. Then when she was at work, I went back to where
she lives and reconnoitered. It's a fourplex; she has one of the
top-floor apartments. There are a lot of kids, and I noticed they
never bother to lock the front door, so I got inside easily. Upstairs, I jimmied the lock on her door—it really wasn't hard to
do. I let myself in and watched TV until I heard her car. I hid in
her bedroom closet and waited."

"Where is the apartment?"

"In Astoria."

"The address?"

"Crane Street. I'm not sure of the number."

"Yes, you are."

McDermott reconsiders. He doesn't want to appear derelict
in his confession.

"Twenty-seven."

"Apartment?"

"2A."

It's my address. *Fuck.*

"Tell me about the woman."

"Late twenties, attractive, blonde, medium build. Not skinny,
not fat, either."

"You killed her?"

"Yes."

"How?"

"She came into her bedroom. I watched her take off her clothes. When she was naked, I came out of the closet and shot her. Oh, I forgot, I put a pillow in front of the pistol, so it would muffle the sound."

"And then?"

"You mean what did I do next? I waited to see if anyone heard the shot, then I put her on the bed."

He waits for my reaction. I give him nothing.

"Would you like to see the gun? I brought it with me, but I had to leave it at the desk."

"Do you have a permit for this gun?"

"No, it's a family heirloom."

I get up.

"I'll be right back."

I meet Tessa outside in the hall.

"He just confessed to killing you," she says.

"I think he's crazy and he's planning to kill me, but he thinks he already has. Maybe there's a psychosis called *wrong tense disorder.*"

"What do we do with him?"

"He said he left a gun at the desk. He doesn't have a permit for it," I say.

"We can arrest him for possession and see if we can get this guy some help."

"Or toss him out. I can take my chances he is harmless and just a pain in the ass."

"Up to you. It's your ass."

"Keep the gun, toss him out. I don't have time for this."

CHAPTER 40

There is a new odor in my basement room. A trace. Subtle. Sweet. Flowery, honeyed. A perfume, shampoo, or deodorant—can I give it a name? My knowledge of perfume is limited to the generic underarm deodorant I get from CVS and keep in my police locker. I check my possessions; they appear undisturbed. Everything is in order except that someone upstairs has been in my space. It won't be hard to sniff them out at dinner. I'll sniff like a dog. Above me, doors shut, feet trod, the clang of the triangle signals dinnertime.

Amanda and I set the table. The delivery boy from Mama Carmela's in Woodside has left three eighteen-inch pizzas—vegetable, meat, and a cheese pie with spinach. There is an extra-large chopped salad and bread sticks, all the food a gift from an anonymous supporter. "There're others," Amanda tells me. "Besides the pizza lady, there's the one who drops off all her hotel shampoos and soaps, another one who pays the cable bill. Phyllis says they're people who lived here, left, and got their lives together—it's how they show their appreciation."

"Do you know who pays the rent?"

"Nope."

I'd like to know the answer. Is the person who pays the rent also the one who arranges the killings?

Sharon, the "new arrival," comes into the dining room. She's in her midforties; her left arm is wrapped in a cast covered by a blue sleeve. If a broken arm is her ticket to Artemis, she must have a seriously nasty and abusive partner. Her face shows the strains of a hard life, cheeks lined with parallel creases, vertical lines between her lips and nose. It is a pleasant and friendly face; she radiates kindness and generosity that suggest that no matter how bad her situation is she would still find time to help you. I imagine she is the kind of woman who would watch your kids, drop by for coffee and collect your mail and papers if you went away. You would want her for a neighbor. Her hair is thick reddish brown, and it looks like it hasn't changed since her high school yearbook photo: bangs droop over her forehead, side flaps drape her temples. Sharon is one of those women who hit a certain age and lose their former frame; their bodies acquire mass and become squared. You could draw a straight line from her shoulders to hips. These women aren't obese. They aren't soft or flabby; they project strength, and their faces retain their beauty as their bodies change.

"Everybody say hello to Sharon," Phyllis says.

We know what to do: we introduce ourselves, first names only, and wait for Sharon to respond. The children eye the pizzas hungrily. *Could you make this fast, please?*

After our introductions, she says, "I just got here. To tell you the truth, I'm kind of in a daze, so I don't have really anything to say right now, if you all don't mind."

Did she say *you all*, or the Southern *y'all*? I'm not sure which one I heard. If it's the latter, what's she doing in Queens?

"Let's eat," Phyllis says. "Sharon, we just help ourselves." Sharon smiles weakly at the sight of the opened pizza boxes with their flattened melted cheeses, slices of sausage and vegetables, and shiny drops of olive oil. Sharon holds up her plate. "May I just have a little bit of salad, please?"

I look around the table. We are all thinking the same thing:

we want to hear Sharon's story, her nightmare, how she got here, who beat her, was it a husband present or ex, a boyfriend, a crazy neighbor, a boss—*Come on, girl, give it up, share*. We want to assess her chances of survival if she leaves and ours if she stays. Will her husband hunt her down and kill her if she leaves Artemis? We are a nosy, gossipy, intrusive group with little respect for boundaries or privacy. We want to know her business. We want her secrets, laid out for our inspection, and then she will get our support, sympathy, and love. Tell us a horror story about *that bastard* and what he did to you, or a funny one about *what an asshole he is* that will make us feel better or worse about ourselves.

I'm not sure what I'm playing anymore. I'm a spy, an impostor, in this house of truly abused and fearful women. I don't have a husband who points a finger in my face with one hand and makes a fist with the other that makes my bladder empty. I'm not afraid to step outside the shelter. I don't look for my husband's car. I can go to a supermarket, a movie, a bank, pick up my child at school if I had one, walk my dog if I had one, call my mother if I had one, be on Facebook, have a Twitter account. What I don't have is someone who wants to hurt me. It was already done. I have that in common with the other women in this shelter. We are sisters. And the bottom line is I don't want to betray them.

Sharon stands and pushes her chair back from the table. "Please excuse me. I'm feeling awfully tired."

As she passes me, her shoulder brushes my cheek and I smell honey.

The new arrival has been in my stuff.

I knock softly and wait, then knock again.

"Minute." A thin strip of light appears at the bottom of the door. A few moments later, Sharon opens the door. She wears a long-sleeved nightgown.

"Oh, hi," she says, friendly enough.

"I'm Lucy."

"Yes. I don't have the names down yet."

"You will. Takes some time." I hand her a baggie with a cheese sandwich and an orange. "You didn't eat anything. This is in case you get hungry."

She nods thanks and takes the baggie. I look past her into the room. There is a four-wheeled suitcase on the floor, next to it a faded JanSport backpack; they both carried the possessions of a woman who is fleeing. I can only imagine what she has left behind.

"Come in," she says.

Inside, I see relics of Haneen's life that Phyllis has left undisturbed: her magazines, *Forbes*, *Vanity Fair*, and *Vogue*; family photos; a framed picture of Haneen and her boyfriend, Teddy, at the Grand Canyon; and taped to the wall, two Knicks ticket stubs. A contemporary New York life snuffed out. Subscription canceled.

"This was Haneen's room," I say.

"Phyllis told me. Such a sad story."

"Everyone here has one."

Sharon allows herself a smile, enough for me to notice the empty spaces where her bottom teeth used to be. Sharon raises her hand to her mouth. "He knocked them out, and I never got around to replacing them. No point. He would just do it again."

"Where are you from?"

"We're army. Sorry, my husband is. Stationed at Fort Dix. Nineteen years in, a lifer about to retire. If I report him for assault, they'll discharge him, and he'll lose his pension and benefits. They're always looking for excuses to kick enlisted men out and save money. I guess I didn't want to be one. But I knew if I stayed, if I called the MPs, filed charges, he wouldn't make it."

"I'm sorry," I say.

"Well, now you know."

"Almost. What were you doing in my room?"

I meant to take her by surprise to gauge her reaction. Expecting a denial, a lie, I instead get a sigh, a big exhale, and tears.

"I'm sorry. You aren't the only one. I've been in everyone's room."

"Why?"

"You know how in an airplane they tell you to take note of the exits? Wherever I am, I want to know the way out. I want to know the best way. If my husband is at the front door with a gun, is it the window in this room, or is it another, or do I want to know the best place to hide? I liked your bathroom in the basement."

Reasonable.

CHAPTER 41

A week later at the station house, Lieutenant Hagen summons Claude Ito, Linda Fuentes, and me to her office. We will be the lead detectives conducting the sting operation against Phyllis. Hagen tells Ito and Fuentes that I have been undercover in the shelter and have provided her with enough information to suspect at least three murders may have originated there.

Linda sneaks a text to me: No shit, girl. I forgive u. I'll ask her later if she's forgiving me for my insults or for manipulating her into the beating that got me into Artemis.

Linda and two teams of plainclothes detectives from the vice squad will follow Phyllis when she leaves the shelter. Ito's cops will protect Bobby, my abusive, dangerous "husband." My job is to stay in the shelter, keep everybody on the outside informed of Phyllis's movements, try to monitor her calls, and convince her my situation is getting more desperate. I tell everyone about the exit route through Myra's house and not to bother watching Artemis's front door.

Claude has a question. "Do we have any idea of what we're looking at in terms of this woman being armed?"

Lieutenant Hagen looks at me. "Nina?"

"I don't think so. She's the facilitator. My feeling is she has people on the outside doing what needs to be done."

I correct myself. "What *she* thinks needs to be done."

Anyone notice? I scan the detectives for tells. Ito? Did he blink? Fuentes. No, I'm okay. Everyone is focused on Lieutenant Hagen.

"Nina," Lieutenant Hagen says, "any way to make this happen faster?"

"I can ask Bobby to show up at the shelter, make a scene outside, wave a gun, then drive away before anyone calls the police."

"Nice. Tell him to make it convincing."

"He'll need a blue Camaro, if Phyllis remembers what I told her."

"We'll find one for him. What year?"

"I didn't say."

"Okay."

We are investigating the murders of Ronald, Derrick, and Joey. They were on track to kill or maim their spouses. Then, for the first time, I hear another voice. It is my father, and he is telling me to do my job.

CHAPTER 42

This morning I am giving math lessons to Ben, Frankie, and Tiffany. When Sofia left the shelter, she handed over her materials with descriptions of each child's math level. I've got three different ages and levels. Tiffany is precocious for a seven-year-old; she can solve algebraic second-degree equations. Frankie is just behind her but struggles with mixture problems, while Ben is doing long division. Sofia downloaded math games to the computer that keep them occupied; Tiffany and Frankie sit at their makeshift desks, doing exercises in their workbooks. I confine the class time to thirty minutes. The children are under enormous stress. They rarely leave the shelter, though occasionally we take them out to the zoo, a museum, or just to a McDonald's—anything that resembles a "normal" life. If the weather is good like it is today, we go outside. Phyllis and some of the mothers come out of the house, and we all play a crazy game of backyard soccer. We have our own rules and equipment. We use a volleyball instead of a soccer ball, and the tin garbage can lying on its side is the goal. Frankie has the ball. He's an expert dribbler; he easily sidesteps me and whacks the ball into the can for a goal. The ball bounces around, making hollow *bong*s that are suddenly echoed by a furious banging on the front door. Phyllis shoos the kids back into the house, grabs a footstool. She climbs on it for a view over the wall to the front of the shelter.

"Stop banging on my door," she yells.

"Let me in, you stupid cunt."

The voice is male, drunk, and it belongs to Bobby.

"I want to see my wife. Her name is Lucy Booth. Tell her to come out or I'm coming in. I know she's in there," he says.

"Go away before I call the police," Phyllis says.

"Call 'em. I don't give a shit. Lucy!"

Phyllis steps down from the footstool to the sounds of Bobby banging his fists on the door.

"Take the kids inside. He's got a gun."

"I'll call 911."

"No, not yet. Get the kids in the house and stay with them. I'll deal with this fool."

On my way to the house, I see Phyllis climb back on the footstool. Her voice is calm and even.

"Listen very carefully. I don't know who you are, but there is no Lucy here. You leave right now, or I am going to call the police and my security company. I will tell them you are armed, and when they arrive they will blow your fucking brains out and then ask me who you are. You understand?"

"Fuck you, lady," Bobby says.

"Okay, mister, we're done."

In the house, I count heads.

"Where's Frankie?"

"His usual. Upstairs bathroom," Tiffany says.

A moment later, Phyllis enters. "He went away. Everybody okay?"

The children nod.

Phyllis says, "Frankie upstairs? Good."

She sits down on the couch and draws Ben and Tiffany into an embrace.

"It's okay. The man went away. I scared the hell out of him. He's gone." Phyllis waits for nods from each of them. "What do you say to watching television now, and I'll get McDonald's for lunch?"

The children know they are being offered a distraction, a palliative to take their minds off the incident; they nod in response.

Today, there will be little joy in funny cartoons and Happy Meals. But they will take whatever they can get. These children live in a house where their mothers tell them they are safe from violent and angry men. And now, just a few minutes ago, one of them showed up with a gun and created more nightmares, and they will consider their lives and their mothers less secure. Phyllis senses it.

"Kids, the man who came today? He won't come back."

"What if he does?" Tiffany says.

"I'll call the police. Have him arrested."

"The police don't do shit," Ben says.

"Then we'll sic Bobo on him. Right, Bobo?"

Bobo thumps her tail on the couch. She makes the kids smile.

Phyllis says offhandedly, as if nothing strange has happened, as if this man with a gun was like a mistaken UPS driver, "Tiffany, will you write down what everybody wants?"

"Can we get Cokes, too?"

In keeping with normal, Phyllis says, "Nope. No Coke."

And to me, "Lucy, can I see you in the kitchen?"

As I go, Tiffany asks, "Was that your husband?"

"Yes."

"Does he want to kill you?"

"He says he does."

"Then he might, right?"

"No, he won't."

In the kitchen, Phyllis hands me a coffee.

"Son of a bitch."

Her face is crunched in a determined rage. The kindness, the gentleness, and the warmth that marked Phyllis's behavior to the children is gone. Her mouth is tight, her eyes narrowed, and for a moment I am afraid of her. It's rage. It's familiar. It's like mine. She is going to get this *cowardly bastard* who showed up at her house and threatened her women and children. She is going to kill him. She is me.

"Are you calling the police?"

"No, I'm not calling the police. I don't want them involved." She stares at me. "Now, you tell me where I can find him."

"He's not a cop. He's not dangerous."

"How do you know that?"

"He's not my husband."

Phyllis cocks her head.

"We'd better sit down," I say.

My words are impulsive, unplanned. As they come out of my mouth, I realize I am ending my career as a police officer.

"I'm here undercover, Phyllis. I am a police officer working for Long Island City homicide. I lied my way in here. We're trying to solve the murders of three people whose partners were in this shelter. We think you, or someone you know, aided by people you know, killed them. That's Ronald Steevers, Joey Savone, Derrick Matthews. That man who was outside is not a dangerous husband. He's part of a sting operation to convince you to hurry along in an attempt to kill him. The plan is to entrap you into trying to kill him. When you set out to do this, we would arrest you for conspiracy to commit murder, and get you to confess to the others."

Phyllis nods. There is no point in outrage, scenes, or histrionics. "You know what you are doing?"

"Yes."

"Why? Why are you telling me this?"

Before I can answer, there is a knock on the door. Sharon steps in.

"Hi, sorry to interrupt. Is everything all right? I heard there was a disturbance outside. A man. Somebody's husband."

"Mine," I say.

"It's under control," Phyllis says. "We chased him off."

Phyllis lets the silence linger, a signal to Sharon that we want to continue our conversation alone.

"It kinda freaks me out," she says.

"Understandable," Phyllis says. "But we took care of it. All's well."

Sharon wants more.

"Really, Sharon. We're safe. We need to be calm. For the children."

"Yes. I see."

Take a hint, Sharon. Leave.

"I'm cooking tonight," Sharon says. "Can I have a count, Phyllis?"

Phyllis closes her eyes and does a mental calculation. I can read her mind; she is thinking, *Do I have to do this now?*

She takes a breath. "Usual."

I look at Phyllis and shake my head.

"Lucy, stay for dinner. Spend one more night. You can say goodbye to the children in the morning."

"You're leaving us?" Sharon asks.

"Yes."

"Oh, my. I do envy you," Sharon says.

"I wouldn't."

"Oh."

"He knows where I am. It's better that I leave."

"Where will you go?"

I just shake my head.

Sharon nods sympathetically. "I'll miss you," she says.

I think, *You'll miss me? Why? I hardly know you. All I know about you is that I caught you in my room. Maybe I'm a cynical cop and I don't believe you were paranoid and checking escape routes.*

Maybe you're a thief, or maybe I just don't like you despite your down-home, sweet mama personality.

Sharon goes to the door. "Well, see you all tonight."

She gets two nods. Phyllis gets up and shuts the door behind Sharon.

"What am I supposed to do now?"

"Nothing. That's the point."

"You want to tell me why you told me all this?"

"I don't want you in jail. I don't want the shelter closed."

"And these so-called murders, your theory is that I had something to do with them?"

"Yes."

"Go fuck yourself."

She says it with a smile.

CHAPTER 43

Sharon's dinner is meat loaf, mashed potatoes, biscuits, carrots, and peas. Dessert is apple pie. She brings in slices from the kitchen, three plates at a time; she must have worked as a waitress. There is no mention of Bobby's intrusion as not to upset the children. The three kids who did see it will boast, exaggerate, and reenact the event for the ones who missed it. Before the children are sent up to bed, I announce that I am leaving tomorrow. I thank everyone for their support, friendship, and love, but since my presence here in the shelter is known to my ex-husband, I don't want to make life any more dangerous. It's a lie, but the truth can't be told. Amanda already knows, and the other children are used to women coming and going.

"I have a new safe place to go where no one can find me."

"Are you going to hide in Europe?" Tiffany asks.

"How did you know? Now I'll have to go somewhere else."

"I won't tell," she says.

"I know you won't."

We all exchange hugs and kisses. Nobody makes any promises to "stay in touch."

I help Sharon in the kitchen.

"I've always been a clean cook. I like to wash pots as I use them. Less work at the end."

"I'm the opposite," I say. "I leave a mess."

I'm tired. I don't want to make small or large talk. I just want to go down to my basement and crash. I'll pack tomorrow.

"Are you all right, Lucy? You look a bit pale."

"I think I'm beat. It was a hard day."

"Then you go. I'll finish up."

"Thanks. If I don't see you tomorrow . . ."

"Oh, you will. I'm an early riser. Sweet dreams."

CHAPTER 44

My dreams aren't sweet. They are revelatory. I dream solutions to problems, I solve crimes that have eluded me, I learn who killed my father, I know where Artie Crews's son's cat is hiding, I realize I know who McDermott will kill, and I dream about a connection between Afghanistan and Long Island City. I am all-knowing. I make a dream note to remind me that when I wake to be sure I remember my dreams and all that is revealed to me. I won't because I am dreaming under the influence of a drug I didn't take. When I wake up, I remember nothing. I am left with only the questions and none of the answers.

And I realize I am not alone. There is someone in the room; another mass occupies my space. It breathes my oxygen, absorbs my heat, and radiates its own. There is a familiar odor; it is the one I smelled last week—sweet, honeyed—and now it is attached to a person. As the odor moves, its intensity swells and fades. *Fee-fi-fo-fum, I smell the blood of an Englishman . . . Cyclops smells Ulysses, Hector smells Ajax, Red Riding Hood smells a wolf. Stop. Concentrate.* The odor belongs to a woman, her perfume, her soap, her shampoo, honey pleasant, unlike the nostril-burning industrial smells of my basement home: heating oil, paint, and the Comet that refuses to erase the yellow stains in the sink. I reach for the lamp switch, but my arm won't move. I try to sit up, but I can't; my back muscles won't work. No part of my body can move. No muscle obeys, no nerve feels. Only smell and sound. I hear air inhaled, a breath taken in. I can hear. I can smell, I can feel, I am alive.

"Would you like some light?" The accent, like the smell, is honeyed; a Southern inflection.

Of course it's Sharon.

"Here you go."

Like a flare exploding in my face, a powerful beam burns through my eyelids.

"It's called Rohypnol. I put some in your food. You can't move. Your muscles are disabled. But it wears off, so I had to tie you down. You won't be going anywhere."

I open my eyes. Sharon stands over me. I am her prisoner, her victim, and I cannot speak. There is duct tape across my mouth. I try to move. I can't. There are restraints around my wrists and my ankles. Smooth, not painful. I glance up to the basement window. Outside it is pitch-black. I have no idea of the time. Sharon, a shadowy presence behind the powerful flashlight beam, sits on the chair next to the cot. She leans in closer, speaks in a low voice. "I know who you are. I know all about you. Let me tell you who I am."

Yes. Talk. Keep talking. As long as you speak, I am alive. Be Scheherazade. I try to nod my head. See? I am interested.

"I am a miracle. Anita Turner, my mother, was a sixteen-year-old high school senior in Matthews, Texas, known as 'The Friendliest Town in the West.' That's a matter of debate, 'cause there sure weren't many friendly people to turn to when she got pregnant by her boyfriend who raped and abandoned her. Mama said he would have come around; the rape was something he wouldn't ever admit or acknowledge. It happened behind the high school, after a dance. There was too much Lone Star and weed, and he wouldn't take no for an answer—as he'd learned in movies, if you kiss a girl hard enough sooner or later, she will melt and give in, and if not, just keep going. There will be time to forgive and forget. Mama didn't forgive, and her periods stopping made it impossible for her to forget. So there.

"I don't know much about him, this rapist father of mine. I

am told I have his nose, his hair, and his temperament, which tended to volatile. He died as young men often do in Central Texas, driving his pickup truck under the influence. Drunk, I guess. Too bad he took a couple of teenagers coming in the opposite direction with him. Since he died before his ambitions were realized, his legends created, and memories deposited in me, his daughter, there's not much for me to say about him.

"I'd rather tell you about my mama's family. They came to Texas from Oklahoma during the Dust Bowl depression, ran out of gas and money in Matthews. My grandpa found ranch work; my grandma had bookkeeping skills, got a job in the local bank. They made a home, had kids—one was my mother. She was the smart one, read a lot, knew life after high school in Matthews meant minimum wage in fast food—if you were lucky, construction, or a doctor's receptionist, and, depending on your success in high school, the chance of a Texas state scholarship to a community college, assuming you or your family could afford books and food. Or the military, my mother's way out. She planned to enlist in the United States Air Force after graduation, and if she couldn't get into their pilot program, she would learn everything she could about airplanes and then use her saved money and veterans' benefits to pay for flight school to become a commercial airline pilot.

"Getting pregnant was an obstacle to that plan, but she could overcome that obstacle by having an abortion. Otherwise, she would be a single mother living at home, fair game for men married and not, in a dusty rural hell.

"There was an abortion clinic in Harlington, a hundred miles from Matthews, but those miles weren't easy for a sixteen-year-old without a car, and whose boyfriend suddenly wasn't talking to her. Planned Parenthood had clinics in Austin, San Antonio, and Dallas. There was always a bus across the border from Brownsville to Matamoros in Mexico, where she could walk into a pharmacy, buy misoprostol over the counter, and give herself a medically induced miscarriage. But it's a dangerous and often unsuccessful solution. It was her great-grandmother Caroline Allen who came to her rescue. She handed Mama the ungodly sum of fifteen hundred dollars in a roll of one-hundred-dollar bills that paid for a round-trip bus ticket to San Antonio, a hotel room at the DoubleTree, and an appointment at the Whole Woman Clinic.

"Two days later, according to plan, my mother would, with the help of a doctor, abort and legally murder me. Then, miracle of miracles, God chose me to express his love for the world. I am here and alive because on her way to have me aborted, Mama got in a taxicab driven by Father Martin, a Catholic priest and a volunteer in the Christian Life Society. The hotel desk clerk would tip off Father Martin when women ordered taxis to drive them to the abortion clinic. Instead of taking them to the Whole Woman Clinic, he drove them to the Life Saver Mission, where they would be counseled, prayed over by beautiful women, and persuaded not to have the abortion. In my mama's case, they were successful. She changed her mind and brought me to birth. If it weren't for Father Martin and those women, I would not be here. I would not be the loving mother of my two beautiful children, Agnes and Martin, I would be a three-month-old fetus incinerated in the ovens of the Whole Woman Clinic. And thirty-three years later, on the anniversary of my birth and the death of our Lord Jesus Christ, my husband, Clyde Fairbrother, and I burned that building to the ground."

Clyde Fairbrother. The man I killed.

"We talked about you, whether we should find you or let you

find us. We knew you had become a policewoman, we knew you were looking for us, but we never considered you would murder Clyde. We thought you were only concerned with finding him. It was a mistake that cost my husband his life."

Take this tape off my mouth.

Sharon reads my movements, shakes her head.

"Can't. I know your questions. You want to know how I found you, how I worked my way into this place, and what do I plan to do to you."

No, I know everything. I want to find a way to get free, disarm you, and then kill you.

"Clyde didn't shoot your father—you know that, don't you?"

Of course I know. Clyde was too smart to do it.

"I did. I was the one who shot him."

He made you the killer. Like your mother, you were raped, only this time by your husband.

"Clyde taught me. Your doctor father was a murderer. He killed hundreds of babies that could have been like me: miracles. He had to be stopped. Clyde knew they would suspect him, so we decided I would do it. He would have an alibi for the night I shot your father. No one would think I did it. I was home with the children, helping them with their homework, and they would swear it so. We are a family; we all do God's work. We taught the children what to say: their answer would be, 'Daddy was racing his car. Mama put us in her bed, and we all slept together.' Clyde and I worked it out like it was a military operation. Once a week, we would drive downstate in my car, using the back roads, to Grahamsville, hike into the woods, and watch you and your family."

Cowardly bastards.

"We studied what time you had dinner, where you each sat. We noticed how he always washed the dishes in front of the kitchen window while you kids ate dessert or did homework. That would be our cleanest shot."

Sammy.

"We picked out the best firing position. We always used the tarp so there would be no clothes fibers on the ground. We wore hospital booties over thick socks so there would be no footprints. We practiced exit routes. Clyde taught me everything about the rifle: how to clean it, how to lock it on the tripod, aim it, adjust the sight, correct for wind and the thickness of the window glass, and pull the trigger."

My father.

"I learned how to break the rifle down so I could carry it in pieces in my backpack in case anybody spotted me. I was just another hiker. Clyde knew his beans, I'll tell you that. He turned me into a first-class markswoman, said if I was younger and we didn't care about being in the news he would have put me up for the Olympics. I was that good."

My mother.

"And then on that afternoon, I hiked into the woods behind your house in Grahamsville and waited for him to come home, for your mother to cook dinner and your baby-murdering father to stand perfectly framed in front of the kitchen window washing the dishes, facing me. One bullet. Now many more babies will live. Praise God."

Me.

"I see the fear in your eyes. It is beautiful to me."

Beautiful?

I see the glint of steel. Sharon is holding a short folding combat knife. I recognize it from a blade weapons lecture at the Police Academy. It's the Hotshot, a Marine Corps weapon, five inches and razor-sharp out of the box.

"It was Clyde's. He won it for being best recruit at Quantico. He was so proud of it. I carry it now in his memory."

She holds the knife in front of my eyes for a closer look.

"What I am going to do now is make two slices in each wrist and let you watch the blood flow out of your veins until you are dead. I am not a cruel person. I think it will be a painless death, but I do want you to die. I want to see the life flow out of you. Then this cycle of death will come to an end. Your father killed babies, I killed him, you killed Clyde, and now I will kill you. I don't think there is anyone who loves you enough to come after me. Not your boyfriend. If he does, I will be long gone and impossible to find. You have five minutes left in your disgusting life."

For all her protestations of miracles and God's love, Sharon has my hate. We are perfectly matched.

She pulls the blanket down to my waist. My wrists are bound to the metal frame of the cot with plastic zip ties. I struggle. I have enough adrenaline energy to lift a Volkswagen, but the weight of my body keeps me locked to the bed. I have no leverage. I get a smile from Sharon. She is proud of her work.

Fuck you.

She cuts a neat vertical slice on my left wrist.

"There. That didn't hurt, did it?"

She is right. There is almost no pain; the blood begins to flow. What will I think about in these last five minutes of my life? I don't believe in an afterlife, so I won't be joining my parents and brother in Elysian Fields, heaven, Valhalla, or hell. My lifeless body will be discovered when I miss a meal, and then another meal, or Phyllis needs to get something out of the basement.

Sharon will have left the shelter. She will be the suspect, but she won't get far, no matter how careful or smart she thinks she is. She will have left too many markers behind. There are videos. Her fingerprints are all over the place. It will be only a matter of time before she is arrested. I am a police officer, and nobody gets away with killing one. If she makes it out of Queens, she will be lucky. She thinks she was the clever one—she wasn't. It was Clyde who planned and carried out the shooting. She just pulled the trigger. I shake my head back and forth, mouthing words unformed, straining against the duct tape. I know I could talk Sharon out of this. She knows it, too, so the tape on my mouth is more for her than for me. She would be vulnerable to mentions of Christian forgiveness, offers of mercy, and threats.

What will happen to your children when you are in prison?

"Now the other wrist. It'll make it quicker."

We both hear the noise. The door at the top of the stairs opens and shuts. *Click-click.* Sharon switches off the flashlight. Pitch-black again.

"Lucy?" Amanda says.

I thrust my hips up with every ounce of my strength. It moves the cot, enough to make the metal legs scrape against the concrete floor.

"Lucy?"

Sharon pushes down on the cot with her free hand. Her weight is sufficient. I can't move it.

"Lucy?"

"It's Sharon. I'm here with Lucy. Would you mind, honey? We need to be alone. We're having a private conversation."

"Sure, no prob." It *is* a problem, but she's only twelve, and she doesn't have a reply.

A wet tongue is licking my ear. Bobo. Floppy mutt.

"Amanda, call Bobo," Sharon says.

"Bobo, come on up."

Bobo's head is on my lap. She whines at the smell of my blood. She senses something is wrong.

"Bobo! Come Bobo."

"Bobo, shoo," Sharon says. "Amanda, call her again."

"Here, Bobo."

The flashlight goes on again. Sharon pulls the blanket over me, hiding me from Amanda.

"Call her, Amanda."

Sharon grabs Bobo's collar and drags her away from me, the blanket falls off.

"Go, Bobo. Go to Amanda."

Bobo whines. She senses something is wrong. Sharon aims the flashlight on Amanda. She is revealed in a spotlight, like an actress making an entrance. She is wearing sneakers, torn jeans, and a T-shirt. She blinks in the powerful beam of the flashlight, raises her hand to her eyes, trying to block out some of the beam, trying to see who's behind it.

"Lucy?"

"Leave us alone, Amanda."

"Sharon?"

"Yes."

"Where's Lucy?"

"She's not feeling well, honey. I'm just sitting with her. Will you go away and take Bobo with you, please? Do not make me ask you again."

Sharon uses a stern, commanding voice. It is a threatening one. Amanda has heard worse.

"Lucy? You okay?"

"For the last time, go away, Amanda."

Amanda doesn't move.

"I want to talk to Lucy."

"If you don't leave, I will have to hurt you. I don't want to, but I will."

Sharon releases her grip on the cot. I shake and scrape the legs on the floor. Now Sharon has to deal with the flashlight in one hand, the knife in the other, and still try to prevent me from jerking my body and causing the cot's legs to scrape the floor.

"Lucy, why aren't you answering me?"

I can see the reflection of the knife blade. She wouldn't kill a child.

Sharon stands. She moves the flashlight to the knife. Holds it up for Amanda to see. Amanda backs up the stairs.

Good girl, there's distance between you and the knife. Get out of here, get help.

Amanda switches on the light at the top of the stairs. Light floods the basement.

What does Amanda see?

She sees Sharon standing at the side of the cot. I'm lying on it, a swatch of duct tape across my mouth, my wrists in plastic restraints, and my blood dripping out of one of them, staining the sheets. She sees Bobo next to me, unwilling to leave, yet wanting to obey her. The dog is torn between us.

Blood on the floor. Mine.

Then: another voice. Phyllis.

"What is going on here?"

What does Phyllis see?

Me on the cot. She sees blood dripping out of my wrist. Bobo, sitting on the floor, panting, tail knocking on the floor. Amanda, a few steps farther down the stairs in front of her, and Sharon standing next to the cot, holding a flashlight and a knife.

"What?!"

Sharon lowers the flashlight and puts the knife against my throat.

"Put that knife away!" Phyllis shouts as she pushes past Amanda and strides toward us. Sharon spins; the blade meets Phyllis and disappears into her chest. There is no sound. Phyllis jolts and drops to the floor on her knees. Amanda takes a tentative step down the stairs.

Run, Amanda.

Sharon raises the knife and faces Amanda. She's a witness.

Amanda, run!

Sharon shakes her head as if to say, *I'm sorry I have to do this*, and moves to the stairs. Amanda backs up, misses a step, loses her footing, falls on her back, and slides down the stairs. She comes to a stop next to Sharon. Sharon raises the knife. In the dim light, I can see Sharon's face, scrunched up, red in splotches like some kind of eczema, her forehead washed with sweat.

"I told you. I warned you to go away. You wouldn't listen. This is your fault."

"Bobo! Attention!"

Bobo snaps her head toward Amanda. Her body stiffens, her tail stops thumping, and every muscle is alert; her whole being is focused on Amanda. She waits for the next command. Amanda raises her arm, stiffens it, and points her index finger at Sharon. Bobo's eyes follow Amanda's finger to Sharon.

"Bobo, secret word!" Amanda says.

From deep in her chest, Bobo growls a low rumble, almost a humming sound. I have never heard it before.

"Bobo! Attention! Secret word! Secret word!"

The dog fixes on Sharon. No more a slobbering mutt, she's a tense, loaded animal. Sharon turns defensively to Bobo, raises the knife.

"Bobo! Secret word! Kiki-kiki! Attack!"

Have you ever been bitten by a dog? Gotten a nip, a warning snap? It's painful. If the dog clamps its jaws tight, it can numb the nerves without breaking the skin.

This is what happens when a seventy-pound trained attack dog does her work:

Bobo leaps into the air, spins, and grabs Sharon's wrist in her jaw. The knife drops to the ground. Sharon screams and slams Bobo on the head with the flashlight. Stunned, Bobo releases her grip on Sharon's wrist. I can see the damage. Her wrist is a mess of blood and flesh. Sharon lifts the flashlight for another blow, but Bobo snatches Sharon's other wrist in her mouth and twists her head back and forth, fast. The flashlight drops to the floor. Bobo wrestles Sharon's arm as if she was playing with a rag doll. Sharon's body jerks left and right. Sharon tries to use her other hand, but she can't—the nerves are severed, the muscles shredded. It won't work. It is a mangled stump.

"Bobo, stop!"

The dog releases her. Sharon stares at her wrists. The left one has the white of her radius bone exposed; the right one is a blur of blood and torn flesh. The color drains from her face, her eyes roll back, and she sinks to the floor in shock. Bobo straddles Sharon's chest, her front paws on the sides of her head, her mouth inches from her throat, growling as she waits for another command from Amanda. If it comes, the dog will tear out Sharon's throat and kill her. I shake my head, making whatever sounds I can through the duct tape. Amanda takes Bobo's collar, gently pulling her away from Sharon.

"Come, Bobo."

The dog's jaw is dark with Sharon's blood.

"Sit, Bobo."

Amanda picks up the knife, cuts the plastic handcuffs on my

wrists and ankles. I manage to pull myself up and peel the duct tape from my mouth.

Phyllis.

I slide out of the bed, drop to the floor next to Phyllis, rip open her blouse. There is a saucer-sized circle of blood just below her breast.

"Amanda, my phone is on the table. Call 911. And then give it to me."

I tear the case off a pillow and apply pressure to Phyllis's knife wound. On the floor, Sharon writhes in agony.

Fuck her.

"Lucy?" Amanda says.

"It's Nina."

"Huh?"

"Nina. It's my real name."

"Whatever. You're bleeding."

"I need your belt."

"I know what to do. A tourniquet."

Amanda removes her belt and ties it around my arm.

"Thanks. Now call 911."

"Wow, this place looks like an emergency room."

Which is where we all end up.

CHAPTER 45

Dear Mom and Sammy,

It's all done. Done.

You know what? In the basement, we were all female—me, Amanda, Sharon, Phyllis, and Bobo. Three females and a bitch, but the real bitch wasn't a dog. The paramedics from 911 and the crew from Long Island City Police Department arrived simultaneously. Phyllis survived, thanks to some talented paramedics in her ambulance; she's in intensive care for now, but the doctor said they'll move her in a couple of days. She will need a long time in recovery. I lost a lot of blood but got it back via transfusion. I now have a fancy row of black stitches on my arm.

Sharon was touch-and-go but they managed to keep her alive. She may lose the use of her hands. There are three of us who will testify against her, so if she doesn't go away for killing Daddy, she is looking at a lot of time for attempted murder and assault with a deadly weapon. I promise she will spend the rest of her days in prison.

Are you wondering about the present state of my mind? Not my mind, my feelings, and where they reside. In my stomach? The back of my skull, my heart? I'm like a rubber ball bouncing off a wall landing on guilt, regret, sadness, then I get this feeling of satisfaction because I did it and then the ball bounces against the wall and I go through the whole thing again.

Sammy, it turns out there were two. We got them. I say we because you were my silent partner, my inspiration. You never let me down. We got her husband, too. He was just as guilty, and we got him. We have been avenged.

I'm sorry you couldn't be around to see it, but wherever you or your sweet spirit are, you can rest now. Mom, I know after Daddy died you were completely focused on making sure we were safe. All that time, you must have been trying to stay sane. Did you have time to mourn? Did you have time to find peace? You said in your last letter: "The death of someone you love, for me, doesn't get better. The only thing you learn to do is navigate. In the beginning, you just think you are going to drown. That's the only way I can describe it. There is a change, but it doesn't get better."

I know your love protected me. I survived; I know how much it pained you that Sammy didn't, despite it. Maybe, like me, you don't trust any feelings. As I said, they come and go. I see Clyde bent on his knees, about to die. I see Sharon holding up her shredded hands. I feel pleasure. I ask, Who am I, that I could feel that? *There are victims of my actions—their children. I killed one parent, and another one is going to spend the rest of her life in prison. Who will take care of them? Will they grow up to be like me and want revenge? Was Clyde a good father? Was Sharon a loving . . . ? Loving? She was a cold-blooded murderer. Can I rationalize their children's loss by saying it is the fault of their parents, not me? They shouldn't have killed mine. These are not easy questions; they will accompany me for the rest of my life.*

When I learned Clyde didn't kill Daddy, it never occurred to me that his wife would be the shooter. Men kill, women die.

How did Sharon know I was in Artemis? Someone told her, of course. I suspected Keller.

In the later investigation, Lieutenant Hagen was able to access Sharon's phone records, her emails and texts. There were plenty of them, and they weren't from Keller; they were from

Detective Higgins. My pal. I remembered Higgins mentioning his Afghanistan combat tour and reading about Clyde's. They were in the same unit, bonded over their shared pro-life beliefs. When he got back to the States, Higgins joined the Army of God but kept his membership secret and used his police sources to get information to Clyde and his followers on clinics, their security, and addresses and phone numbers of abortion providers.

Higgins said it was another part of his rejection of his parents' lifestyle. They thought they had raised a little revolutionary destined to follow them and their politics. Instead, he hated everything they stood for: their radical politics that seemed to care more about the oppressed than him, the hiding, keeping track of new names and identities, moving from town to town. In high school, he found companionship and shared politics with the conservative students. He was drawn to the right-to-life movement. His parents were distraught. They gave him books by Richard Dawkins and Bertrand Russell to no avail, until his politics and religious fervor were no longer topics of discussion. In telling Sharon where I was, he was revealing the identity and whereabouts of an undercover police officer. The DA decided not to charge him. They did make him resign from the force. He will have to find adventure elsewhere.

Sharon waited until it was her turn to cook dinner. She put the drug in my food. It was easy. It just required patience, waiting for the right moment, just as Clyde and Sharon did when they rehearsed and waited for the right moment to kill Daddy. I don't like saying "they were patient," as it gives them a virtue reserved for teaching a child, learning to play the violin, or speaking French. They were patient in planning a murder. It makes me glad I did what I did.

Mom, there it is, my rage coming back. It will never go away.

It will be a part of me. Killing Clyde and sending Sharon to prison won't change that. It is no small thing to kill another human being. Bobby says the feelings will fade; they will become old and only return in odd dreams or nightmares. He says it won't be a part of everyday me. I don't know. I hold on to things. Like my anger. I never let it go, did I? I fed it, and when it started to go away, like just before I went to Hawaii, I found ways to keep it alive.

You know what, Mom? When I feel bad, or guilty, I think of Sammy asking me if I found him. I say, "Yeah, Sammy. I did."

I can live with that. Did I tell you I am not a policewoman?
Love,
Nina

I was coming out of the emergency room; I see a woman in a wheelchair. Not so uncommon in a hospital, I thought, but . . .

I glance at her, take a police mental photo just in case, add it to my collection. I note a grim square-jawed expression that could be pain or discomfort, or she could just be pissed to be in a wheelchair. I don't blame her for any of the above.

"Detective Nina Karim?"

"Yes."

A better look now, as she wheels around to face me. She's pretty, this blond, frizzy-haired woman, wearing an expensive leather jacket and soft leather pants. Her feet, in Manolo Blahnik boots I couldn't afford, rest lifelessly on the footstep of the wheelchair.

"Can I walk you to your car? A figure of speech." She looks at my bandaged wrists. "Or give you a ride? I have a car waiting."

"I can drive," I say. "Let's talk here."

I walk over to an empty couch in the waiting room and sit. She follows me.

"What can I do for you?"

The woman opens her purse, removes a silver case, and hands me a business card: VALI LOPEZ, CERTIFIED PUBLIC ACCOUNTANT. No address, just a phone number.

"I work for Artemis. I'm their accountant."

I realize who she is just as she tells me. She's the one whose cigarette-flicking husband set her on fire.

"I'm also president of a little club called Friends of Phyllis. I believe you have met one or two of our members. I won't mention their names. I will simply say when called upon, they donate their time."

I know their names. Karen the bartender; Janet, widow of a football player; Susan, Ronald's widow?

"I assume it's a pretty elite group. What's the requirement for membership? You have to participate in a murder?"

"Not unlike yourself. We know all about your journey to Malone."

"Will I be blackmailed?"

"We don't do blackmail. We don't want anything from you except silence. We expect the same."

"I have nothing on you or anyone else. I'm not a cop anymore."

"Good."

"Anything else?"

"Phyllis is retiring. Would you like the job?

What the fuck?

CHAPTER 46

Our "new arrival" came in this afternoon. Her name is Cheryl. She's twenty-six, medium height, and has thick brown hair, except for the round patch on her left temple where her husband, Larry, ripped out a handful. She's young, kind of punk, with two metal bolts in her left earlobe and a whale tattoo on her shoulder. Her right ear is caked with dried blood where the matching earrings have been torn out. She carried twin girls, asleep in blankets.

Dr. Iskin came over after her rounds at Flushing Hospital and examined Cheryl. Aside from the torn ear, the missing teeth, the bald patch, the cigarette burns, and the abrasions around the neck, where Larry, had been choking her for the last five hours in between punching, kicking, and then raping her while her children screamed in their cribs, Cheryl was in fairly good shape—that is, still alive. Ruth dressed her wounds and gave Cheryl some painkillers. I helped her up the stairs. Amanda and Frankie followed behind us, each carrying one of Cheryl's little girls.

The police arrested Larry at Starbucks. The judge set bail at one hundred thousand dollars. The DA asked him to deny bail to keep him in jail and away from Cheryl. Larry's lawyer swore he would obey the judge's restraining order. He was able to borrow ten thousand to post bond and is now free to find Cheryl—in violation of the restraining order and the ankle bracelet he must wear as a condition of his release. None of this means shit to Larry. When he finds Cheryl, as he will if she ever leaves Artemis, he'll resume beating and torturing her until she is dead.

We are all sure of this: Karen, Phyllis, and me. Cheryl told us Larry drives a black Jeep Renegade to LaGuardia Airport, where he works as a ticket agent for Alaska Airlines. He gets off at nine. Bobby leaves his book club early and follows Larry to his favorite bar on Ditmars Boulevard. They get into a friendly conversation; two beers take them from the Mets to the Knicks to the new *Star Wars*. Bobby learns Larry plans to fly-fish Sunday on the Esopus Creek near Saugerties. It's close to Grahamsville, my hometown. What a coincidence. Bobby stops off at the Bum Bum Bar, talks to Karen Marschner about fly-fishing. She says it will be easy and calls one of her Tenacious Dames buds.

Sunday, on a deserted stretch of the Esopus Creek, Larry will meet two novice fly-fisherwomen. One is thin and wears glasses; the other is stocky with a bright white smile. They are weekenders from Brooklyn. While Larry is showing the woman with glasses how to tie a Woolly Bugger, the other will take a can of Mace out of her L.L.Bean bait bag and spray him in the face. Larry will be blinded; the woman with glasses will loosen his waist waders and push him backward into the creek. His waders will fill with water and take him under. He will drown.

It happens.

Later, in Artemis, I will say to Cheryl, "You can go home now."

ACKNOWLEDGMENTS

First, heartfelt thanks to Sara Nelson, my editor at HarperCollins. Quite simply, she did what editors are supposed to do: she made the book better. Also, Jonathan Burnham at HarperCollins, who was always encouraging and accessible. Mary Gaule, for getting me through the stations of the text and Janet Rosenberg for her forensic eye where mine failed.

I had real assistance from writers and friends who read and improved successive drafts: Lily Anolik, Jessica Anya Blau, Deborah Blum, Constance Borde, Sheila Malovany, Bianca Roberts, Ruth Rogers, Ken Brown, David Freeman, Dale Herd, Patrick McGilligan, Dennis Roberts, and my son, Fred Elias, who kept me current in music, technology, and graphic novels. Any lapses in those areas are mine, not his.

I am in debt to Martine Bertea, my agent in Paris who started the ball rolling and brought it to the excellent Carla Briner of Editions du Masque. Finally, my London agent, Caroline Michel of Peters Fraser + Dunlop. My champion always. I am lucky to have her.

ABOUT THE AUTHOR

MICHAEL ELIAS is a screenwriter, novelist, and playwright. Screen credits include *The Jerk*, *Envoyez les violons*, and *Lush Life*. His first novel, *The Last Conquistador*, was published by Open Road Media. Paul Mazursky directed his play *The Catskill Sonata*. It was named one of the best plays of the year by *Los Angeles Weekly*. He lives in Los Angeles.